FATAL REMAINS

By

TE HOLT

Contents

SYNOPSIS

BROOKS

Brooks Meeker swore she'd never return to Ennis. But after a bullet to the back ended her career as a crime scene investigator, she has nowhere else to go. When a local woman is found murdered—her body staged with a chilling message—Brooks realises the nightmare she left behind in Chicago has followed her home.

Detective William Jett came to Ennis for a quieter life, but murder has a way of upending even the best-laid plans. The town isn't ready for the truth, and neither is Jett when he realises Brooks might be the killer's true target. She's reckless, infuriatingly stubborn, and impossible to ignore—but she also might be the only one who can stop the bloodshed.

As more bodies turn up, the case becomes terrifyingly personal. A killer is playing a deadly game, one that began long before Brooks came home. And the only way to end it? Step back into the shadows she barely escaped… before she becomes the next victim.

PROLOGUE

I took one hand off the wheel to flip off the "Welcome to Ennis" sign as I sped past it, my middle finger standing tall in the late evening sunlight.

Dramatic? Maybe. Petty? *Absolutely.* But after everything this town had put me through, it felt earned.

I cracked open the Red Bull tucked between my thighs and took a long sip, the sickly-sweet bite of artificial energy burning down my throat. The rock playlist I had blasting—heavy on the *Green Day* and *Metallica*—wasn't doing much to drown out the voice in my head reminding me that this wasn't just a visit.

I was *moving back.*

To Ennis.

A town I'd spent my entire life trying to get the *hell* away from.

I tightened my grip on the steering wheel, my fingers aching slightly from the effort. It was a habit now — clenching my hands when they started to tremble, trying to force them *steady.*

Didn't work, but I did it anyway.

I exhaled through my nose, forcing myself to focus on the stretch of highway ahead of me. The familiar roads, the endless fields and forests, the distant outline of town creeping closer in the haze of the setting sun.

This wasn't forever.

Just a pit stop.

A temporary detour until I figured out what the hell came *next.*

Because my old life? *That* was over.

I'd spent the last eight years building a career I loved. Busting my ass through school, through training, through the endless nights of working crime scenes in Chicago, chasing the high of piecing together the worst moments of someone's life and finding a way to make it *make sense*.

And then, in a matter of *seconds*, it was all gone.

One bullet to the back.

Two shaky, unsteady hands.

This goddamn *tremor* that I couldn't control, without the help of drugs.

I'd tried to push through it, to pretend that it didn't matter—that I could *compensate* for the way my hands refused to cooperate, for the way my fingers fumbled with the camera, for the way my entire body betrayed me at the worst possible moments.

But I knew.

And worse—so did everyone else.

I could still see the pity in my supervisor's eyes when she sat me down and *gently* suggested early retirement. Could still hear the *careful* way my coworkers started talking to me, like I was some fragile thing that might break apart at any second. And the cover-up. They wanted me out to cover up how badly that setup went. They wanted me out of there so I would stop being a constant reminder of how bad it all got fucked up.

So, I left.

Packed up my shit, signed the papers, and turned in my gun before they could officially take it from me.

And now?

Now, I was heading *home*.

Back to the place I swore I'd never come back to.

Back to the people I hadn't seen in years, to the town that would never stop feeling *haunted*, to the town so small it practically *choked* the life out of you.

I could already feel the walls closing in.

I took another long sip of Red Bull, letting the caffeine settle in my veins, pretending like it might actually help.

It wouldn't.

But at least it was something.

The road into Ennis stretched ahead; the old pavement cracked and empty except for the occasional truck speeding by. My hands tightened on the wheel as I drove, the hum of the engine steady beneath me. I shouldn't be focusing on the case, on the mess I was leaving behind, pissed that it had all gone cold, but my mind kept drifting—back to the case, and back to a time before I ever held a badge, before I ever knew what it was like to step onto a real crime scene.

✝

The lecture hall smelled like old textbooks and stale coffee. I sat near the front, my notebook open but untouched. The crime scene photo projected on the screen made my fingers twitch, a shiver running down my spine. It was always the same—the first glance was fine, but then the flashes would come, amplified anytime by eyes closed, even a blink. Disjointed images, like pieces of a film reel, flickered too fast for me to catch.

Breathe. Keep your face neutral. No one can know.

"Classic overkill," Professor Dawes said, tapping the laser pointer against the victim's torso on the screen. "The wounds tell us more about the killer than the victim. What does this pattern suggest?"

A few murmurs from the class. A chair shuffled behind me.

"Crime of passion," someone in the back answered.

"Possibly. But look here." Dawes clicked to the next slide, zooming in on the body. My vision blurred, my stomach rolling. The light felt too bright, too sharp, like a spotlight burning into my skull.

And then it happened.

I saw it. Not the photo. Not the dead woman on the screen. But the moment it happened. The murder flashed behind my eyelids. A shadowed figure stands over the victim. The metallic glint of a blade. The way the blood sprayed, hot and red, coating his hands.

I flinched. Just a little. Just enough.

"Brooks?"

My head snapped up. Professor Dawes was watching me expectantly.

Shit.

"I—uh—" I swallowed. My throat felt raw. The taste of copper lingered on my tongue, even though it wasn't real.

Another chair creaks behind me.

"It's not passion," I managed, clearing my throat. "It's control. He didn't just kill her—he staged her." I pointed to the way the body was positioned, legs straightened, arms placed just so. "He wasn't in a frenzy. He was careful. Intentional."

Dawes gave a nod of approval. "Good eye."

I exhaled slowly, forcing myself to take notes, trying to shake off the lingering unease.

A light elbow nudged my arm.

"Damn, Brooks," Joseph whispered from the seat beside me, a grin tugging at his lips. "You always gotta show the rest of us up?"

I huffed a laugh, though it came out a little shaky. "Hardly."

He tilted his head, studying me. Unlike the others who were caught up in the lecture, he actually seemed to notice something was off.

"You good?"

I hesitated. Joseph and I weren't exactly close, but we'd worked together a few times—group projects, late-night study sessions in the library, that one time we grabbed coffee before an exam when we both looked like we hadn't slept in days. He was one of the few people in class who wasn't overly competitive or constantly trying to one-up everyone else. He was just… normal. A little quiet but easy to be around.

"Yeah," I said finally. "Just spaced out for a second."

Joseph nodded like he believed me, though there was a flicker of something uncertain in his expression. But then he smirked, shifting back in his chair.

"Well, if I ever get murdered, I want you on the case. You'd have it solved in five minutes."

I rolled my eyes. "Let's aim for neither of us getting murdered, how about that?"

"Fair deal."

He grinned before turning his attention back to the professor, and I let out another breath, relieved to have the moment pass unnoticed by the rest of the class.

But the flashes were getting worse. More frequent. And sooner or later, someone was going to notice.

Now, years later, driving toward Ennis, I couldn't shake the thought that maybe someone already had.

CHAPTER ONE

Nothing ever happened in this town.

Somehow, in the past two years, I've demoted myself from big-city undercover detective to small-town babysitter. I'd traded dead bodies and drug rings for stolen shopping carts and speeding tickets.

And it pissed me off some days. I came here to slow down, sure. But not stop. I felt like I was in a constant standstill.

"Brennan, this coffee pot is officially busted," I said, watching as my best friend—and my boss—walked through the front door of the sheriff's office.

"Then fix it, Jett," he shot back without looking up, disappearing into his office and slamming the door behind him.

I blinked. Well, damn.

"Don't take that personally," Skyla said, stepping inside right behind him.

She handed me a coffee, a paper cup from the café down the street, like she'd somehow predicted the machine in the office would die today. I took it without question, muttering a half-assed thanks as I peeled back the lid.

"He seems pleasant," I observed dryly, taking a sip.

Skyla shrugged. "I have a feeling he's going to be like that for a few days."

She hesitated, like she wasn't sure if she should continue, but I waited her out.

Finally, she sighed. "His sister just moved back to town."

I raised a brow. "And that's a problem?"

Skyla huffed a quiet laugh, shaking her head. "Let's just say, if you think Brennan's a headache, you haven't seen anything yet."

That caught my interest.

I knew Brennan had a sister—he'd mentioned her in passing—but in the months we'd been friends, he'd never said much about her. I wasn't even sure he'd told me her name, just that she'd been working in Chicago.

Now, suddenly, she was back, and judging by Brennan's mood, he wasn't thrilled about it.

Interesting.

I was about to ask more, but the phone on Skyla's desk rang, yanking her attention away. She snatched it up, speaking in her usual no-nonsense tone.

The rest of the morning passed in a blur of routine calls, mostly petty nonsense that barely warranted a report. A noise complaint from old Mrs. Teller, who claimed her new neighbors were throwing a "rock concert" at noon. A minor fender bender outside the grocery store. A teenager was caught shoplifting a pack of gum.

Nothing serious. Nothing exciting.

By the time noon rolled around, I was tempted to call it a day. But instead, I found myself at the diner, picking at a plate of fries while Skyla and I swapped stories about past cases—most of them from my time in New York, since she seemed to like hearing about the chaos of the city. Brennan, still brooding, sat at the counter, absently stirring a cup of coffee but not drinking it.

I watched him for a minute before turning back to Skyla. "So, this sister of his. She as much fun as he is?"

Skyla smirked. "Oh, Brooks is way worse."

I raised a brow. "Brooks?"

She nodded. "Brooke, Brooklyn, technically. But everyone's called her Brooks since we were kids."

I took a sip of my drink, considering that.

"So, she's trouble?"

Skyla laughed. "You have no idea."

Before I could press for details, my radio crackled. A routine check-in from one of the deputies patrolling the outskirts of town. I listened absently, but nothing sounded urgent. Just another slow night in a slow town.

I sighed, stretching back in my chair. "Remind me why I left the city?"

Skyla grinned. "Because you were tired of getting shot at."

"Right," I muttered. "Good times." But that was maybe only half the reason.

The first time I thought about leaving New York, it had been just a passing thought—something that flickered through my mind during another late night at my desk, watching my phone light up with a text from Michelle.

Home late again?

Yeah. Don't wait up.

She didn't respond after that. She rarely did anymore.

At first, she'd tried. *We* had tried. We made time where we could, stole weekends away when our schedules aligned, and promised that *next month would be easier*.

But next month never *was* easier.

One day, I looked up and realised I barely knew the woman I'd married.

So, I quit.

Walked into my captain's office, turned in my papers, and went home to surprise her—*to fix things*.

Only to find out there was nothing *left* to fix.

"I thought it was the job," she had admitted, standing in the kitchen with her arms crossed, her ring still on her finger but barely worn in anymore. "But I was just using that as an excuse."

I stared at her, uncomprehending. "What?"

Her shoulders sagged. "I just… stopped loving you, Jett."

That was it.

No big moment. No affair.

Just a quiet, slow death of something that was supposed to last forever.

I had never been good at standing still.

So, I ran.

Took the first job that would get me as far away from New York as possible.

Which is how I ended up here—chasing down farm animals, breaking up bar fights, and refereeing grocery store disputes in a town that didn't need me.

The sound of two old ladies screaming at each other over a shopping cart made me wonder, *not for the first time*, if I'd completely lost my mind moving here.

"She took it right out of my hands!" one of them huffed, jabbing a bony finger at the other.

"It was *empty!*" the accused shot back. "I thought she changed her mind!"

I pinched the bridge of my nose, inhaled slowly, then exhaled even slower. "Ladies, I'm sure we can find another cart—"

"I *don't want* another cart!" the first woman snapped. "I want *my* cart."

I resisted the urge to look up at the sky and ask why the hell I was being punished.

This was my life now.

Not homicide. Not organised crime. Not anything that required the years of experience I'd built in New York.

Just shopping cart disputes and speeding tickets.

I sighed, running a hand over my jaw. "Alright," I muttered. "Which one of you wants to press charges? Anyone?"

Both women immediately scoffed.

"Well, *not* when you put it like that," one grumbled.

"Good," I muttered. "Then sort it out and don't call me about it again."

I turned and walked back to my truck, ignoring their bickering as I climbed into the driver's seat.

As soon as the door shut, I slumped back against the headrest, sighing.

What the hell was I doing here?

This wasn't my life. This wasn't what I was *supposed* to be doing.

And yet, here I was.

Because running away had been easier than facing reality.

I scrubbed a hand down my face, my fingers gripping the steering wheel tighter than necessary.

I'd meant to call Michelle before I left New York. *Not to fix things—* not anymore—but just to say goodbye. Maybe to prove to myself that I could.

But I hadn't.

Because some pathetic part of me had still been hoping she'd call *me*.

She didn't.

And now I was in Ennis.

I exhaled, glancing at the clock and back at my desk.

The hours dragged on. Darkness settled over the town, quiet and uneventful. Brennan left first, mumbling something about an early morning. Skyla followed not long after. By midnight, I was alone in the office, flipping through old case files just to pass the time.

Brennan didn't usually set hours for Skyla and me. One of the three of us was almost always at the station or just a phone call away if one of the other cops needed our help. And because I was wedded to my work, I could often be found here late at night.

✝

I must've dozed off at some point because when my phone rang at 4 AM, I jolted awake, my heart hammering. It was Brennan. This couldn't be good.

"They found a body, Jett." Brennan sounded strained, almost distraught. "Murdered." He added, like he couldn't believe the words himself.

I swung my feet off the desk, shaking off the fog of sleep. "Where?"

"Off the main hiking trail in Tall Pines," he said. "Skyla's already there. We need to move."

"I'm on my way." I grabbed my jacket and keys, and I bolted out the door.

The roads leading up to the trailhead were narrow, winding through dense forest. It was the kind of place people came to clear their heads, not to die. My headlights barely cut through the thick mist clinging to the trees as I pulled up beside Brennan's truck.

Skyla stood just beyond the trail entrance, flashlight in hand, her face set in hard lines. She glanced up as we approached, expression unreadable.

"It's bad," she said simply, then turned, leading us into the woods.

The body was just off the trail, crumpled among the fallen leaves. Blood soaked into the earth, dark and glistening under the weak beam of Skyla's flashlight. The victim's face was nearly unrecognisable—whoever had done this had been brutal. This wasn't just a killing. It was rage.

Brennan stood stiff beside me, not looking at the body, arms crossed tightly over his chest. I knew that look. He wasn't just disturbed—he was overwhelmed.

And for good reason. The Ennis Sheriff's Office wasn't built for this. We handled drunk disputes, the occasional break-in. A murder like this? It was beyond our means. No forensic unit, no real crime lab, nothing but a handful of officers who weren't trained for anything like this.

Skyla knew it, too. I saw it in the way she looked at Brennan, jaw tight, like she was preparing for a fight.

"We need help," she said, voice quiet but firm. "You know we do."

Brennan didn't respond right away. His fingers curled into fists at his sides, his entire body tense. "Not her."

Skyla exhaled sharply. "We don't have a choice. You and I both know it."

I frowned, glancing between them. "Who are we talking about?"

Brennan ignored me, staring hard at Skyla. She didn't back down. Whatever silent conversation was happening between them, she was winning.

Finally, he let out a slow breath, his jaw ticking. "Damn it."

Skyla pulled out her phone. "I'm calling her."

CHAPTER TWO

"What?" I grumbled into my phone, barely managing to fish it off my bedside table before it stopped ringing.

"It's Skyla." She announced, like her name hadn't been glaring at me on the screen. "We need your help. Please."

"We?" I doubted Brennan would ask for my help. I grabbed the nearest bottle on my nightstand, hoping for water but finding flat beer instead.

"Pretty sure Brennan knows how to get a hold of me if he needs something."

I was about to hang up when her voice tightened with urgency.

"Please, Brooks. We have a body."

I swore under my breath. "Text me an address."

I ended the call and dug through the overflowing hamper in the corner of my room, pulling out a passable pair of jeans and a flannel to throw over my sleep shirt. No time for coffee. A Diet Coke from the fridge would have to do.

The address was near the hiking trails. Not long before early-morning joggers would be out, trampling over what little evidence there might be.

Nobody dies here. Not like this. Not in a way that requires waking up a semi-retired crime scene investigator at 4 a.m.

"Fuck's sake," I muttered, climbing out of my car. I parked next to Brennan's cruiser at the trailhead, grabbed the toolbox that lived in my trunk, and made my way toward the crime scene tape.

Before I could duck under, a uniformed officer put a hand up, like he was about to question why I was here as if we hadn't gone to high school together.

"Fuck off, Smit," I said, ignoring his attempt to stop me. I flashed my old, expired, useless badge from my back pocket just to shut him up and pushed forward.

Brennan, Skyla, and a tall officer I didn't recognise stood between me and the body.

"Too many people here, Brennan," I said, setting my kit down to pull on a pair of gloves. "Send some of them away."

"Brooks—"

"No, seriously. Too many bodies in a crime scene contaminates evidence. At least push them farther down the trail to keep hikers away." My hands trembled as I struggled with the gloves. I hadn't taken my pills.

"Brooks—"

"I'm fine. I'll take them when I get home. Just clear this area."

"Brooks!"

I looked up, ready to snap at him for raising his voice, but then I saw it—the crack in his expression, the way his weathered face buckled under emotion.

"It's Darby."

Oh.

That part hadn't occurred to me that I might know the body.

I'd taken photos of more crime scenes than I could count, but those bodies had been just that—bodies. Not people I grew up with. Not people I knew.

"There are too many people here, B," I said quietly. "Get them out."

Skyla moved fast, clearing out the extra officers. But the tall one next to Brennan didn't budge. I wasn't in the mood to repeat myself, so I just shot him a glare.

"Detective William Jett." He offered a hand.

I didn't take it. "I didn't ask."

"I used to work homicide in New York."

"And now you're a benchwarmer in this shithole. Congrats. Get out of my crime scene."

"Not your crime scene, sweetheart."

He plucked the glove from my fingers and held it open for me to slip my hand in. I considered smacking him with it instead, but I had a job to do.

I fixed the right lens onto my camera and looped it around my neck. Brennan still hadn't moved.

"B," he called as I stepped past him. "It's not pretty."

"I've seen worse."

And I had. But at that moment, I didn't think I'd ever seen anything that made my stomach turn quite like this.

"Christ, Darby, who did you piss off?" I muttered behind my camera.

Her blonde hair was matted dark with blood from a deep gash along the side of her face. Her clothes were ripped and ruined. One foot twisted unnaturally, missing a shoe. The stab wounds across her torso—those were likely the cause of death. But the shreds down her arms? Post-mortem. The kind of personal, rage-fueled mutilation that came after.

Acid burned the back of my throat. I closed my eyes for a second but immediately snapped them back open when flashes of her final moments played behind my lids.

"Where's Greg?" I asked Brennan, needing the distraction.

"He's trying to find someone to take his kids. Sherry's working the night shift at the hospital."

"Fuck's sake." My right hand twitched, making it hard to steady the camera. "Can't he just bring them?"

"To a crime scene?"

"Dad would've brought us." And look how we turned out.

"Did you need some help?" Jett's voice cut in.

"No, former homicide detective William Jett, I need a fucking medical examiner."

Brennan finally turned toward me, probably about to tell me to play nice with his detective, but his gaze landed on my hands—shaking so badly I could barely grip the camera.

"B," he started.

"I'm fine."

"You can't work like this, Brooks." He sounded like Dad.

"There's a bottle in my car. Glove compartment."

Skyla, who had just returned, was already moving towards where we had parked.

"You have to start taking care of yourself," Brennan said. "This is serious—"

"Listen, I get that you need to focus on something other than Darby's body right now, but I don't need a lecture. I've been doing just fine on my own this past year."

"Oh, have you? Then why'd you move home, Brooks? It wasn't for the job opportunities; that's for damn sure."

"With you as sheriff, seems like there's plenty of work."

"Oh, you would blame this on me—"

"Could you two keep your shit together for one minute?" Skyla whispered harshly as she returned. "How many?" She asked shaking my pill bottle in front of me.

I held up two fingers, and she popped the pills into my mouth before tipping the can of Diet Coke to my lips so I wouldn't contaminate my gloves.

"So sorry, Sheriff," a voice interrupted. Greg. "I got here as soon as I could. What do we have?"

"Female victim- "I started to say but the fucking detective was talking over me, spewing the same information I would've to our ME.

"Who the fuck is this guy anyway?" I asked Skyla in an annoyed tone.

Hearing my voice, Greg turned from Jett to look at me. "Brooks! I didn't know you were back in town." He exclaimed, as if there wasn't a body under our noses right now.

"Are you fucking kidding me, Greg? Do your job."

I went back to work, tuning out whatever incompetence Greg was demonstrating and ignoring whatever bravado the big New York detective was flaunting as he expertly made his way around the scene, almost as deftly as me. Almost. I was immersed in my job, capturing every little bit of potential evidence on camera. But as I finished, I caught the tail end of a conversation.

"I know she's your sister," Jett was saying to Brennan. "But we have to do our due diligence." His sharp features were unreadable in the early dawn light. "I'll question her at the station, and we'll be done."

"Really?" I pulled off my gloves, hands steadier now.

"It's formality."

"You think I killed Darby?"

"It's a little convenient. You've been back a week, and we have our first murder."

"Oh, convenience, is that how they taught you to solve murders in New York? In Chicago, we liked to look at the evidence first."

"I'm not saying you did it, sweetheart."

"Say 'sweetheart' one more time, and I'll show you exactly what it looks like when I murder someone."

Skyla sighed, stepping between us. "Can we focus? We have a murder to solve."

Jett scoffed. I glared. "I couldn't murder her. There isn't enough strength left in my hands to plunge a knife that deeply into someone without their being more evidence of hesitation." And under my breath I added, "Keep pissing me off and I'll try though."

"Come with me, Brooks," Skyla said. "I'm going to go speak to Darby's parents."

"I'm not good at comforting people."

"What a surprise," Jett muttered.

I ignored him, and Skyla and I made our way to my car.

The drive to the Richards' house was too quiet.

Skyla sat in the passenger seat, her fingers tapping against her knee, her shoulders drawn tight. I could tell she was trying to psych herself up, running through the words in her head, figuring out how to deliver them.

I should've volunteered to do it.

But this was her first time handling a murder, and she needed to learn how to do this part too—the part that never got easier.

I tightened my grip on the steering wheel, jaw locked as we turned onto the familiar street. I'd been here before. Not often, but enough.

Darby and I had gone to high school together.

She'd been a year younger, a little quiet, always carrying a book around, always quick to smile. I hadn't known her well, but I *knew* her. Small towns worked like that.

Now she was gone.

And we had to be the ones to tell her parents.

I pulled up in front of the house and killed the engine.

Skyla inhaled sharply. "Okay."

I glanced at her. She looked pale but determined.

"You sure you're good?" I asked.

She nodded quickly. "Yeah. I mean—no, but yeah."

I let out a breath, rubbing my hand over my face. "Take your time. Just be direct."

"Right." She straightened her spine. "Direct."

Neither of us moved.

Then Skyla muttered something under her breath, squared her shoulders, and climbed out of the car.

I followed.

The Richards' house was small, with white paint peeling along the front porch railing. Wind chimes clinked softly in the breeze. The whole place felt still, too peaceful, like the world hadn't gotten the message yet that something terrible had happened.

Skyla knocked twice.

A few seconds later, the door opened, and Mrs. Richards blinked at us, eyes puffy, like she'd been crying *before* she even knew why we were here. Maybe she'd felt it already, the way mothers sometimes did.

She saw me first, recognition flickering through her grief. "Brooks?"

I swallowed hard. "Hi, Mrs. Richards."

Her gaze shifted to Skyla, and her expression twisted with unease. She knew.

She didn't *know*, but she *knew*.

Still, she stepped aside, letting us in.

The living room smelled like cinnamon, like she'd just been baking only last night, as if going through the motions of normal life could stop the inevitable from crashing down.

Mr. Richards sat in his recliner, a newspaper open in his lap. He looked up, his brow furrowing. "What's this about?"

Skyla swallowed, her fingers curling into fists at her sides.

"There's no easy way to say this," she started, her voice steady but too careful. "Darby—" She hesitated, exhaled sharply. "Darby was found this morning."

Mrs. Richards' breath hitched.

Mr. Richards sat forward, newspaper forgotten. "Found?" he repeated.

Skyla nodded, her throat working. "I'm so sorry."

The words barely left her mouth before Mrs. Richards let out a sound that shattered the air—part gasp, part sob. She stumbled back, one hand covering her mouth, the other bracing against the couch like her legs weren't strong enough to hold her up.

Mr. Richards looked between us, his face going pale. "No."

Skyla stood frozen for half a second too long. Then she quickly stepped forward, lowering herself onto the couch beside Mrs. Richards, murmuring something soft.

There were no right words.

Mr. Richards's hands curled into fists. "What happened?"

Skyla hesitated, flicking a glance at me.

I met Mr. Richards' gaze, my voice coming out rougher than I meant. "We're still investigating."

His jaw was clenched. "Someone *did* this?"

I nodded.

His whole body tensed, shoulders shaking as he inhaled sharply.

Mrs. Richards wiped at her face with trembling hands. "She never hurt anybody," she whispered. "Why would someone do this?"

I didn't have an answer for her.

Because I'd been asking myself the same thing.

Skyla took a deep breath, her voice softer now. "We're going to do everything we can to find out who did this."

Mr. Richards' eyes snapped to mine. "You *promise*?"

I held his gaze.

"I promise."

CHAPTER THREE

I was royally fucked.

Skyla trailed in behind Brennan's sister, shutting his office door behind her, leaving us all crammed into the tiny space. Brennan looked like he wanted to be anywhere but here, pacing the narrow gap between his filing cabinet and where Skyla stood, arms crossed, in the corner. He could barely look at his sister. Meanwhile, Brooks stood in front of his desk, eyes fixed on me like I'd better make this worth her time.

I snatched the small plastic evidence bag from Brennan when he passed close enough.

"This was in Darby's mouth." I flattened the bag against the desk so Brooks could read it. "Care to explain?"

Welcome home, Brooks.

Even after reading it a dozen times, the scrawl still felt sinister. Brooks's right hand trembled as she smoothed over the plastic, like she might be able to erase the words if she tried hard enough. She switched the bag into her steadier left hand, staring at it for a long moment.

"'Scuse me." Her voice was quieter than I'd ever heard it. She didn't look at any of us as she moved around the desk, weaving past Skyla and Brennan. "Sorry," she muttered, barely brushing against me as she reached for the desk phone.

She dialed a number and pressed the receiver to her ear. "Can you transfer me to Detective Lynch, please?"

With no regard for personal space, she wedged herself between me and the filing cabinet, her front pressing into my side. She rifled through one of the drawers, then pulled out a half-full bottle of whiskey. The cap came off with her teeth, and she took a long drink. "Caleb? It's me," she said, barely waiting for the call to connect. "My phone's dead. I'm using Brennan's. Listen, I need you to send me some case files."

A muffled voice grumbled on the other end. Brooks took another drink, and this time, both her hands shook—one gripping the bottle, the other clutching the phone.

"He's here." Her voice was ominous, like she was speaking a truth no one wanted to accept.

Brennan and I exchanged glances.

"No, Caleb, I'm very fucking serious. He followed me."

I reached over and hit the speakerphone button. I needed to hear both sides of this conversation.

"-hasn't shown his face in months, Reaper. What's got you all spooked?"

Brooks gripped the whiskey bottle tighter.

"He left me another note. In a dead girl's mouth."

Silence. A chair creaked, then footsteps, followed by the sound of a door shutting on the other end of the line.

"Brooks... arc you one hundred percent sure it's him?"

She stared at the note again, her jaw tightening. "Yes."

A long exhale. "Shit."

"Please, Caleb. Send me the files."

"I'll do what I can, Reaper. Lock your doors, okay?"

Brooks hung up, cursed under her breath, and took another pull from the bottle. I looked over at Brennan, who was pale and gripping the edge of his desk like it might be the only thing keeping him upright.

Yeah, he hadn't known.

And now I had a sinking feeling I was in way over my head.

"I think you need to explain what the hell is going on," I finally said.

Brooks blinked, like she'd forgotten we were even there. Her gaze flicked to me, then away just as fast. She stepped back like the two inches of space between us was offensive.

As if this investigation wasn't enough of a headache, now I had the unfortunate realisation that I liked having her this close. I ignored the urge to pull her back.

She exhaled sharply. "Eighteen months ago, we had a serial killer in Chicago. Started with sex workers, then moved on to anyone he could get his hands on. He was inconsistent—always changing weapons, locations, times. Hard to pin down. Then he started leaving notes. For me. The bodies were for me to photograph."

Brennan swore under his breath.

Brooks squeezed her eyes shut for a second, then took another drink, like she was trying to block something out. "Long story short, he found me alone one night. I tried to draw my gun, but not fast enough. I got shot. Lost my job, went through months of PT, moved back here… and now he's followed me."

The room was too quiet.

I should've asked something useful, but all I could think was: *If the Chicago PD couldn't stop this guy, what chance did this department have?*

Still, I had to try.

And looking at Brooks, exhausted and furious in front of me, I *wanted* to try.

†

Brennan had gone home hours ago, dragging his furious little sister with him. Skyla had knocked off about half an hour later.

I should've left too, but sleep wasn't happening tonight.

I sat at my desk, staring at the report in front of me, barely reading it. Something gnawed at me. Something I couldn't shake.

I grabbed my phone and dialed a familiar number.

"It's midnight here, Jett," came a groggy voice on the other end. "Which means it's, what, ten o'clock there? You're working past your bedtime again."

"Like you're one to judge, Neil."

There was a pause before I spoke again. "I need some information."

A sigh. "Who died?"

"Darby Richards. But that's not what I need. I need you to dig into someone for me."

Another pause. "Okay… who?"

"Brooks Meeker."

Neil made a noise of recognition. "Isn't that—"

"It is," I cut him off. "It's a long story."

"Oh, is she a suspect?" More typing came from his end.

I hesitated. No. She had convinced me of that. So why was I still digging?

"I'm not sure yet," I lied. "Just doing my due diligence."

"Okay, let's see…" More typing. "Brooklyn Elizabeth Meeker, twenty-seven years old, born and raised in your little town, Ennis. Daddy was sheriff, now consults for public safety in D.C. Big brother took over as sheriff after he retired. Mother died in childbirth. Graduated early, honors student. Flew through the academy, fast-tracked CSI training. Worked for Chicago PD for two years before being let go for failing a physical."

A beat.

"Any details on that injury?" I asked.

Neil whistled. "Gunshot. In the back. Jesus, I'm surprised she can still walk."

I clenched my jaw. I already knew that part.

"Anything in the record?"

"Huh." More typing. "That's weird." Click. Click. Click. "The entire record is wiped."

I gripped the phone tighter.

"Oh, for fuck's sake."

BROOKS

I sat on the cold garage floor, my back against a half-unpacked box labeled *SHIT I DON'T NEED BUT REFUSE TO THROW OUT*, staring at the mess I'd made. Files, crime scene photos, a hastily drawn timeline—all spread out in front of me like I could force the pieces together if I just stared hard enough.

The laptop screen cast a pale glow in the dim garage, highlighting the records I'd pulled—Darby's finances, her social media, old emails. I'd scraped through every part of her life that wasn't locked behind a damn paywall, hoping to find something, anything, that linked her to Chicago. To him.

Nothing.

No distant relatives. No trips. No weird connections.

And yet—she was killed the way he used to kill them. The same level of overkill, the same precision, the same fucking signature. Stabbing and a note, his favourite.

My stomach twisted.

Because the only thing that connected Darby Richards to that monster was me.

I let out a dry, humorless laugh. *Jesus Christ. Am I just a fucking bad omen now?*

I reached for my coffee, barely remembering when I made it. Cold. Of course. Everything in my life was half-finished, half-functional, half-falling apart. I needed something stronger, but every beer bottle out here was empty, and my whiskey bottle was still on the counter inside, and I wasn't about to go back in there just to get judgmental looks from my reflection.

My phone buzzed.

I ignored it.

It buzzed again.

I groaned and snatched it off the ground, my annoyance only slightly outweighing my dread.

Brennan.

I debated letting it go to voicemail, but at the last second, I swiped to answer.

"You home?" His voice was tight. Stressed.

"Why? You coming over to yell at me some more?"

A pause. Too long.

Then, softer than I expected: "No."

That threw me.

Brennan didn't just *not* argue with me. That was like the sun refusing to rise.

I shifted, pushing some papers aside. "Yeah. I'm home."

"I'll be there in five."

And then he hung up before I could ask why.

I stared at the screen, then at my notes, then at the empty doorway like I could somehow get an answer from the air.

Instead, I shoved the laptop shut and waited.

Brennan stood in the garage doorway, hands braced on his hips, looking like he'd rather be anywhere but here. His eyes flicked to the floor, taking in the papers, the photos, the chaos. His mouth pressed into a hard line.

I leaned against the tables in the middle of the room, crossing my arms. "Well? Go ahead. Say whatever lecture you rehearsed in the car."

He exhaled sharply through his nose. "I don't have a lecture, Brooks."

"Bullshit."

His jaw tightened. "I don't." He dragged a hand down his face, looking absolutely *wrecked*. "I just… I don't know what to do with you."

The words shouldn't have hit as hard as they did.

I looked away, picking at the peeling label on a nearby beer bottle. "You don't have to do anything with me, B. I can handle myself." I then pointed to myself. "Big girl. Remember?"

"Yeah?" He let out a humorless laugh, gesturing to the mess crime scenes spread at my feet. And then to the empty alcohol bottles cluttering the garage. "Because this looks like you're handling things real well."

I clenched my jaw, shoving past the sting in my chest. "Darby had no connection to Chicago." My voice came out sharper than I intended. I pushed off the table and stepped closer. "None. But the way she was killed? The way she was left? It's the same pattern."

Brennan frowned. "You're saying it's the serial killer from Chicago."

"I'm saying that or… nope, that's what I'm saying."

His frown deepened, the muscle in his jaw twitching. "Then why, Darby?"

I didn't answer right away. Instead, I bent down, picking up a crime scene photo I'd been staring at for the past hour.

The bloody pile of flesh that used to be a blonde-haired, beautiful, kind girl..

I tossed the photo at his chest. He caught it, barely.

"That's why. He got our attention, didn't he?" I wanted to scream into a void, not at my brother. "His victims *never* made sense, Brennan. Everything was to make a scene." I gestured widely at the photos around me. "A literal scene."

Brennan stared at the photos on the ground, his fingers flexing in and out of a fist like he wanted to crush something. His throat bobbed as he swallowed hard.

"I need you to be honest with me, Brooks." His voice was tight, controlled. "Is there any chance you know who did this?"

I let out a sharp, humorless laugh. "Yeah, B. That's the problem. I do. I know exactly who he is and he's a fucking ghost."

His jaw tightened. "You're saying—"

"It's him." The words tasted like iron, bitter and sharp in my mouth. "I'm certain, Brennan."

Brennan went still. "Brooks—"

"I know how it sounds, okay? But I spent months staring at his crime scenes. I *know* his work. He's here." I gestured wildly at the photos on the floor. "He's here," I repeated.

Brennan shook his head. "That doesn't make sense. He disappeared. No arrests, no new bodies—"

"He stopped because I left my job. I wasn't there to witness his work anymore." The realisation hit me even as I said it. I exhaled sharply. "That's what this is. He wasn't *gone*; he was waiting. And now that I'm back here—"

"He's making sure you remember him."

"He's making sure I know, wherever I go, he follows."

I met Brennan's gaze, and for the first time since this all started, I saw the flicker of fear in his eyes.

He believed me.

I swallowed, my throat tight. "You need to prepare for the fact that this won't stop with Darby."

Brennan ran a hand down his face, exhaling hard. "Christ."

For a long moment, neither of us spoke. The garage felt too small, the air too heavy.

Finally, he looked at me again, jaw set. "You're not investigating this."

I scoffed. "Oh, so we're back to this bullshit? What did former homicide detective William Jett tell you to say that?"

"I mean it, Brooks." His voice was edged with something I didn't hear often—fear. "This guy *fixates*. He targeted you in Chicago, and now he's escalated. You being involved is exactly what he *wants*."

I felt my fingers curl into fists. "You really think I can just sit this one out?"

"I think you *have to*."

I shook my head. "I can't."

Brennan swore under his breath, looking like he wanted to punch something. "You are the most stubborn—" He cut himself off, exhaling sharply. "Fine. But stay safe. No one will be able to do their job if we're all too worried about you being reckless."

I smirked. "No promises."

He muttered something under his breath but didn't fight me on it. Instead, he scrubbed a hand through his hair and gestured to the crime scene photos.

"I'll put more officers on night patrols. And I'll warn people to be careful, but we can't tell the town we have a serial killer on the loose unless we have actual proof."

"We *do* have proof." I gestured to the note.

"We have a *theory*," he corrected. "And I need more than that before I set this town on fire."

I clenched my jaw but didn't argue.

Brennan sighed, rubbing his temples. "Look, just—be careful. Keep your doors locked. And for God's sake, try to lay low."

I snorted. "Yeah. Sure."

Brennan shot me a look, clearly not buying it, but he didn't push it further. Instead, he muttered something about getting some sleep and headed for the door.

I watched him go, waiting for the sound of his car pulling out of the driveway before exhaling slowly.

He was wrong.

Laying low wasn't an option.

Because the Phantom wasn't just killing again.

He was killing *for me*.

And that meant I was the only one who could stop him.

CHAPTER FOUR

Despite the shower and fresh clothes, I still felt worn. Ragged, even. Two hours of sleep at my desk didn't do much for me, but I'd gotten up, gone home, showered and changed, and was now on my way back to the station—with a stop to make first.

It wasn't hard to figure out where Brooks was living. Houses rarely went on the market in this town, and when they did, it was the biggest news since the last county fair. God, small towns were weird.

At the end of a cul-de-sac, on the last subdivision before the town gave way to endless forests, sat a small brown house built against the rock face. Trees flanked it, shielding it from the neighbors. Her car was parked outside the single-car garage. I took the steep walk-up along the side, past the garage, and knocked loudly.

No answer.

I knocked again.

The door swung open on the side of the garage below me, and Brooks stood there, eyes heavy, mouth already curled into a scowl. "Can I fucking help you?"

For reasons I couldn't explain—not logically, at least—that angry little bite in her voice sent something hot through me.

I shoved those thoughts aside, locked them down behind a neutral expression, and jogged back down the stairs to where she stood at the garage entrance. She looked me over like she was debating whether to slam the door in my face. Then, with an annoyed sigh, she yanked it open wider.

I stepped inside and immediately understood why her car wasn't parked in here. Boxes lined the walls, stacked four deep, floor to ceiling. In the center, two plastic folding tables sat pushed together, covered in papers, empty beer bottles, and scribbled notes. Behind her, a whiteboard bloomed with a chaotic mess of black ink—bullet points, arrows, frantic writing.

"You have thirty seconds to tell me why you're here, former New York homicide detective William Jett." She crossed her arms over an oversized T-shirt, her stance defensive.

And for some fucking reason my brain reverted back to being a caveman and was temporarily derailed by the unmistakable fact that she was not wearing a bra. I redirected my attention to the grocery list being weighed down on the table by a beer bottle.

- Bread
- Red Bull
- Those sticky notepad things
- Eggs

"You know, you can just call me Jett like everyone else. Less of a mouthful." I barely stopped myself from saying what else I had that was a mouthful. Something told me she'd punch me, and something else told me I might like it.

She arched a brow. "Tick tock."

"Why'd you lie about how you got shot?"

No flicker of surprise. Just a narrowing of her eyes.

"Because it's not relevant." She turned away, moving to the table to gather up the bottles like she didn't want me seeing them.

"Was it him that shot you?"

That made her stop. She spun to face me, setting her shoulders—something she always seemed to do around me, like it made her feel taller. "Yes." But it sounded like a lie.

"If you had your weapon drawn, why was your back turned to him?"

A flicker of something in her gaze, sharp and assessing. Like she was reading my interrogation script off my face.

"My back wasn't to *him*." Her voice was quieter now. "It's not relevant."

I studied her for a moment, debating how much more I could pry before she shut down completely. She looked like she'd slept as little as I had. Her hair was gathered into a messy knot at the base of her neck; her shirt was wrinkled like she'd rolled out of bed and grabbed whatever was closest. Her eyes were dark and heavy with something beyond exhaustion, but I noticed—her hands weren't shaking. Not as much as they had been the last time I saw her.

"I need to know what happened to decide if it's relevant." And I needed to know why the case file was wiped from the system.

"If I don't tell you now, are you going to find a way to turn this into formal questioning where I have to tell you?"

I shrugged.

She let out a sharp breath, her jaw ticking in irritation. "Fine. Everything else I told you was true—there are files to back it up." A hollow laugh. "Or at least, there were." She gestured vaguely to herself. "A few senior detectives thought it would be a good idea to draw him out. Give him what he wanted."

A sick feeling settled in my gut.

"They thought it would be best if I wasn't aware of the plan," she continued. "That way, I wouldn't give up the ruse." A bitter smirk. "Sent me to a scene alone. At night. Missed when they tried to take him down."

She turned around, reaching for the back of her shirt, pulling it up just enough to expose the raised, pink scar between her spine and right shoulder blade.

"He got away. They covered their asses—fudged paperwork to make it look like the plan never existed. Put me on desk duty when I got out of the hospital, then essentially forced me to leave when they got scared people would start asking questions. Figured that must've scared him off, too. No activity. No bodies." She pulled her shirt back down and turned to face me again. "Until yesterday."

"That's—" I cut myself off, too pissed to finish the sentence.

She shrugged like it was old news. Like she was over it.

I wasn't.

"Anyway," she said, "your time's up, and you've overstayed your welcome."

I stepped into her space, crowding her against the table. Partly because I wanted to make what I was about to say very fucking clear. Partly because I was a selfish bastard.

"Don't touch this case anymore, okay, spitfire?"

She lifted her chin. "Oh, have I graduated from sweetheart?"

She didn't back down. Instead, she squared her shoulders, closing what little space was left between us. The fabric of her T-shirt barely grazed my chest. Not nearly enough contact to satisfy the need clawing at me.

"Don't tell me what to do, Jett." She spat out my name like it tasted bad.

"I'm serious. Stay out of it." My hands clenched at my sides, itching to tangle in her hair.

"Or else what? Are you threatening me?"

Did I sound threatening? Maybe. Maybe that would make her listen. But the fire in her eyes said otherwise. She wasn't scared of me. She was pissed.

"If I was, would you listen?" My voice dropped lower, barely more than a breath.

The glint in her eyes told me all I needed to know.

She lifted her hands, pressing them to my chest like she meant to push me away. But I caught her wrists, her pulse fluttering against my fingers. There—just the faintest tremor in her palms.

"Just trying to keep you safe and do my job, okay?"

Despite how much it fucking killed me, I let her go and turned for the door.

A few muttered words followed in my wake. Something along the lines of, "Fucking asshole."

I grinned.

†

By the time I made it to the station, Brennan was already in his office.

Which had never happened before.

Skyla was right behind me, and she caught what I was staring at. "Yeah," she started, a little grimly. "He's pretty certain this is the end of the world. Or at least the end of quaint little Ennis."

I couldn't dispute that fact, unfortunately. Quaint little Ennis would always be tainted by this murder now. And if we couldn't catch this fucker, the town would be haunted by it forever.

If I couldn't catch this fucker, I'd be haunted forever too.

The phone rang on the desk next to us, the sharp sound cutting through the tense silence. My hand shot out before Skyla's did. "Ennis Sheriff's Office."

"This is Mayor Little's office. She would like to speak with Sheriff Meeker, please."

Oh, this was going to go over well. Without a word, I transferred the call to Brennan's office. Through the glass, I watched him stare at the blinking light on his phone for a long moment, jaw tight, fingers flexing against the desk like he was debating letting it go to voicemail. At the last second, he snatched up the receiver, his expression darkening as he muttered a terse, "Sheriff Meeker."

Skyla and I exchanged a glance, then turned our attention back to him. He was pacing now, as far as the corded phone would let him in that tiny, cluttered office, looking like a caged animal ready to bite the first hand that reached for him.

I folded my arms. "Ten bucks says he hangs up on her."

Skyla smirked. "Nah. Five says he just grunts his way through it and slams the phone down."

A minute later, Brennan did exactly that. I sighed and stepped inside.

"She's freaking out," he huffed, gesturing toward the phone like it had personally offended him.

"Naturally." I leaned against the doorframe, crossing one ankle over the other. "First killer on the loose in Ennis? That'll do it."

"She's breathing down my neck about it," he went on, running a hand over his face. "Worried we'll have to cancel the Halloween Fest if we don't catch the killer before then. Says holding the festival would be like rounding up the town for slaughter. And, of course, it would be my fault if we canceled and flushed all that money down the drain."

He scoffed, but there was something beneath his frustration—something heavier. Exhaustion. Pressure. The weight of knowing that, right now, he wasn't just responsible for upholding the law. He was responsible for the town's sense of safety. For their belief that life in Ennis could go back to normal.

The problem was it couldn't. Not until we caught whoever did this.

I studied my friend for a moment, then pushed off the doorframe. "So, what's the plan, Sheriff?"

Brennan exhaled sharply. "The plan?"

"Yeah. Do we lock this town down? Cancel the festival? Send people door to door with pitchforks?" I shrugged. "Because if we don't have a plan, people are going to start making their own. And that's usually when things get messy."

His jaw ticked. He knew I was right. "We'll call a meeting. Update the town. Make it clear we're handling this."

Skyla leaned in. "And if we don't catch the guy by Halloween?"

Brennan didn't answer right away. He just stared at the map pinned to the wall behind his desk, his fingers drumming against his thigh. Finally, he muttered, "Then we have bigger problems than a damn festival."

CHAPTER FIVE

My garage smelled like cold concrete and stale beer, but all I could smell was blood.

My blood.

I squeezed my eyes shut, pressing the heels of my palms against them, but it didn't help. The memories came anyway, slamming into me like a freight train.

I wasn't in Ennis.

I was in Chicago.

It was raining that night—because, of course, it was. The kind of rain that turned streets slick and made the city feel claustrophobic, water pooling in gutters, neon lights reflected on wet pavement.

I was on an assignment I hadn't even wanted. A supposed lead—some anonymous tip about a possible connection to the Phantom.

I should have known better.

The alley was empty when I got there, the damp air thick with the scent of rot and gasoline. I kept my back against the brick, fingers curled around my gun, my pulse steady. I was alone—apparently the rookie was good for all the shitty jobs.

But something felt off.

A rusted fire escape loomed above me, water dripping from the metal. The street behind me was quiet, too quiet for a city that never really slept.

Then—movement.

A shadow peeled away from the darkness.

I raised my weapon, breath tight in my chest. "Chicago PD! Hands where I can see them!"

The shadow stilled. And then I saw it—the glint of a blade.

Not a gun.

A knife.

The air shifted, and suddenly the alley was too small, too closed in. But before I could react—

A gunshot.

Pain exploded through my back, white-hot and searing, stealing the breath from my lungs.

My body locked up, then buckled, knees slamming into the wet pavement. The world tilted, the alley spinning sideways as my gun clattered from my grasp.

Not from the Phantom's knife.

From a bullet.

From behind me.

I gasped, trying to suck in air, but my body wasn't listening, my fingers twitching uselessly in the puddle beneath me.

There was shouting. Chaos.

I barely registered the voices—orders being screamed, tires screeching on wet pavement.

And the Phantom?

Gone.

Boots pounded against the pavement, and then someone was kneeling beside me, hands pressing hard against the wound.

"Stay with me, Meeker," a voice muttered—one I recognized, but my brain was too sluggish to process it. "We've got an officer down! Get medical!"

I tried to focus, to make sense of what had happened.

I had been shot.

From behind.

I wasn't even facing my attacker.

Which meant—

I sucked in a sharp breath, agony ripping through me. Someone cursed and pressed down harder, but the world was already darkening at the edges.

Somewhere in the distance, sirens wailed.

I tried to hold on.

But then everything went black.

The memory slammed into me so hard I nearly doubled over.

My breath came in short, sharp gasps.

I pressed a hand against my lower back—phantom pain, a reminder of how close I'd come to dying in that alley.

I hadn't even seen the shooter.

But I knew it hadn't been the Phantom.

And I knew the truth, even if no one would say it out loud.

"Need me to fly over there?" Caleb asked. He had been quiet on the phone for so long I had figured he had hung up or fallen asleep, but his voice brought me right back into the present and away from my nightmares.

I had only called to ask about the files—what he had managed to pull together for me—but his offer told me everything I needed to know about what was in them. It was surprisingly a lot, considering how badly that case had gone to shit. I figured the brass would've been reluctant to let Caleb share just how spectacularly we had fucked up.

Now, Caleb was more concerned about the competency levels of the officers here.

"What could you do down here that I couldn't?" I muttered, scanning the pages scattered across my table like I hadn't spent months pouring over them already. "You don't have any jurisdiction here. You'd be just as useless as I am."

"Why stabbing?" I asked, mostly to myself.

"Why stabbing? Why shooting? Why suffocating? Why killing? Why you?"

"I know, I know all that." I blew a breath upward, pushing a stray hair from my face. "But why does he keep reverting back to stabbing? First murder: stabbing. Between every new method: stabbing. I move home—"

A knock at the garage door cut me off. I swore under my breath.

"Hang on, Caleb."

I left my phone on the table and yanked the door open. "What the fuck do you want now?"

Jett took up the entire doorway, leaning against the frame like he was waiting for an invitation.

"Just driving by," he said smoothly. "Saw your light on. Thought I'd check in."

"Driving by?" I snorted. "I live at a dead end."

I considered slamming the door in his face, but I figured it might go quicker if I just let him in. I left it open and went back to the table, picking up my phone.

"Caleb, I'll call you back," I said. "I have to entertain a home invader disguised as a concerned detective."

"Okay, lock your doors," Caleb reminded me like always. Then, after a pause: "Be safe, Reaper."

Jett's head tilted at the name, but his attention had already shifted to the whiteboard covered in crime scene photos.

"Reaper?" he echoed.

"When a serial killer murders fourteen people for you, Reaper ends up being an appropriate nickname." I paused, glancing at the photos. "Fifteen people," I corrected.

"Jesus." He exhaled sharply. "Chicago sent this down pretty fast. Why didn't it go straight to the sheriff?"

"Because this isn't from Chicago." My voice felt distant. My gaze locked onto the photos, the stark black-and-white stills of mutilated bodies. "These are my personal records."

I knew what was coming before it hit, but I couldn't stop it. The flashes.

Suzanna—the first victim. A quick stab to the gut. He walked up to her in the alley, the knife hidden in his pocket. Close enough to touch. He pulled it out. The blade sank into her flesh—shallow, messy. He was scared. A quick stab, then he ran. She fell, clutching the wound, trying to—

"You good, Spitfire?"

Jett's voice cut through the haze, yanking me back.

I turned to find him watching me, moving closer. His dark eyes held something sharp, something unreadable. I'd be the world's biggest liar if I said I didn't love the way he looked at me—like I was prey, like my defenses meant nothing to him.

"I'm fine." I snapped, dragging the sleeves of my too-big sweater over my goosebumped arms. My hands were still shaking. "Are you going to tell me why you're here? For real this time?"

His expression hardened. "I know Darby's parents asked you to investigate. Skyla told me."

I exhaled through my nose. "And?"

"I know you've been going around digging into this." His tone shifted, low and menacing. He took another step forward, backing me toward the folding table. I was starting to think this was the only move he had.

"I'm a licensed private investigator now. I'm not doing anything wrong." I crossed my arms, defiant. The movement pressed them against his lower ribs. I almost felt the way his jaw ticked at the contact.

"I told you to stay off this case."

"And what made you think I'd listen?"

"I figured you had an ounce of common sense."

"Clearly, you figured wrong."

His hand flexed at his side, but he didn't move away.

"You're the center of some demented obsession," he said darkly. "If you aren't careful, you're going to wind up like one of them." He jerked his chin toward the board.

"Looking into suspects doesn't make me any more likely to end up dead than sitting around and waiting for it."

His body flinched—an instinctive, full-body reaction—like the thought of my death physically rattled him.

I should've said something, but my mouth had gone dry. His stare lingered too long, too heavy. It made my pulse skip. I could feel the heat radiating off of him, feel the tension humming between us, sharp and unspoken.

Then, our phones rang simultaneously.

Jett stepped back first, answering his. I grabbed mine.

"What?" I snapped.

"Can you—" Brennan's voice cracked. He cleared his throat four times before he could finish. "Can you come here?"

"Where, Brennan?" A sharp edge crept into my voice. I glanced up. Jett was finishing his call, his expression darkening.

"The lake."

My stomach dropped.

"There's a body."

His voice wavered, unsteady.

I swallowed hard. "Be there soon."

I didn't wait for Jett. I jogged up the stairs to the house, grabbing my kit from the living room before detouring to the kitchen. Pills first. I shook two into my palm, the familiar weight of the orange bottle grounding me. Toolbox in one hand, can of Red Bull in the other, I made my way back down to the garage.

Jett was still there, leaning against his truck.

"You're still here," I noted.

"Thought I'd give you a ride." His gaze flicked to my hands. He didn't trust me to drive.

I considered arguing, but we didn't have time.

The inside of Jett's truck was exactly what I expected—black interior, spotless, like he'd just driven it off the lot. Of course, he kept it pristine. The man probably ironed his socks.

"Here."

Before I could protest, he snatched the Red Bull from my hand, using his index finger to pop the tab.

"I can do it myself," I said, snatching it back and using it to take my handful of pills.

"What do you do when no one's around to open shit for you?"

"I manage."

"Right." His tone was flat. "Like I keep watching you manage not to take your meds at all."

I turned to the window, choosing to ignore him.

The parking area by the lake was overflowing with cruisers. The sun was setting, staining the water a deep orange.

Greg had actually shown up on time for once.

Without a word, I climbed out of Jett's truck and slammed the door. Hard.

Jett cringed. Good.

Brennan was bracing himself against his car, staring at the ground like it might anchor him. His hands were shaking.

"Get your shit together," I snapped. "Or get out of here."

Skyla met my eyes. "We don't know who it is."

I flexed my fingers, steady now. The pills were kicking in.

Jett hovered by the shoreline. The body lay half-submerged, the gentle waves lapping against it.

Motherfucker.

A scrap of paper peeked from the victim's pocket.

Jett eased it from the pocket with a gloved hand, unfolded it, reading in silence before slipping it into an evidence bag.

I exhaled through my nose. "Do I want to know what it says?"

He met my gaze. "It's for you."

I closed my eyes only for a split second, but long enough to witness the slashes that would have been delivered to our victim.

I shook my head, muttering to myself under my breath. I forced myself back to the present. I would not let him win.

Not tonight.

CHAPTER SIX

The smell of damp earth and lake water clung to the air, mixing with something heavier—something metallic. Blood had a way of sinking into a place, seeping into the ground, and staining the air long after the body was gone.

I crouched near the water's edge, flicking my flashlight across the patch of soft rounded rocks where the victim had been found. The crime scene was officially cleared, but that didn't mean I wouldn't find something here, something that was missed.

Because they *always* missed something. Even if it wasn't physical evidence.

The tide had risen slightly since last night, lapping at the shore, erasing the last traces of disturbance. I frowned, scanning the mud for footprints, for drag marks, for anything that told me how the killer got here—and how he left.

Nothing.

Which meant he still knew what he was doing. He was still under control, despite the mutilated bodies that demonstrated anything but control.

I exhaled through my nose, pushing back the frustration. **Focus.**

If I were him, where would I have gone next?

I straightened, flicking my flashlight toward the tree line. It was still early—just before sunrise—but the forest was thick, dark enough to keep secrets.

And I was in the mood to dig them up.

I adjusted my grip on my flashlight and stepped into the woods. The ground was soft underfoot, the scent of wet leaves strong in my nose. I moved carefully, scanning for anything that looked out of place.

Then—something caught my eye.

A photo, just a blurry Polaroid, almost like the person that took it was running.

I crouched, shining my flashlight over it. Fresh, barely damp from the morning dew. Someone had been standing here *after* the rain stopped.

Watching.

I felt the prickle of unease at the base of my neck.

I stood, heart thumping, scanning the shadows between the trees.

Nothing.

But I wasn't stupid.

I knew I wasn't alone. With him still out there, still hunting, I was never alone.

"Are you following me, Spitfire?"

The deep voice came from behind me, cutting through the quiet.

I spun, my pulse spiking, already to defend myself before I registered the silhouette leaning against a tree.

Jett.

The tension in my shoulders didn't ease. "Jesus Christ, do you *always* sneak up on people?"

He smirked, pushing off the tree, stepping closer. He was dressed like he hadn't even gone home yet—same clothes as last night, shirt rumpled, badge clipped to his belt. He probably hadn't slept either.

Good.

"Didn't sneak up on you," he said easily. "You were just too focused on playing detective to notice me."

I rolled my eyes, tucking my knife away. "You should try being useful instead of just lurking, *detective*."

His smirk faded, replaced by something sharper. "You shouldn't be here, Brooks."

I arched a brow. "Oh? And you *should*?"

"I'm *on* this case."

"So am I."

"No, you're not."

I crossed my arms. "Darby's parents asked me to look into her murder, and guess what? That doesn't just mean *her* murder. It means *all* of them."

Jett's jaw ticked. "That's not how this works."

"It's how it works *for me*."

His gaze darkened, sweeping over me, taking in my stance, my expression. "You don't listen to a damn thing anyone tells you, do you?"

"Not when they're wrong."

His eyes narrowed slightly, like he was assessing me—like he was trying to decide if he should argue or just let me burn myself out.

I took the choice away from him.

I turned my back on him, heading deeper into the woods.

Jett cursed under his breath.

And then, like the stubborn bastard he was, he followed.

"I don't need a babysitter, Jett."

"Yeah? Tell that to Brennan."

I stopped walking so fast he nearly ran into me. I turned, staring him down. "You talked to *Brennan* about me?"

Jett crossed his arms, clearly unimpressed with my outrage. "He's the *sheriff*, Brooks. And he told me to keep you the hell away from this case."

I scoffed. "Oh, and you just *do* what you're told? That must be *new* for you."

Something flickered behind his eyes—something unreadable.

"Even if he hadn't told me to, I'd still be here telling you the same damn thing Brooks."

I pushed past him, my fingers twitching at my sides. I *hated* this. Being watched. Being controlled. Being treated like some reckless wildcard who needed to be handled.

Jett's voice came from behind me, lower now. "You ever stop to think maybe people don't want you involved because they *don't want you dead?*"

I clenched my jaw. "I don't need saving, Jett."

His hand wrapped around my wrist, stopping me mid-step.

I sucked in a sharp breath, pulse spiking at the contact. His grip wasn't tight, but it was *there*, his fingers warm against my skin. I turned slowly, my eyes locking onto his.

The tension between us crackled, sharp and electric.

"You don't get it, do you?" His voice was quiet, rough. "This guy isn't playing games. He's *fixated* on you."

I exhaled slowly. "That's exactly why I *can't* back off."

His grip tightened, just slightly.

My breath hitched.

I wasn't stupid.

I saw the way he looked at me—like I was something dangerous, something unpredictable. Like I was an open flame, and he couldn't decide if he wanted to put me out or let me burn.

I hated how much I *liked* it.

Jett let out a slow breath, his gaze flickering to my mouth before snapping back up.

I smirked. "Let go, Jett."

He didn't. Not right away.

His thumb brushed against the inside of my wrist, barely there, but enough to make my stomach flip.

Then, finally—he let go.

I stepped back, putting distance between us, even though some reckless part of me didn't want to.

His expression had hardened again, back to the stoic, infuriatingly unreadable detective. "Go home, Brooks."

I tilted my head. "Make me."

His jaw was clenched.

And just like that, the moment was gone.

Jett exhaled sharply and stepped back, shaking his head like I was the most frustrating person he'd ever met.

Maybe I was.

I turned and walked away.

And this time—he didn't follow.

Jett

Brooks disappeared into the trees, her dark silhouette swallowed by the early morning mist.

I stood there longer than I should have, my fingers still flexing from where I'd touched her.

She was going to get herself killed.

She wasn't wrong about one thing—the killer was *fixated* on her. Every move he made, every message he left, it was all meant for her. And if we didn't find him first, she was going to end up as his grand finale.

I turned away and ran a hand through my hair, exhaling sharply.

I needed to focus.

I pushed down whatever the hell that moment was between us and turned back to the case.

The medical examiner's office was quieter than usual when I walked in, the air thick with the sterile scent of disinfectant and decay. Greg was already there, hunched over a report, flipping through pages with slow, deliberate movements.

He barely glanced up when I entered. "You look like hell."

I snorted. "Appreciate it."

He set the file down and stretched, his joints popping. "You here for the autopsy report on Wilson?"

When I paused before answering, he added, "We identified him this morning, tattoo on his leg."

"Yeah. What've you got?"

Greg gestured toward the metal slab in the center of the room. The body had already been cleaned up, the worst of the blood and dirt scrubbed away, leaving behind only the cold, lifeless remains of whoever Wilson was before the killer got to him.

"Time of death was roughly between eleven and two," Greg said, flipping a page. "Cause of death—multiple stab wounds to the torso, just like the others. But here's where it gets weird."

He turned the file toward me, tapping his pen against a set of notes.

"The injuries weren't all inflicted at once. There are two separate patterns—one at the time of death, the other *post-mortem*."

I frowned. "You're saying the killer came back?"

"That's my guess. Some of the wounds are too clean, like they were made after the body had stopped bleeding. No struggle, no defensive wounds—he was already dead by the time those were inflicted."

A chill ran down my spine.

He wasn't just killing anymore. He was *playing*.

I scanned the notes again, my mind turning over the details, trying to find something—anything—that gave me an edge.

Then I saw it.

A note in the margins, Greg's usual shorthand, but with one detail that made my stomach twist.

'Brooks said stabbing = signature.'

I narrowed my eyes. "When the hell was Brooks here?"

Greg raised a brow. "You mean *before* or *after* she pissed off half the hospital staff?"

I dragged a hand down my face. "Jesus Christ."

"She was here at the crack of dawn," he said, flipping to another page. "Asking about cause of death, checking the wounds, making a damn mess of my paperwork."

Of course, she was.

I clenched my jaw, irritation spiking through me.

She hadn't just ignored Brennan's orders—she'd gone out of her way to get ahead of me.

Greg smirked. "You two need to just sleep together already and get it over with."

I shot him a look. "Shut up."

He barked out a laugh. "Seriously, man. The whole 'I hate her, but I can't stop looking at her' act? It's exhausting to watch."

I ignored him, flipping through the report again. "Did she take anything?"

Greg shrugged. "Nope. Just poked around, asked questions, and left looking pissed off."

That sounded about right.

I snapped the file shut and turned for the door.

"Where you going?" Greg called.

"To deal with a goddamn problem."

I let myself into her garage to find her, shockingly, not in it. But her car was parked outside, so I knew she had to be here. I let myself up the stairs from the garage to the living room and was immediately met with her scowl that was wavering between angry and smug.

"What the hell were you doing at the M.E.'s office?"

She exhaled slowly, watching me with those sharp, assessing eyes. "Investigating."

I took a step closer, invading her space, my patience wearing thin. "You think this is a game, Brooks?"

"Do I look like I'm having fun?"

I clenched my jaw. "You went behind my back."

She let out a sharp, humorless laugh. "Oh, cry me a river, Jett. You were gonna get the same report *eventually*."

I narrowed my eyes. "You're reckless."

"And you're slow," she shot back.

Something snapped in me.

I grabbed her wrist—not hard, not tight, but enough to make her look at me. "You keep pushing like this, you're gonna get yourself killed."

She arched a brow. "You worried about me, *Detective*?"

I was.

More than I wanted to admit.

I let go of her wrist, stepping back before I did something stupid.

CHAPTER SEVEN

Jett hovered over me like he was trying to be intimidating. It wasn't working.

That stiff posture, squared shoulders, the clench of his jaw—I bet it was the same look he gave suspects when he was fishing for a confession. Too bad for him, I wasn't one of his cases.

I crossed my arms. "I'm not staying out of this."

Jett exhaled sharply, his jaw flexing as if he were chewing back all the names he wanted to call me. "You are infuriating. Do you know that? So goddamn stubborn. I could just—"

His hand twitched at his side, like he wanted to grab me again but thought better of it.

"You could just what?" I stepped in closer, making sure he either backed off or let me invade his space. He didn't move. "What're you gonna do, Jett? Tell my brother on me?"

His nostrils flared, but he didn't take the bait. Instead, he stepped forward, pressing me back toward the wall, boxing me in with his arms.

My pulse pounded, but not from fear. He was too close, his scent— leather, soap, something distinctly Jett—was too damn distracting. I should've shoved him away. Instead, I stared at that infuriatingly square jaw, the tension there, the way his lips were just slightly parted—

A voice called from the garage.

"B!" Brennan.

We jerked apart, moving so fast we might as well have been caught committing a felony. Jett retreated to the opposite side of the room, raking a hand through his hair. I turned to the door just as my brother let himself in, hoping my face didn't betray anything.

"What's up?" I asked, ignoring the heat still lingering in my chest.

Brennan glanced between Jett and me but didn't press. "Dad's coming over for dinner. Fifteen minutes. He's bringing takeout."

I blinked. You have got to be kidding me.

"Are you—Brennan, what the hell? You couldn't have warned me sooner?" My house was a disaster. There were empty beer bottles on the coffee table, dirty dishes in the sink, and files spilling across every available surface. I wasn't exactly presenting an image of stability.

I didn't even have time to yell properly before I sputtered, "Bottles."

Brennan—bless him—understood immediately and started gathering the evidence of my questionable life choices. That gave me just enough time to rush to my bedroom and yank on a blouse that wouldn't make our father think I was an unemployed alcoholic. Semi-alcoholic.

I was pulling my hair into a ponytail when I called back, "Why the fuck is he coming here?"

"He said he wanted to see what you've done with the place."

I groaned. "I haven't done anything to the place."

Which meant that excuse was bullshit.

I caught sight of my hands in the mirror—trembling.

"Pills," I muttered to myself and rushed toward the kitchen.

But I didn't get far before I spotted the mess on my kitchen table. "Shit." Files, folders, evidence of everything I'd been working on, all out in the open. I swept them up, shoved them under my pillows, and yanked my duvet over them for good measure.

Before I could do a final sweep of my disaster zone, a familiar gruff voice carried up from the garage.

"Brooks? Brennan?"

I took a steadying breath, squared my shoulders, and opened the door. "Hi, Dad."

He barely looked at me as he passed over a takeout bag. Brennan took it, while I kept my fingers interlocked behind my back so he wouldn't notice the slight tremor in my hands. I didn't get a chance to grab my meds before he entered the kitchen.

Brennan, ever the dutiful son, made introductions. "Dad, this is Detective Will Jett."

Jett stuck out a firm hand, already knowing the type of man my father was. "Nice to meet you, sir."

Dad gave him a curt nod, then took a seat at the head of the table like it was his damn house. Brennan sat beside him. Skyla arrived just in time, slipping into the chair next to my brother. I ended up between Dad and Jett, which meant I had nowhere to hide.

As long as I moved slow, I could keep my hands steady enough to avoid suspicion. But I felt like a countdown timer was ticking in my head, waiting for my father to start his interrogation.

He didn't make me wait long.

"So, Brooks?"

Here we go.

"What's the plan for the house? Looks lived in. You getting any renovations done?"

I reached for the container of chicken balls, struggling to pry off the lid. "No, I like it the way it is. Feels cozy."

Jett reached to help me, but I cut him off before he could touch it. "Don't."

Dad barely blinked at the interaction, like he was making notes for later. "You should at least replace the exterior doors. Any idiot with a screwdriver could break in."

"Yes, sir."

The lid finally popped off. A chicken ball rolled out of the container and onto the table. I saw Dad's gaze zero in on my hands.

Brennan, mercifully, redirected his attention. "How was the drive, Dad?"

That bought me time. I managed to finish most of my meal, shoving it back quickly, without drawing too much attention, but when Dad turned back to me, I knew I wasn't getting out of this unscathed.

"Now," he said, leveling me with that unreadable stare. "Why did you leave that job I got you in Chicago?"

My throat tightened. "I wanted to move home."

"I pulled a lot of strings to get you that job. You shouldn't have been in the field for at least another three years."

I wasn't sure if he was bragging about his influence or putting me down for being green. Either way, I had nothing to say that would change his mind.

"I know, sir. Thank you for the opportunity."

I reached for my water, but my hand knocked against my plate, making a loud clang. I froze. Dad noticed.

Jett must have noticed, too, because when Dad asked me to pass the pitcher of water, he moved to grab it first.

Dad stopped him. "Brooks."

My breath caught.

I grabbed the nearly full pitcher. The second I lifted it, the water sloshed. I adjusted my grip, trying to keep it steady—

Jett reached out to help.

"Stop," I snapped, pulling it away from him. The movement sent water sloshing over the rim, drenching my shirt.

"Fuck!" I slammed the pitcher down, rattling every dish on the table. The room fell silent. My pulse pounded in my ears.

Jett moved to hand me a napkin, but I shot to my feet. "Fuck off! Stop trying to help me! Stop grabbing shit out of my hands!"

"Brooks—" Dad started.

But I wasn't done.

"I got shot, Dad! I got shot, and now I can't use my goddamn hands. That's why I lost the job in Chicago. That's why I had to move back to this shithole town. Is that what you wanted to hear?" My voice shook, fury blurring my vision. I lifted my trembling hands like it was a cool trick. "Look, Dad. Can't hold them still. Happy now?"

He knew.

He had known this whole damn time.

I didn't wait for his response. I left the table, stormed down the hall, and slammed my bedroom door behind me.

✝

Half an hour passed before it creaked open again.

Brennan stepped inside, holding out an orange pill bottle like a peace offering. "If I knew he knew…" He sighed. "I wouldn't have let him do that."

I took the bottle, my hands still shaking. "Of course he knew."

Brennan hesitated. "Could you cut Jett a break?"

I said nothing.

Brennan nodded. "Just… think about it. He's only trying to help. And he's just trying to keep you safe because he's my friend." Then he left, shutting the door softly behind him.

I stared at the pill bottle in my hand.

I hated that I needed it.

I stared at the pill bottle in my hand, my fingers curled so tightly around it that my knuckles ached.

I *hated* this.

Hated the way my father still had this hold over me, like I was some kid waiting for his approval. Hated the way my hands wouldn't cooperate, how I couldn't even get through a goddamn dinner without turning into a spectacle. Hated that, and no matter how much time passed, I still felt like I had something to prove to him.

I'm fine.

That's what I wanted to scream. I was fine. I was surviving. I was—

A quiet knock interrupted the spiral of thoughts unraveling in my head.

Not Brennan.

Jett.

I clenched my jaw and didn't answer, but that didn't stop him from opening the door anyway, pushing it just far enough to step inside.

I didn't look at him. Just sat on the edge of my bed, legs drawn up, the pill bottle still gripped in my hand.

He closed the door behind him. No words. No smartass comments. Just the quiet weight of his presence filling the space between us.

After a long moment, I sighed. "I don't need a lecture."

"I wasn't gonna give you one."

I finally turned my head toward him, studying his face in the dim light. His expression was unreadable, but his eyes—those dark, steady eyes—held something I didn't know how to deal with.

Jett walked over and sat beside me on the bed, the mattress dipping slightly under his weight. He didn't reach for me, didn't try to force anything. He just sat there, waiting.

"I meant what I said," I muttered. "I don't need help."

Jett scoffed lightly. "Yeah, Brooks. You're *real* convincing."

I huffed out a sharp breath, somewhere between frustration and exhaustion. My grip tightened around the bottle, the plastic biting into my palm. "I don't want him to see me like this."

Jett was quiet for a second, and then his voice came, low and even. "You think he doesn't already know?"

I flinched.

Jett exhaled slowly. "I get it. You don't want to look weak in front of him."

I turned to snap at him, but Jett was already shaking his head. "And before you bite my head off, I don't think you're weak. Not even close." His voice dipped lower. "But you gotta stop acting like struggling with something means you're broken. You got shot, Brooks. And you're still standing. You're still fighting. That's not weakness."

I swallowed hard, my throat tight. I *wanted* to believe him.

Jett nodded toward my hand. "Take the damn pills."

I hesitated.

Jett didn't push, didn't try to force them out of my hand. He just looked at me, waiting.

Finally, I sighed and twisted the cap off, shaking one into my palm. Before I could second-guess myself, I tossed it back and swallowed dry.

Jett didn't gloat. Didn't say *I told you so.*

He just stood, running a hand through his hair. "Get some sleep."

I didn't say anything as he left, shutting the door behind him.

Silence settled over the room.

I sat there for a long time, staring at the pill bottle in my hands, my thoughts a tangled mess.

I hated that I needed them. Hated that I needed *help.*

But more than anything, I hated that Jett had been right.

CHAPTER EIGHT

I knew something was wrong the second I pulled into my driveway.

For one, the porch light was on, even though I never left it that way.

For two, someone was sitting on my front steps, their legs crossed, hands folded neatly in their lap, posture way too poised for someone in this town.

I groaned the second I recognized her. Claire Kensington.

Bright-eyed, blonde-haired, pastel-wearing, always-smiling Claire.

The same Claire who had once cried over a Hallmark commercial but could somehow inhale three tequila shots without blinking.

The same Claire who had been my roommate in Chicago.

The same Claire I'd specifically told to stay the hell away from my life here.

She grinned and shot up to her feet the second I stepped out of the car. "Brooks!"

I gripped the car door and took a slow breath. "Jesus Christ."

Claire practically skipped down the steps, her oversized pink suitcase bumping along behind her. "Surprise! I took some time off work and came to help!" Claire worked as an admin assistant in a high-end law firm back in Chicago.

I stared. "What?"

She beamed. "Well, technically, I cashed in all my vacation days, but it's fine! Totally worth it." Sometimes, I wondered what Claire's purpose was at the law firm, other than putting bright sticky tabs on case files.

I blinked. "Why?"

She scoffed. "Um, because you're dealing with a murder investigation, and you obviously need help?"

I scrubbed a hand down my face, exhaustion pressing against the back of my skull. "How the hell do you even know about that?"

Claire's smile faltered, just slightly. "Uh—Caleb told me."

That snapped me awake.

I narrowed my eyes. "Caleb."

She nodded quickly. "Yep! He mentioned you were in over your head and could use some backup, and I figured, why not?"

I stared at her, my mind racing past the part where Claire had taken an impromptu murder-solving vacation and landing squarely on the part where Caleb was the reason she was here.

I had explicitly told him to stay the hell away from Claire.

And yet, somehow, they were talking about me?

Claire shifted, suddenly looking uncertain. "Are you…mad?"

I inhaled slowly. Exhaled even slower. I wasn't going to dwell on Caleb right now.

I had a more immediate problem standing directly in front of me.

"You can't be here," I muttered.

She made a face. "Well, that's rude."

I let out a short, humorless laugh. "Claire, you're too—" I gestured vaguely at her. "—you for this."

Her hands went to her hips. "Excuse me?"

"This isn't a weekend getaway," I snapped. "This is a murder investigation, and you—"

"I know what it is, Brooks," she cut in, surprising me with how firm her voice was. "I know this is serious. I know you hate accepting help, but guess what? I'm already here. So, you can either waste time arguing with me or let me do what I came here to do."

I pressed my lips together.

Damn it.

She was still annoyingly stubborn.

I sighed, dragging a hand through my hair. "Fine. But we need some ground rules."

Claire gasped dramatically. "Like an official murder-solving pact?"

I ignored that. "One—you don't go anywhere alone."

She rolled her eyes. "Obviously."

"Two—stay away from crime scenes."

She opened her mouth, then shut it again, looking vaguely guilty.

I narrowed my eyes. "Claire."

"Okay, okay! I promise."

I wasn't convinced, but I kept going. "Three—if anything feels off, you call me."

Claire tilted her head. "Like, emotionally off? Because I get weird vibes from people all the time, and—"

I clenched my jaw. "Claire."

"Right, right—dangerous off."

I exhaled slowly. "And four—if I say run, you fucking run."

For the first time since she'd opened her mouth, Claire looked serious.

She nodded. "Okay."

I studied her for a second, debating whether I should tell her to pack up her pink suitcase and get the hell out of town before she got caught in something way bigger than she realized.

But she was already here.

And I wasn't going to shake her.

Claire perked back up. "Oh! I forgot to tell you—I found the cutest little bed and breakfast in town! Mrs. Hendricks, the owner, is an angel, and she makes the best scones. I already made a list of places we should check out for the case over breakfast tomorrow!"

I groaned. "Of course you did."

She grinned. "You still drink way too much black coffee? Perfect, I'll bring you one every day. I'll be like your murder solving assistant; I can help you organize all your files. You know I'm so good at colour coding."

†

I knew it was a mistake letting Claire into my life again.

I should have slammed the door in her face yesterday and told her to get on the next flight back to Chicago. Should have called her boss and told them she was absolutely essential to the office and needed to return immediately. Should have done anything but let her think she could stay and be part of this.

Because now she was showing up at my house with coffee.

I stared at her through the kitchen window as she bounced up my driveway, a too-bright smile on her face, carrying two cups from the café down the street like she belonged here.

I sighed, bracing myself before going to open the garage door before she could try to scrape open the door on the back porch. I doubted Claire would even be able to push the damn jammed thing halfway open.

Claire beamed. "Good morning! I brought coffee!"

I crossed my arms. "How did you even remember how I take my coffee?"

"I remember things," she said proudly. "Unlike some people."

I rolled my eyes and took the cup from her, lifting the lid to check. Black. At least she got that right.

Claire, of course, had some kind of sugar-loaded monstrosity topped with whipped cream.

She waltzed inside like she lived here, looking around the garage. "Alright. Let's get started."

I narrowed my eyes. "Started on what, exactly?"

She set her cup down, pulled a tiny pink notebook from her purse, and flipped it open. "Murder-solving, obviously."

I groaned. "Claire—"

"I already made a list of things I can help with!" she interrupted, tapping her notebook with a glittery pen. "Research, organizing, tracking details, looking into potential connections—"

"Jesus Christ." I ran a hand down my face.

"—and, of course, making sure you actually eat and sleep, because judging by your face, you are failing at both."

I shot her a glare. "Claire."

She smiled sweetly.

I was this close to kicking her out.

But my stomach chose that moment to betray me, letting out a loud, hollow grumble.

Claire's eyes lit up.

"Oh, perfect!" She clapped her hands together. "Let's go to the diner. We can plan over breakfast."

I sighed heavily, but arguing wasn't worth the effort.

"Fine," I muttered, grabbing my jacket. "But I swear to God, if you start asking people in town about the case, I will drag you back to the airport myself."

Claire just hummed happily and linked her arm through mine like this was a fun little girls' trip and not a serial murder investigation.

I had a very bad feeling about this.

The bell jingled as we stepped inside, the scent of coffee and fried food thick in the air. I steered Claire toward a booth in the back, away from too many ears, and slumped into the seat.

Claire slid in across from me, already flipping to a fresh page in her notebook.

"Okay," she said, pen poised. "Tell me everything."

I scoffed. "No."

Claire pouted. "Brooks."

I sighed, flagging down the waitress for coffee refills before leveling a look at her. "You don't need to know everything."

"But I can't help if I don't know what's going on." She gestured around us. "I mean, I know there's been murders, obviously. And I know you think they're connected. But you haven't told me anything about what's actually happening."

I hesitated.

Because, yeah, Claire didn't know the half of it.

She didn't know about the notes. About how the killer wasn't just randomly killing people—he was doing it for me.

She didn't know that every time I closed my eyes, I saw the crime scenes burned into my brain, the way he posed them, the eerie familiarity of it all.

She didn't know that I could feel him watching.

And I wasn't sure I wanted her to.

I exhaled slowly, running a hand through my hair. "Fine," I muttered. "But you do not repeat any of this to anyone. Got it?"

Claire nodded so fast I thought she might give herself whiplash.

I sighed again. "The killer doesn't leave evidence. None. No DNA, no footprints, no fingerprints. He knows how we investigate, how we think. He makes sure there's nothing to find."

Claire scribbled in her notebook. "So, he has a background in forensics?"

I shrugged. "Or he he's been at this longer than we know. Either way, he's not some random psycho. He's smart. Careful."

Claire tapped her pen against her chin. "And he left a note at the last crime scene?"

I tensed slightly.

Then I nodded.

Claire frowned. "What did it say?"

I hesitated for half a second too long.

Her eyes widened. "Oh my God—it was for you, wasn't it?"

I clenched my jaw. "Claire—"

"Brooks!" She smacked the table. "Are you kidding me?"

I sighed, rubbing my temples. "This is why I didn't tell you anything."

She huffed, scribbling furiously in her notebook. "And you didn't think this was an important detail?"

"It doesn't change anything."

She gawked at me. "It absolutely changes everything!"

I shook my head. "I already know he's watching me. Leaving a note just confirms what I already suspected."

Claire stared at me like I'd lost my mind. "How are you so calm about this?"

I wasn't.

But I'd gotten good at pretending.

I took a sip of coffee instead of answering.

Claire sat back, arms crossed, scowling. "Well, now I definitely have to help."

I sighed. "You can help—just not with the dangerous parts."

She narrowed her eyes. "Define 'dangerous.'"

I ignored her. "You're good at organizing, right?"

She perked up instantly. "The best."

"Great. Then you're on information duty."

She narrowed her eyes. "This feels like busy work."

I smirked. "It is busy work. But it's necessary."

Claire huffed but didn't argue. "Fine. But if you keep anything from me, I will find out."

I smirked into my coffee cup. "Noted."

Our food arrived, and Claire let the case go long enough to drown her pancakes in syrup.

I took the opportunity to scan the diner, my guard slipping just slightly.

I wouldn't say it out loud, but having Claire here—really here—made something in my chest unclench just a little.

Even if she was annoying as hell.

Jett

The mic stand squealed with feedback, sending a sharp pulse of irritation down my spine.

The community center was packed, bodies crammed together, the air thick with burnt coffee and tension. Town hall meetings in Ennis were usually about property taxes or why someone's neighbor had too many junk cars in their yard.

Not murder.

I adjusted the mic higher, scanning the crowd. Half of them looked pissed. The other half looked scared.

Brennan stood beside me, arms crossed, jaw set. Skyla sat on the other side of him, clipboard balanced on her lap, looking a lot calmer than I knew she actually was. It was her first time dealing with something like this, and now she had to sit in front of half the town and act like she had it under control.

She was holding her own so far. A lot better than Brennan was, but I wouldn't tell him that.

Brennan stepped forward first. "Alright, let's get started."

The low murmuring died down, and all eyes shifted to us.

"As most of you know," Brennan continued, "we've been dealing with an ongoing investigation regarding the recent murders." He let that settle before continuing. "I know people are worried, and I know there's been a lot of speculation, but I want to make one thing very clear—we *are* doing everything in our power to solve this."

A woman near the front crossed her arms. "And what does that mean, exactly?"

"It means we're working the case," I said, keeping my voice steady. "We're following leads, increasing patrols, and putting precautions in place to make sure everyone stays safe—especially with the festival coming up."

A man in a faded baseball cap shook his head. "You mean you *still* don't have a suspect?"

I kept my expression unreadable. "If we had a suspect, you'd know."

"That's what we're *supposed* to believe," another voice piped up from the middle of the crowd.

Brennan's jaw twitched. Before he could snap, Skyla stood and spoke.

"I understand that tensions are high," she said, voice calm but firm. "And I know how frustrating it is to feel like you're not getting answers fast enough. But we can't jeopardize the investigation by throwing out unconfirmed details."

She was handling this better than I expected.

Brennan stepped back in. "Here's what we *can* tell you: this is likely the work of a single individual."

The room stilled.

I let the silence stretch just long enough before I spoke. "We have reason to believe the killer is methodical. He has experience, and he doesn't make mistakes."

A quiet curse came from somewhere in the back.

I scanned the crowd again, watching the way people reacted. The way fear twisted into suspicion.

Then my eyes landed on *her*.

Brooks.

She was sitting near the back, arms crossed, legs stretched out in front of her, the picture of relaxed indifference. But I wasn't stupid. She was listening to every word.

What did surprise me, though, was the woman sitting next to her.

Blonde, dressed in soft pastels, completely out of place in a room full of weary locals.

I hadn't met her, but I knew there was no chance she was from around here.

Brooks caught me looking, *staring* at her, and arched a brow, the corner of her mouth tugging up in a smirk.

I clenched my jaw and looked away.

I'd deal with *that* later.

Someone in the front row cleared their throat. "What about the festival?"

Brennan nodded. "As of now, yes, the festival is still happening. But we're implementing some changes."

Skyla pulled out her clipboard. "There will be a strict curfew—events will end by ten, and no one should be out alone after that. We'll have extra patrols on duty, and certain areas will be restricted."

A man scoffed. "And you *really* think that's enough?"

I leaned into the mic. "What's the alternative? Cancel it and send the whole town into a panic?"

Silence.

Because *that* was the truth.

Ennis was the kind of place that thrived on routine. Disrupting it would only make things worse.

Brennan gave a sharp nod. "If you see anything suspicious, you report it. If you feel unsafe, you get inside. And until we catch this guy, you *don't* take unnecessary risks."

I scanned the crowd again.

Brooks was still watching me, chin resting on her hand, like she was waiting for me to slip up.

The blonde next to her whispered something in her ear, and Brooks rolled her eyes before responding.

I exhaled through my nose, gripping the mic stand.

This town had no idea what kind of storm was coming.

But *I* did.

The room shifted with uneasy murmurs, the tension stretching tight like a live wire. People wanted to believe us, wanted to trust that we had things under control—but we didn't.

Not yet.

I could see it in their faces.

The skepticism. The fear.

They wanted a guarantee. A promise that no one else would die.

And I couldn't give them that.

Brennan glanced at me, jaw tight. I gave a small nod—his cue to wrap this up before someone really lost it.

"We'll be increasing patrols near the festival grounds," Brennan continued, voice steady. "There will be additional officers stationed throughout town, including at the entrances and exits. If you have concerns, come to us directly. But I'll say it again—stick to the curfew, don't walk alone, and if you see something, report it."

That should have been the end of it.

But of course, it wasn't.

A woman stood near the middle of the room, her dark hair streaked with gray, a deep frown pulling at her face. Mrs. Jenkins.

She crossed her arms. "You say all this, but what happens when you *don't* catch him before the festival? What then?"

The room went still.

I felt Brennan stiffen beside me, but I was the one who answered.

"Then we adjust," I said simply. "We keep people safe, and we keep moving forward. What do you expect us to do? Shut the whole town down?"

She didn't back down. "I expect you to do your *damn jobs.*"

A few voices in the crowd murmured in agreement. The irritation at the back of my skull flared, but before I could say anything, another voice cut through the room.

"They are."

The tone was sharp, unwavering, and it made people turn.

I followed their eyes to the back of the room.

Brooks.

Arms crossed, one brow arched, her expression somewhere between unimpressed and *completely over this shit.*

"If you think they aren't doing enough," she continued, standing slowly, "then maybe you should tell us all exactly how you'd solve a case with no witnesses, no evidence, and a killer who knows exactly how to cover his tracks."

Silence.

Mrs. Jenkins opened her mouth, then shut it again.

Brooks let out a humorless laugh. "Yeah, that's what I thought."

A few more murmurs rippled through the crowd—some surprised, some agreeing, some just entertained by the fact that someone had said what most of them were thinking.

I had to fight back the urge to smirk.

Brooks wasn't the type to play nice just to keep the peace, and I shouldn't have been surprised that she couldn't just sit there while people ran their mouths.

"Look," she continued, her voice calmer now. "You don't have to like the way they're handling this. Hell, you don't even have to *like them.* But trust me when I tell you that catching this guy isn't as simple as wanting it bad enough."

A beat of silence passed before she added, "And if you *really* want them to do their damn jobs, maybe stop wasting their time by making them stand here and listen to the same complaints over and over instead of actually letting them work the case."

Mrs. Jenkins muttered something under her breath but sank back into her seat.

Brooks sat down too, like nothing had happened, but I didn't miss the way the blonde next to her leaned in and whispered something to her, probably scolding her for making a scene.

I cleared my throat, adjusting the mic stand. "Well," I said. "Couldn't have said it better myself."

That got a few quiet chuckles from the crowd, and the tension loosened just slightly.

Brennan let out a breath. "If there are no more questions, that'll be all for tonight. If you need to speak with us, we'll be here for a while."

People started filing out, some lingering to whisper in hushed tones.

I scanned the room again.

Brooks was back to sipping her coffee like she hadn't just verbally shut down half the town.

I shook my head, muttering a curse under my breath.

I didn't know if she was going to make my life easier or ten times harder.

Probably both. Why did I almost like that idea?

CHAPTER NINE

The festival poster sat on my kitchen counter, the edges curling where I'd flattened it out.

It was bright and colorful, the kind of thing meant to draw families and tourists, advertising pumpkin carving, a haunted corn maze, and live music in the square. The kind of thing normal people looked forward to.

But I wasn't normal.

And I wasn't going for the cider and fucking caramel apples.

I was going because *he* would be there.

The Phantom. The killer. The one who was watching.

I didn't know how I knew. I just *did.*

He liked to stalk his victims before he struck, liked to study them, liked to plan. And what better place for him to hunt than a crowded festival full of people in masks and costumes, blending into the crowd?

I exhaled slowly, drumming my fingers against the counter.

Brennan would tell me to stay away. Jett would probably try to drag me out of town himself.

But I wasn't about to sit on the sidelines, waiting for another body to show up.

If he was hunting, I wanted him to see *me.*

I wanted him to know that I wasn't afraid of him.

I wanted him to think I was his next victim.

Because if I played this right—if I was careful—maybe I could turn the tables before he had the chance.

I grabbed the festival flyer and folded it neatly, tucking it into my jacket pocket. If he was going to be watching, then I'd make damn sure he saw exactly what I wanted him to.

The festival was already in full swing by the time I pulled into a side lot near the town square.

Music drifted through the air, mixing with the scent of kettle corn, cider, and something fried. Laughter echoed from the streets, families moving between vendor tents, kids sprinting ahead of exhausted parents, teenagers loitering near the game booths, pretending to be too cool to care.

The whole thing was so *normal*.

It was almost enough to make me forget why I was here.

Almost.

I killed the engine and sat back in my seat, eyes scanning the crowd. The town square had been transformed—string lights crisscrossed overhead, jack-o'-lanterns lined the sidewalks, and fake cobwebs clung to shop windows.

It was the perfect place to disappear.

The perfect place for him to hunt.

I exhaled slowly, gripping the steering wheel.

I shouldn't be here.

That's what Brennan would say. That's what Jett would probably growl in my face before dragging me out by my damn collar.

But I *was* here.

Because if I was right, he'd be watching.

And if I played this carefully, he'd think I was the one being hunted.

I grabbed my jacket from the passenger seat, slipping it on as I stepped out of the car. The air was crisp, cold enough to bite, the early October chill settling in as the sun dipped lower.

I pulled the hood up—not enough to hide, just enough to make him *work* to find me.

A game of cat and mouse.

And I wasn't sure which of us was which.

I melted into the crowd easily, slipping between families and groups of teenagers, moving with the flow of foot traffic but never too fast. I kept my eyes sharp, scanning faces, looking for someone watching too closely, standing too still.

Looking for someone like *me*.

Nothing.

Not yet.

I passed the vendor stalls, ignoring the smell of cinnamon and roasted nuts. The corn maze loomed in the distance, its entrance marked by a flickering lantern and a cheesy *"Enter if You Dare"* sign.

Beyond that, the woods stretched out like a dark mouth, swallowing the last of the sunlight.

That's where I needed to be.

If he was here, if he was hunting, *that's* where he'd wait.

The thought sent a chill down my spine, but I ignored it.

I adjusted my jacket, steadied my breathing, and took the first step toward the trees.

The festival lights faded behind me, swallowed by the dense trees as I moved deeper into the woods. The air felt colder here, damp and heavy, thick with the scent of wet earth and fallen leaves. Somewhere in the distance, laughter and carnival music still carried through the night, but it felt farther away than it should.

I shouldn't be out here alone. I knew that.

But the boot prints leading away from the parking lot had been fresh. Something about them had sent a jolt through my gut—the way the heels dragged slightly, like whoever left them had been unsteady. Something felt *wrong*.

And I couldn't ignore it.

My phone's flashlight barely cut through the darkness, illuminating patches of ground in sharp, shaky circles. The trail I'd been following had nearly disappeared beneath a thick layer of leaves, but I pressed on, listening. Waiting.

Then I heard it.

A crunch.

Not mine.

I froze, heart slamming against my ribs as I held my breath. The sound had come from my left, past the thick tangle of trees. Slowly, I turned, shining my flashlight in that direction, but the beam barely reached past the first few trunks.

Silence.

Maybe an animal. A deer. A fox. Something small.

Or maybe someone.

A chill crawled up my spine, and I forced myself to take a step back toward the festival.

Another crunch. Closer this time.

Every nerve in my body locked tight. My fingers gripped my phone harder, my pulse a steady roar in my ears.

I needed to leave. *Now.*

I turned and started walking quickly, trying to retrace my steps. But something was *off.* The path didn't look the same. Had I turned too sharply? I was sure I'd walked in a straight line, but now, everything looked unfamiliar—the trees stretching tall and endless, the darkness pressing in from every angle.

The festival music was quieter now. Too far away.

My breath quickened.

Then—another snap behind me.

I didn't think. I ran.

Leaves crunched beneath my boots as I moved blindly through the trees, my breath coming in sharp, panicked bursts. The flashlight bounced wildly, catching flashes of bark, glimpses of roots. I didn't know which way I was going, only that I had to move, had to get *out—*

My foot caught on something.

I went down hard.

Pain shot through my hands and knees as I hit the ground. My phone flew from my grasp, tumbling into the leaves. The flashlight flickered, the beam spinning before landing face-down, plunging me into near-total darkness.

I bit back a curse, my pulse pounding. My palms stung, my knee throbbed, but I scrambled forward, reaching blindly for my phone—

And then I heard it.

A breath.

Right behind me.

Not mine.

Cold fear crashed over me, but I forced myself to move. I grabbed my phone and rolled onto my back, my hand shaking as I swung the light up—

Nothing.

Just trees. Just empty space.

I was losing it. I had to be.

Swallowing hard, I pushed myself to my feet. My breathing was ragged, my head spinning, but I needed to focus. The festival had to be close. I just had to listen—

Through the trees, I caught a flicker of orange. Faint. Almost hidden. But there. A pumpkin.

The festival.

I ran toward it, crashing through the underbrush, not caring how loud I was, not caring if I tripped again. I just needed to get *out*. My feet hit pavement, and suddenly I was back—back in the warmth of the festival, back where the lights and the noise drowned out the fear still curling around my ribs.

I turned, breathless, scanning the woods.

Nothing.

But I *knew* someone had been there.

And they had let me go.

I forced myself to stay at the festival for a while after getting out of the woods, lingering at the edges of the crowd, trying to steady my breathing. I grabbed a cider from one of the stalls just to have something warm in my hands, something to focus on. But no matter how much I told myself I'd imagined it, that I had let my own paranoia get the best of me, the feeling lingered. That *breath*. The way I *knew* someone had been there.

They let me go.

I swallowed hard, trying to shake it off.

I had to be wrong.

When I finally left, the crowd was still thick, and I stuck close to the festival lights until I reached my car. I hesitated before unlocking the door, glancing around the parking lot, scanning the tree line. The woods loomed dark and quiet behind me. Nothing moved.

Still, I locked my doors the second I slid behind the wheel.

By the time I pulled into my driveway, exhaustion had settled deep in my bones. The whole night had taken its toll—between chasing clues, the panic in the woods, and now the creeping unease that followed me home.

I grabbed my keys and got out of the car, glancing up at my house. The porch light was on, the same as I'd left it. Everything looked normal. I let out a breath, feeling ridiculous for how rattled I still was.

Then I stepped towards the garage.

And saw the door.

The lock was busted, the frame splintered, the door slightly ajar.

A cold chill slid through me.

I stepped back instinctively, my heart hammering against my ribs. The woods. The feeling of being watched. The breath at my back.

Had they followed me home?

I swallowed against the rising panic, reaching for my phone with trembling fingers. I dialed Brennan first. No answer. Skyla. Straight to voicemail.

My breathing came faster.

I knew who I had to call.

I pressed the next number and brought the phone to my ear, my voice barely above a whisper.

"Pick up, pick up, pick up." My voice shook as I whispered into the receiver.

Brennan didn't answer his cell. Skyla didn't either. That left only one more number to call, and I hated how badly I wanted him to pick up.

The phone barely rang twice before his voice filled my ear. "Brooks?"

I almost collapsed with relief. I'd been holding my breath so tight my chest ached. I told myself it didn't matter that it was Jett who answered—that I would've taken anyone. But that was a lie. Now that I'd heard him, I knew. Brennan wouldn't have been enough to calm me down right now.

"Will?" I breathed his name, my body shaking from something deeper than the cold night air. The weight of the night crashed down all at once, and I had to press my lips together to keep from sobbing.

"Brooks?" He sounded sharper now, urgent. "What's wrong? Where are you?" I heard rustling—him grabbing his keys, throwing on his jacket. He was already moving.

"I'm home. Please." My voice cracked, barely a whisper.

"I'll be there in two minutes." His words were clipped, tight. "Just hang on, okay?"

I nodded even though he couldn't see me, pressing my forehead against the doorframe as I waited.

Jett must have broken every speed limit in town because I saw the flash of his red and blues as he tore down my street. The siren was off before he even turned into the driveway, and then he was out of the car, bounding toward me.

"Are you hurt?" His hands were already on me, scanning for injuries before I could shake my head. His eyes raked over me, dark with concern. "What happened?"

I opened my mouth, but nothing came out. Instead, I turned my head toward the garage door—the one I'd found half open when I got home.

Jett followed my gaze, his whole body going rigid. "You didn't go in, did you?"

I shook my head.

His shoulders eased just enough to exhale. "Good girl."

Something about the praise, quiet and relieved, cracked something inside me. The fear in my bones loosened just a little.

"Wait here," he said, stepping between me and the house. "I'll check it out."

On any other night, I would've argued. I would've rolled my eyes, insisted I could handle it myself. But tonight, I didn't have it in me.

I watched as he drew his gun and flicked on his flashlight, announcing himself as he stepped inside. I stayed on the porch, arms wrapped tight around my middle, counting my own breaths to keep from shaking apart.

The minutes dragged. I could see the beam of his flashlight moving through the rooms, shadows shifting behind the curtains. I thought I heard something—something too heavy to be just the wind—but before I could spiral into panic, Jett emerged from the garage, shaking his head.

"Nothing." He stepped back outside, holstering his gun. His voice was steady, but I could see the tension in his jaw. He wasn't convinced. "Let's get inside."

I nodded and followed him in. The broken door scraped against the frame as he shut it as best he could, twisting the deadbolt for good measure.

Nothing. He broke into my house and touched nothing. This was retaliation. I taunted him at the festival, and he wanted me to know that he could play the same game.

I flicked on every light in the house, unwilling to let the dark linger in the corners. Every shadow felt like a threat.

Jett watched me from the doorway, arms crossed over his broad chest.

I cleared my throat, trying to force the tremor out of my voice. "Thank you for coming to check." I tried to sound casual. Like I wasn't unraveling. "I'm just gonna take a shower and go to bed. You can head back to work."

"I'm not on duty," he said. "Just couldn't sleep. Was catching up on paperwork." His eyes swept over me, lingering on my shaking hands. "I'll wait while you shower. So, you don't have to worry."

I should've argued. Should've told him I didn't need a babysitter. But the truth was, I did. And the way he said it—soft, gentle, like it wasn't up for debate—made it easier to nod.

I grabbed clean clothes from my closet, half-expecting someone to jump out at me. Nothing but empty space and hanging fabric. Still, I hurried to the bathroom.

When I crossed the hall, I noticed Jett had pulled a chair from the living room, settling himself at the end of the hallway. He wasn't leaving. He was keeping watch.

I left the bathroom door open just a crack, not wanting to feel completely alone. As I stood under the hot water, I heard Jett clear his throat—just loud enough to cut through the sound of the shower. I don't think he even realized he was doing it. But it was comforting. It grounded me.

When I finally stepped out, dressed in my old T-shirt and sweat shorts, Jett was still in his chair, staring out the window.

"Scared the shit out of me, Brooks." He didn't look away from the street. His voice was quieter now, rough around the edges. "Hearing you like that. Christ, I thought you were hurt."

I opened my mouth to apologize, but he turned then, and the look in his eyes stopped me cold. Haunted.

"I'm not leaving." His voice was steel. "Be stubborn with me, yell at me, I don't care. But you are not staying here alone tonight."

I swallowed hard. "Okay."

I didn't close my bedroom door behind me. Couldn't. Not with Jett sitting out there like a sentry, his presence the only thing keeping the fear from swallowing me whole.

I pulled back my duvet and started to crawl under it, but hesitation stopped me. I walked to the window, yanking the blinds shut, then the curtains, double-checking the locks before turning back toward the bed.

I made it halfway before stopping again.

I turned, padding back into the hall where Jett sat, elbows on his knees, gaze locked on the street outside. He turned his head at my approach, reading my face before I could speak.

"Can you come in here?" I asked quietly.

He stood immediately, but his steps toward me were slow, careful—like he was approaching something fragile.

I hovered near the bed, suddenly unsure what I was asking for.

"I'll grab the chair," he offered, jerking his thumb toward the hallway.

"No." I shook my head. The words stuck in my throat, but I forced them out. "Would you just… lay with me? Please?"

Something shifted in his expression. He didn't answer right away, just turned to shut the bedroom door quietly.

I watched from the bed as he unfastened his belt, hanging it on the closet door. He unbuttoned his shirt next, shrugging it off and draping it neatly over the hook. My eyes tracked his fingers as they worked, slow and methodical, revealing the lean muscle beneath.

I swallowed hard and climbed into bed before I could embarrass myself.

I watched as he placed his gun on my nightstand, hesitating just a second before looking at me again. His expression was unreadable, like he was deciding something.

Then he reached for the spare blanket at the end of the bed.

"You can get in the bed, Jett," I muttered. "We're both adults."

His lips twitched like he wanted to smirk but thought better of it. He pulled back the covers and lay down beside me, keeping his eyes on the ceiling.

I turned onto my side, watching him. His face was softer in the dim light, but there was tension in his jaw, in the way his hands fisted in the sheets like he was holding himself back.

"Thank you for coming tonight," I murmured.

"You don't need to thank me."

I hesitated. "Thank you for staying."

That got his attention. He turned his head to look at me, his eyes dark and unreadable in the soft glow of the bedside lamp.

I hesitated, pulse racing in my throat. My body felt like it was on fire, torn between wanting to push him away and needing him closer. "Will?"

His voice was soft now, almost a whisper. "Yes, Brooks?"

I swallowed the knot in my throat, a quiet plea escaping before I could stop it. "Could you hold me?"

For a moment, I thought he might say no, but his expression softened, his usual walls coming down just enough. Then his arm slid beneath my shoulders, pulling me toward him until our bodies were pressed together, fitting like pieces of a puzzle. His hand settled against the small of my back, the warmth of his palm seeping through the thin fabric of my shirt, sending a shiver through me.

I melted against him, burying my forehead in the hollow of his collarbone, inhaling the deep, intoxicating scent of soap and something that was purely him. His fingers began to trace lazy, absentminded circles along my back, the movement slow and deliberate, grounding me but also teasing.

"We'll find him," he murmured, voice tight, strained, like he was holding onto something—control, restraint—something that made him sound angry, but not in the way I expected.

I nodded, barely aware of the movement, my hand slowly drifting over his chest. My fingertips brushed across the firm plane of his stomach, grazing lower, daring myself to touch more, to feel more.

Jett sucked in a sharp breath, his grip tightening on my wrist in an instant, halting my movement before I could get any farther. "Don't."

The simple command sent a rush of heat between my legs, making me ache for more, for him. I lifted my gaze to meet his, my voice low, almost a challenge. "Why not? I see the way you look at me, Jett. Like you want to devour me."

His grip on my wrist tightened for a fleeting second; then, he let go with a long, slow exhale, his eyes dark with something unreadable. He didn't answer with words. He didn't have to.

Instead, he pulled me even closer, his lips brushing my forehead in a lingering kiss—tender but filled with something so much more intense. So much more charged.

It wasn't the answer I was hoping for, but it was the answer I needed.

†

I should have woken up a hundred times throughout the night, but exhaustion dragged me under, deeper than I expected. Jett had been warm, steady, something solid to anchor me.

And yet, despite the hours of sleep, I still woke up tired.

And alone.

I sat up, blinking blearily, the space beside me empty but still faintly warm. The distant murmur of voices pulled me from bed, dragging me toward the living room.

"I swear to god, Jett, I'll fucking kill you."

Brennan.

Oh no.

"Brennan, can you just take a deep breath and calm down?" Jett's voice was low, edged with exhaustion.

"Take a deep breath?" Brennan snapped. "I show up to find your truck in the driveway, my sister's front door broken, and then you come sauntering out of her bedroom with half a shirt on, pointing a gun at me. I'm not sure what part of that is supposed to make me calm."

I pushed through the doorway just as Jett shifted, blocking Brennan's path. His shirt was unbuttoned, his gun tucked into the back of his pants, looking every bit like someone who had just stepped out of my bedroom.

Honestly? I would've paid good money to see the look on Brennan's face when Jett actually came out of my room half-dressed and armed.

Brennan's eyes snapped to me as I leaned against the wall. "Please tell me you did not sleep with him."

I scoffed. "Oh, please." I strode toward the kitchen, grabbing aspirin. "You know I don't fuck cops, B." I tossed the pills in my mouth and swallowed. "Besides—" I shot a smirk at Jett. "Have you seen the size of his truck? Obvious overcompensation."

Jett made a noise in his throat that might've been a laugh.

Brennan, however, turned red. "Brooks—"

"Anyway," I continued, "he was just playing bodyguard for the evening. Since you were apparently too indisposed to answer your damn phone." I leaned on the counter and crossed my arms. "Hey, B, maybe hire a deputy that isn't your girlfriend, so someone actually picks up the phone while you're getting your rocks off?"

Brennan's face went scarlet. "I— I wasn't—"

"Oh, come on." I rolled my eyes. "You're not subtle."

"It's none of your business," Brennan snapped.

"And who I sleep with is none of yours," I countered.

"It is." He said it fast, petulant, like a child.

I arched a brow. "Oh?"

He hesitated. Then, instead of answering, he muttered, "You're so cranky in the morning."

Before I could respond, a scraping noise came from the back door— someone struggling with the door.

I jumped, slamming into Jett's side, my heart hammering. Embarrassingly obvious.

"I'm really sorry, Brooks!" Claire's voice called as she pushed the door open. "I know you don't like me using this door, but the garage is broken, and—" She stopped short, taking in the scene. "Oh." Her eyes flicked to the coffee mug in my hand. Then to Jett's half-buttoned shirt. "Oh."

"Claire, this is my brother, Brennan. And former New York homicide detective William Jett."

Claire made an audible squeak.

I smirked. "Did you bring the stuff I asked for?"

Claire swallowed. "Uh— the sticky notes?"

Claire stood frozen in the doorway, clutching the bag of office supplies like it might somehow protect her. Her gaze flicked between Jett, still looking half-dressed and unimpressed, and Brennan, who looked two seconds away from pulling out his gun just to shoot the tension in the room.

Jett exhaled, rubbing a hand down his face like he was barely holding onto his patience. "Jesus Christ."

Brennan crossed his arms. "You're telling me."

I just smirked, taking a slow sip of coffee. "Aw, come on, B. It's too early for this much stress. Relax."

Brennan shot me a look. "You really want to test me right now?"

I rolled my eyes. "Calm down. I told you, nothing happened."

His frown deepened, but he must've decided this wasn't the hill he wanted to die on because instead of continuing the argument, he turned to Jett. "You staying here again?"

Jett grabbed his jacket off the back of the chair. "Nope." He nodded toward me. "She's alive, her house is locked up, and she's got enough caffeine to keep her sharp. My job here is done."

I scoffed. "Your job?"

Jett smirked slightly but didn't take the bait.

Instead, he turned back to Brennan while he finished redressing himself. "See you at work." With that, he strolled out the door, leaving a thick silence in his wake.

Brennan stared after him for a long moment, then turned back to me. "You cannot keep doing this, Brooks."

I arched a brow. "Doing what?"

"Running into danger, calling him instead of me—"

I held up a hand. "I did call you. Twice."

Brennan hesitated. His jaw flexed. "...Still."

I smirked. "So it's the Jett part that bothers you?"

He glared.

I shrugged. "Not my fault he actually answers his damn phone."

Brennan let out a frustrated breath, shaking his head. "You're impossible."

I grinned, sipping my coffee. "Not a crime, B."

Before he could argue, Claire, who had apparently been standing there completely frozen in shock this entire time, finally cleared her throat.

"So," she started hesitantly, "just to be clear... this is your brother." She pointed at Brennan. Then at the door. "And that was the former homicide detective from New York."

I nodded.

She exhaled slowly. "Huh."

I narrowed my eyes. "What's that supposed to mean?"

Claire hesitated, then smiled innocently. "Nothing."

"Claire."

"Nothing!" She pressed a hand to her chest, feigning offense. "I'm just... observing."

I groaned. "Jesus Christ."

Claire just grinned. "Anyway," she said brightly, shaking the bag in her hands. "I did bring the sticky notes. And highlighters. And some index cards because I know you never actually plan how you organize things."

I rolled my eyes but took the bag. "You are insufferable."

"Again," she chirped. "Not a crime."

I huffed a laugh, shaking my head.

Brennan groaned. "I can't deal with both of you at once." He ran a hand down his face. "I'm going to work. Brooks, stay out of trouble."

"No promises."

Brennan muttered something under his breath but didn't push it further. He shot one last warning glance at me, then turned and headed out.

The second the door shut behind him, Claire whirled on me, practically vibrating with energy.

"Oh. My. God."

I groaned. "Claire—"

"You didn't tell me Jett… was like that," she hissed.

I frowned. "What does that mean?"

"That he's hot, Brooks!" She smacked my arm. "Stupidly hot. Why did you not mention that?"

I rolled my eyes. "Because it's irrelevant."

Claire gasped dramatically. "Irrelevant? Oh, honey." She shook her head. "You're so in denial."

I ignored her, already digging through the bag for the sticky notes.

Claire crossed her arms. "So… nothing happened?"

I paused.

My brain flashed back to last night—his warmth beside me, the steady weight of his arm, the way his voice had softened when he whispered, *"Good girl."*

I shoved the memory away.

"Nope," I said, grabbing a pen. "Nothing."

Claire squinted at me.

I ignored her. I had work to do.

CHAPTER TEN

The garage was a disaster.

Sticky notes covered nearly every available surface—sprawled across the plastic tables, plastered onto the wall, stacked in neat little piles that Claire had *tried* to color-code before giving up on the idea entirely. Open files sat in messy heaps between coffee cups and granola bar wrappers, and my whiteboard was filled with half-finished thoughts, timelines that led nowhere, and arrows pointing in a hundred different directions.

It was chaos.

And we had gotten *nowhere*.

I scrubbed a hand over my face, sighing. "This is useless."

Claire, who was sitting cross-legged on the floor with a highlighter tucked behind her ear, frowned up at me. "It's not useless."

I shot her a look.

She gestured vaguely to the disaster zone around us. "It's… just *a process*."

"A process," I repeated flatly. She nodded.

I exhaled, stretching my legs out in front of me. "We're going in circles, Claire. None of this is adding up."

It was the same problem I'd been running into since the start. The killer was *too careful*. He left no fingerprints, no DNA, nothing to track. He was either a ghost or knew exactly how to cover his tracks.

And the worst part? He was toying with me. The note in Darby's mouth, the break-in at my house—it was all personal.

He wasn't just killing. He was *playing a game*.

Claire flipped through one of the files, tapping her pen against her chin. "Well, he has to sleep somewhere."

I stilled.

Her words landed heavy, sinking into my skull like a slow, dawning realization.

He had to sleep somewhere.

Somewhere that wasn't a house. Somewhere that wasn't easily traceable. Somewhere, he could come and go without anyone noticing.

I turned my head toward her, sitting up straighter. "Say that again."

Claire blinked. "That he has to sleep?"

"No—the part about *where*."

She hesitated, then tilted her head. "Well… yeah. He's not just wandering around 24/7. If he's not a local, then he has to be *staying* somewhere."

I stared at her.

How the hell had I not thought of that before?

I had been so focused on *who* he was that I hadn't stopped to consider the *where*.

He needed somewhere temporary. Somewhere, no one asked questions.

A motel.

"Holy shit," I muttered, pushing myself up to my feet. "Why didn't I think of that sooner?"

Claire perked up. "Wait, so that's actually helpful?"

"Yes." I moved toward my laptop, flipping it open. "He's not a local. He followed me here from Chicago; he has to be staying somewhere. Probably a motel."

Claire was already pulling out her phone. "Give me a second." Her fingers flew over the screen as she searched, scrolling through results. Then, suddenly, she made a small triumphant noise. "Bingo."

I leaned over her shoulder as she turned the screen toward me.

The listing was for a rundown motel just outside of town—one of those places that looked like it had seen better days back in the *sixties*.

Old Spruce Motel.

Cash only. No ID is required.

A perfect place to hide.

I met Claire's wide-eyed stare.

"We need to check this out," she said.

I was already thinking ahead. *If he was staying there, how long had he been there? Did anyone see him? What name—if any—was he using?*

But I wasn't about to drag Claire into this.

"No," I said, closing my laptop. "*I* need to check this out."

Claire frowned. "Brooks—"

I cut her off with a look. "No."

She crossed her arms. "You *just* said this could be important. That this could actually lead somewhere."

"It *could.*"

"So, shouldn't we go now?"

"We?" I let out a dry laugh. "You're not going anywhere near that motel, Claire."

Her eyes narrowed. "You *cannot* keep acting like I'm useless."

I sighed. "I *don't* think you're useless. I just think that if this guy *is* staying there, the last thing I need is to bring you along and paint a damn target on your back."

Claire opened her mouth, probably to argue, but I shook my head.

"I'm checking it out," I said firmly. "*Alone.*"

She let out a frustrated huff but didn't push it further.

I grabbed my jacket, my mind already running ahead to what I might find.

If I was right—if this was where he was staying—then I was about to get closer to him than ever.

And I wasn't sure if that thought thrilled me or terrified me.

"And don't you dare tell Jett or my brother."

Jett

I should have been able to focus.

I'd spent hours at my desk, pouring over crime scene photos, old case notes, anything that would pull my mind away from her.

It didn't work.

I wasn't sure why I even thought it would.

My pen tapped against the desk, the rhythmic click-click-click of the cap the only thing filling the quiet as I stared at the half-written report in front of me. I hadn't gotten past the second damn sentence.

Every time I tried to focus, my brain kept dragging me back to last night.

To Brooks, standing in the porch light, her voice shaking as she whispered, "Please."

To the way she had curled into me like she needed me there. Like she wanted me there.

To the way I almost lost my goddamn mind when she asked me to hold her.

I barely slept after I left her house. Spent most of the morning telling myself to get my shit together, to push her out of my head and focus on the case.

But it wasn't working.

Because despite every warning Brennan had ever given me about his sister—about how she was reckless, stubborn, and a walking disaster—I still couldn't shake the feeling that she'd gotten under my skin.

And now, after hours of trying to shove it down, I was done pretending.

I pushed back from my desk, standing abruptly. Skyla, who was typing something across the room, barely looked up. "You good?"

"Yeah," I muttered. "Just need some air."

I didn't wait for a response. Just grabbed my keys and walked out the front doors before I could change my mind.

Brooks's driveway was empty when I pulled up.

That was my first sign that something was off.

I had expected her to be home—figured she'd be buried under case files, probably with Claire hovering nearby, trying to make her color-code things.

But her car was gone.

I frowned, climbing out of my truck and heading up to the side door. I knocked twice.

A few seconds later, the door scraped open, and Claire blinked up at me.

She looked startled, which wasn't a good sign.

"Detective Jett," she said, her voice going slightly higher than normal. "What… brings you here?"

I narrowed my eyes. "Where's Brooks?"

Claire shifted her weight. "Uh…"

I crossed my arms. "Claire."

She sighed dramatically. "Okay, fine. She went to check something out."

I already didn't like where this was going. "Where?"

She winced. "You're not gonna like it."

"Claire."

She muttered something under her breath, then finally looked up at me. "A motel. Just outside of town."

My stomach dropped.

A motel.

"Tell me she didn't go alone," I said, already knowing the answer.

Claire bit her lip.

"Jesus Christ." I turned away, already stalking back toward my truck.

"She said she'd be fine!" Claire called after me.

I yanked the door open. "She always says that."

Claire hesitated. "Are you… mad?"

I exhaled sharply, gripping the top of the door. "No." I wasn't mad.

I was fucking pissed.

Because she knew better than this; she knew she had a target on her back. She knew this guy was playing with her. And still, she ran off alone.

I climbed into my truck, slamming the door shut.

I was going to find her.

And when I did, she was going to get a piece of my goddamn mind.

The Old Spruce Motel looked exactly how I expected it to—like the kind of place you either rented by the hour or never checked out of.

The neon sign buzzed faintly in the dark, casting a dull red glow over the cracked pavement of the parking lot. The air smelled like damp wood and cigarette smoke, and the only other car parked in the lot was one I knew too well.

Brooks.

I clenched my jaw, my grip tightening on the steering wheel.

Of course, she was here. Alone.

I threw the truck into park, yanked the keys from the ignition, and climbed out. The air was sharp against my skin, but I barely felt it as I crossed the lot, scanning the motel.

Only a handful of rooms, all ground level, the kind of setup that made for easy getaways.

Brooks's car was parked outside room six, but the curtains were drawn, and the door was slightly ajar.

My pulse kicked up.

I didn't think. Just moved.

The door creaked as I pushed it open, stepping inside.

It was exactly what I expected—a room frozen in time, the air thick with stale cigarette smoke and bad decisions. The floral bedspread looked like it hadn't been washed in years, the carpet was worn down to the threads, and the lamp on the nightstand flickered like it was deciding whether to give up entirely.

But Brooks wasn't here.

I exhaled sharply, scanning the room for any sign of a struggle, any indication that something had gone wrong.

Nothing.

The bed was still made. The dresser drawers were open but empty.

I turned back toward the door, irritation simmering in my chest.

She was fine.

She had to be.

And I was going to kill her for making me think otherwise.

I stepped back outside, letting the door fall shut behind me, and scanned the motel again. If she wasn't in the room, then—

My gaze landed on the front office.

Through the dirty window, I could just barely make out the outline of Brooks, leaning casually against the counter, her head tilted, a smirk playing on her lips.

And the man behind the desk?

Completely entranced.

I clenched my teeth so hard my jaw ached.

She was flirting.

She had run off, alone, to a sketchy motel, and now she was standing there, smiling like she didn't have a care in the world, probably conning that poor bastard out of whatever information she needed.

I was going to lose my goddamn mind.

Without thinking, I moved.

The bell above the door jingled as I stepped inside.

Brooks stiffened instantly.

The man behind the desk flinched, his wide, bloodshot eyes snapping to me as I shut the door behind me.

"Shit," Brooks muttered under her breath.

She turned her head slowly, her expression unreadable, but I could see the flicker of pure, unfiltered annoyance beneath it.

The guy behind the counter looked between us, suddenly wary, his eyes widening at the gun and badge on my belt. "Uh… you need a room?"

I ignored him, my eyes locked on Brooks.

Her lips pressed into a thin line. "What the hell are you doing here?"

"What the hell are you doing here?" I shot back, voice low.

She exhaled sharply, crossing her arms. "I had it under control."

I let out a dry laugh. "Yeah? Looked like he was the one under your control."

The desk clerk made a choked noise.

Brooks's glare sharpened.

I stepped closer, my voice dropping even lower. "You do not pull shit like this, Brooks."

She scowled. "I had it handled."

"You shouldn't have had to handle it alone."

The guy behind the counter shifted awkwardly. "Uh… am I—should I be here for this?"

I barely spared him a glance. "No."

Brooks groaned. "Oh, right. Because nothing puts people at ease like a six-foot-three cop scowling at them."

I exhaled slowly, pinching the bridge of my nose. I wasn't here to fight with her. Not in the middle of a damn motel lobby.

But she had no idea what it had done to me, finding her gone. Seeing her car outside that room, the door open, not knowing what the hell I was about to walk into.

And now, because I'd stormed in like an idiot, the clerk was shifting uneasily, already pulling back.

Brooks' window for getting more information was closing.

She knew it.

I knew it.

And she was pissed.

Her fingers flexed against her arms before she plastered on a tight smile, turning back to the clerk. "Sorry about that, Pete. He gets a little overprotective sometimes."

Pete still looked thoroughly spooked. "Uh. Yeah. No problem."

Brooks shot me one last glare before straightening. "Well. Guess I'll let you get back to work."

Pete nodded too fast. "Yeah. Sure. You, uh, have a good night."

Brooks flashed a strained smile, then turned on her heel and stalked past me, shoving the door open with more force than necessary.

I clenched my jaw, staring after her before following.

The second the door swung shut behind me, she whirled around.

"What the fuck was that?" she hissed, voice low but sharp.

I let out a slow breath, trying to keep my own temper in check. "That was me making sure you don't get yourself killed."

"I had it handled."

"You shouldn't have had to handle it alone."

Brooks exhaled sharply, pressing a hand to her forehead. "You don't get to storm in here and ruin—"

"I thought something happened to you."

The words came out rougher than I intended, my chest still tight with the fear I wasn't ready to admit to.

Brooks hesitated.

I ran a hand through my hair, forcing myself to exhale. "I showed up at your house, Claire told me where you went, and then I get here and find your car parked outside a half-open motel room? What the hell was I supposed to think?"

Brooks blinked at me, something flickering behind her expression—something I couldn't place.

For a second, she didn't answer.

Then, quieter, she muttered, "I didn't think you'd notice I was gone."

My stomach twisted.

I stepped closer, lowering my voice. "Of course I noticed."

She held my gaze, and for a second, I thought she was going to say something.

But then she shook her head, letting out a slow breath. "Well. Congrats, Detective. You just scared my best lead into silence."

I huffed a laugh, running a hand down my face. "Yeah, well. Sue me for wanting to make sure you're still breathing."

She scoffed, but the fight had mostly drained out of her.

I glanced back at the motel. "Did you at least get anything?"

Her lips pressed together. "Not enough."

I sighed. "Then let's go."

She raised a brow. "Oh? And where, exactly, do you think you're taking me?"

"Back to your house." I jerked my head toward her truck. "You're done here."

"No, I am not done here. I'm going to stay until tomorrow." She started making her way back to her motel room.

"Why, just to fucking spite me?" I couldn't believe how much she just *gets* under my skin.

"No, because I already paid for this fucking room and maybe, just maybe I'll be lucky enough to come across a clue."

CHAPTER ELEVEN

The dim light from the motel lamp flickers, casting uneven shadows across the peeling wallpaper. The air smells like stale cigarettes and mildew, the kind of scent that clings, settling in the back of your throat. Outside, the highway hums in the distance, but in here, it's quiet. Too quiet.

I'm pacing again, my shoes scuffing against the thin carpet, adrenaline still buzzing under my skin. The lead I chased here—another dead end. A wasted night. And now, I'm stuck here with Jett because I was throwing a tantrum, and he followed me back to my motel room.

Jett slams the door behind him, his expression tight as he tosses his jacket onto the worn chair in the corner. He's still running hot from the moment in the lobby, and I can feel the tension radiating off him like a storm of his own.

"You want to tell me what the hell that was back there?" His voice is low, clipped, and controlled—but there's something sharp underneath.

I spin to face him, arms crossing over my chest. "You mean how you almost blew my cover by storming in like you own the place?"

His jaw clenches. "I was trying to keep you from getting yourself killed."

I scoff. "Right. Because I need you to save me. Again."

His eyes darken, something flashing behind them. "You don't listen, Brooks. You never listen. You charge in, you push, you take risks without thinking, and one day, that's going to get you killed."

I take a step closer, the frustration boiling over. "I know what I'm doing. I've been in this world, too, Jett. So don't stand there and act like I'm reckless just because I don't do things your way."

"You think that's what this is?" His voice drops lower, rougher. "I don't give a damn how you do things—I give a damn about keeping you alive."

My pulse spikes. "I don't need you to protect me."

He doesn't move, doesn't blink, but something in his expression shifts. His chest rises and falls, controlled, measured. "Maybe not," he says quietly. "But that doesn't mean I don't want to."

I was still breathing hard, my fists clenched at my sides, my entire body buzzing from the argument we'd just had.

Jett stood in front of me, chest rising and falling, his hands fisted at his hips like he was barely holding himself together.

His jaw was tight, his shoulders stiff, his eyes burning into mine with a frustration so palpable it made the air thick between us.

God, he pissed me off.

And yet—

I wanted him.

The heat that had been simmering between us since the moment we met had finally boiled over, and now, it was threatening to consume us completely.

I swallowed, my pulse pounding in my throat.

Neither of us spoke. Neither of us moved.

Then Jett let out a rough breath, muttered a quiet, "Fuck it."

And then he grabbed me.

His hands fisted in my shirt, his mouth crashing into mine, claiming, demanding, unyielding.

The force of it sent me stumbling back, my spine hitting the motel wall with a thud, but Jett only pressed harder, his body pinning me in place, his hands everywhere at once.

I gasped into his mouth, and he swallowed it, his tongue sliding against mine, coaxing, taking.

The kiss was violent, all of our pent-up frustration, anger, desire— every unspoken thing between us, crashing together in a storm we couldn't escape.

I clawed at his shoulders, tugging him closer, and he groaned, low and deep, his hands sliding down my waist, my hips, gripping me like he was afraid to let go.

"Jett," I whispered, my breath ragged, my fingers tangling in his hair, pulling—

He growled, his teeth skimming my jaw, my throat, nipping, soothing, claiming.

"You drive me insane," he muttered against my skin, his voice low, wrecked, desperate.

"Good," I shot back, my nails digging into his back, feeling the heat of him, the weight of him pressing me down.

He let out a choked laugh, but then his hands were on my thighs, lifting me, wrapping my legs around his waist like he couldn't stand the space between us anymore.

I gasped as he carried me across the room, tossing me onto the bed with a force that sent a thrill down my spine.

Jett stood over me, his chest rising and falling, his eyes dark and unreadable, his lips wet and swollen from kissing me.

"Tell me to stop," he murmured, his voice like gravel, like a warning.

I didn't hesitate.

"Don't you fucking dare."

A sound rumbled deep in his chest, and then he was on me.

He kissed me hard, his hands shoving my shirt up, yanking it over my head, his lips following the path of exposed skin, tasting, taking, claiming.

I arched beneath him, my body burning, my fingers frantic as they pushed at his shirt, shoving it up, needing to feel him, skin on skin.

Jett let me, pulling back just long enough to tear his shirt off, tossing it to the floor before coming back down on top of me, all heat and muscle and desperation.

I could feel him rock-hard against me, pressing right where I needed him most, and a whimper escaped my throat before I could stop it.

Jett's head snapped up, his gaze fixing on mine, sharp and hungry.

"You sound so pretty when you beg," he murmured, his hand slipping between us, fingers dipping beneath my waistband, teasing, exploring. "You're so wet." He growled.

I gasped, hips jerking into his touch, but it wasn't enough.

"Jett," I groaned, digging my nails into his back, feeling his muscles tense beneath my fingertips.

He smirked, dragging my pants down, down, leaving me bare to him, his eyes dragging over every inch of my exposed skin.

"You're perfect," he muttered, his voice almost reverent.

I rolled my eyes, but the heat in his gaze made my breath hitch.

He stripped off his jeans, and suddenly, there was nothing between us but air and too many layers of built-up tension.

Jett braced himself over me, his forehead dropping to mine, his breathing uneven, controlled.

"I don't have a condom," he admitted, his voice gritted, rough.

I should have cared. I should have hesitated.

But I didn't.

I cupped his jaw, tilting his face toward mine, pressing my lips to his softly before whispering, "It's okay. I have an IUD. I want to feel you. Nothing between us."

Jett groaned, his hand gripping my waist, his jaw clenching like he was barely holding it together.

"Christ, Brooks," he muttered, pressing his forehead to my shoulder, his breath ragged.

Then, without warning, he lined himself up, pressing the tip of him against my entrance, waiting, giving me one last chance to stop this.

I didn't.

I arched up, wrapping my arms tighter around his neck, pulling him in.

That was all it took.

Jett slammed inside me, burying himself to the hilt, stretching me wide, the shock of it stealing my breath.

I gasped, my body clenching around him, adjusting, needing more, always more.

"Fuck," he groaned, his fingers digging into my hips, his forehead dropping to my shoulder.

He was huge, the stretch almost too much, but it was perfect, exactly what I needed.

I dug my fingers into his back, tilting my hips to take him deeper, to feel all of him.

Jett's breath hitched, his control hanging by a thread.

"I'm not gonna be gentle," he warned, his voice tight, dark.

"I don't want gentle," I shot back, wrapping my legs tighter around him, pulling him deeper, harder.

Jett cursed under his breath, and then he snapped his hips, thrusting deep and rough, making the bed slam against the wall.

I cried out, but Jett's hand was already there, clamping over my mouth, muffling the sounds threatening to give us away to the empty motel.

"Shhh, sweetheart," he murmured, his lips teasing my ear, his pace punishing.

I whimpered, my body tightening around him, my nails dragging down his back, leaving red welts in my wake.

Jett let out a deep, wrecked groan, his movements turning frantic, desperate, and perfect.

I was right there, so close, so overwhelmed, the heat between us threatening to swallow me whole.

Jett's fingers found my clit, circling, pressing, teasing, and that was it—

I shattered beneath him, my body tensing, clenching, and unraveling completely.

Jett followed me over the edge, burying himself deep, groaning my name, filling me, marking me, claiming me.

The room is quiet now, save for the sound of our labored breathing. My heart is pounding in my chest as I lie there, my body still trembling from what just happened. Jett is lying beside me, his arm heavy around my waist, pulling me into the warmth of his chest. For a moment, I let myself relax, let myself feel the weight of his body against mine.

It's strange how quickly the world has changed. One moment, I was filled with anger, frustration—determined to keep my distance—and now, I'm here, in his arms, in bed, tangled in something I can't untangle.

I try not to let myself think about it. I try to ignore the way my heart is still racing, the way my mind is spinning. This was reckless. I know that. But right now, as I lie here in the aftermath, it feels... right. And I hate myself for it.

Jett shifts beside me, pulling me closer, his warmth seeping into my skin. I try to push the thoughts away, but they linger, gnawing at the edges of my mind. What does this mean? What happens now?

I don't get the chance to answer myself. His voice breaks the silence. "You okay?"

I nod quickly, my throat tight. "Yeah. Just… trying to figure this out."

His hand brushes over my back, and I can feel the warmth of his fingers against my skin. I don't know what it means, but I don't know how to stop this, either. It's too much.

We lie there for a while, the silence stretching between us, but it doesn't feel awkward. It feels comfortable. Almost peaceful, in a way that makes me question everything I thought I knew about myself.

†

The soft rustle of the sheets wakes me up, and for a moment, I forget where I am. The room is still dark, only the faint light from the streetlights filtering through the blinds. Jett's arm is still around me, his grip firm but not tight. He's holding me like he doesn't want to let go.

I'm not sure how long we've been asleep, but it's long enough that the air in the room feels cooler now. I blink, trying to shake off the grogginess, but I feel it—the weight of his arm across my waist, the steady rise and fall of his chest against my back.

I shift, trying not to wake him, but he stirs, his grip tightening slightly as if he knows I'm trying to move. His voice is a low murmur, "Where do you think you're going?"

I freeze, panic flooding through me. My heart skips a beat, and for a moment, I think he's already awake—already figured me out. I don't know how to respond, don't know what to say. The guilt is already starting to creep in, the realization of what we've done and what it could mean.

I don't say anything. I can't.

He just pulls me closer, pressing a soft kiss to the back of my neck, and I'm not sure if it's a reassurance or a warning. Either way, I feel the pressure building inside of me. I can't stay here. Not now. Not like this.

His breathing slows again, and I wait a moment, letting the sound of his steady breath settle me, before I slip out of his grip, careful not to wake him. I move as quietly as I can, my heart thumping in my chest as I gather my clothes and pull them on. I don't look at him. I can't.

When I reach for the door, I hear him stir again, a soft groan escaping his lips. My stomach tightens, guilt settling heavily on my shoulders. I hesitate, my hand on the door handle, but then I push it open, stepping into the cool air of the motel room.

I don't look back.

I just leave.

CHAPTER TWELVE

Claire's rental car was parked in its usual spot in front of my house, but so was an unfamiliar SUV with Illinois plates. My brain quickly filtered through the possibilities of who from Chicago might show up unannounced, and only one terrifying thought stuck: Had he come for Claire? Or was he here for me?

If Claire got hurt just because I had to find out exactly how Jett's dick felt inside me, I'd never forgive myself.

I grabbed the tire iron from my trunk and approached the house, creeping up the stairs from the garage, weapon pointed low at my side but ready. I paused at the top, straining to hear any signs of distress.

"She'll probably be here in a couple minutes anyway." Claire's voice, distant and calm, floated from the kitchen.

I didn't see anyone in the living room, so I pressed forward, quiet as a shadow. "Let her go, you freak!" I shouted, rounding the corner, tire iron raised.

"Jesus, put that away, Reaper! Are you fucking nuts?"

I blinked. "Caleb?"

My former partner sat comfortably at my kitchen table, making himself at home. A suitcase sat behind his chair.

"What the fuck?"

"They were dragging their asses getting these files to your brother, so I thought I'd deliver them personally. Cash in on some of those vacation days I never use."

Caleb had always looked older than he was—not in his hair, which was still deep black, or his taut skin, but in his expression. Worn and aged with stress. And in the few months since I'd last seen him, he seemed to have aged a decade. "You look like shit," I told him, grabbing my usual coffee that Claire had brought over.

"Back atcha, Reaper."

"My brother won't be at the station this late." I checked the stove clock and debated. "We should just take them to his house. No room for that shit at the station." Too many idiots at the station, more like. I paused for a moment, feeling guilty for some reason. And then I wondered if they could smell the motel room and the sex on me from across the kitchen. "Just give me a couple minutes to shower first.

"Fine. Got a guest room I can unpack in while you shower?"

I laughed coldly. "You're kidding?" But his face told me he wasn't.

"Fucks sake, this isn't a hotel," I called over my shoulder as I headed for the bathroom.

†

Caleb took some time to get settled in the usually empty spare room. It had literally no furniture, so I let him drag in the seldom-used couch from the living room to sleep on.

We had to pack the boxes in around Claire to make room in the SUV. I didn't warn Brennan we were coming—I didn't want to give him time to invite Jett over. My hasty, cowardly retreat was still rattling in my skull.

"Fuck," I muttered under my breath as we pulled up to Brennan's house. It didn't matter. Jett's truck was already there. Karma was a bitch.

"Special delivery!" I called, following Claire inside with a stack of boxes nearly as tall as me.

Brennan and Jett sat in the sunken living room, a football game on TV. A relaxed evening, ruined by murder.

"Caleb, this is my brother, Brennan. B, this is Special Agent Caleb Lynch. And that's former New York homicide detective William Jett."

Brennan barely acknowledged the introductions. "What is all that?" He eyed the stacks of boxes I was unloading onto the dining room table.

"Chicago PD's case files on the Phantom Killer," Caleb announced, dumping more onto the table.

"We didn't name him," I added. "They couldn't print what I wanted to call him. Apparently 'Fuckwad psycho' was inappropriate."

107

Jett's attention snapped to one of the boxes labeled with my name. He plucked the top off, retrieving a note encased in an evidence bag.

"'My Sweet Brooks,'" I began reading. "'Have you ever heard someone struggle to catch their breath inside a plastic bag? It's not as stimulating as the sound of them choking on their own blood when I slit their throat.' Do I have it right so far?"

Jett's eyes lifted from the note, dark and unreadable. Anger rolled off him in waves, as if the files and the presence of others did nothing to dampen it. Was he pissed at me or the killer? Likely both, but which had him angrier?

"I'm not going to like what's in these boxes, am I?" Brennan muttered.

"You thought the body at the lake was bad?" I scoffed. "Wait till you see this shit."

Brennan's house transformed into a war room; every flat surface was covered in files. Caleb and Claire occupied the sunken living room, him typing notes on his laptop, her marking pages with sticky tabs, fixing everything with colour as usual. Skyla had replaced Brennan when he left for patrol a couple hours in. Jett stood opposite me at the kitchen island, silent. The flaw in his silent treatment? I would always out-petty him.

"Why stabbing?" I muttered for the thousandth time.

"If I ever have an answer, you'll be the first to know, Reaper," Caleb said, cracking his stiff neck. He checked his watch. "Jesus."

Jett glanced at the time, then abruptly dropped his file. "I should go to the station." He turned to Skyla. "I should've gone in with Brennan." Without another word, he was gone.

I ignored his departure and rummaged in Brennan's fridge, catching Caleb's smirk. "What?" I snapped.

"Nothing. Just happy to see you can piss off detectives in any state."

Skyla suppressed a laugh.

"I didn't do anything," I protested.

"It's probably their egos," Claire yawned.

Hours passed. When I emerged from Brennan's room, now in a fleece shirt I'd stolen from his closet, my brother had come back from the station. There was nothing there that was more pressing than the work being done here. Jett had returned as well—freshly changed into his usual dark-button up that he wore to the station, still ignoring me.

I took my seat at the dining table. My eyes blurred over the words I'd memorized, so I kept refilling my coffee. When Caleb stood, stretching, I barely noticed—until he crossed the room, pulled a blanket off the couch, and gently draped it over Claire.

He smoothed the fabric over her, tucking it in around her shoulders. Then, without thinking, he brushed a strand of hair from her face.

I felt my blood turn to ice. His sheepish smile when he realized I caught him doing it only pissed me off more.

I stood so abruptly that Jett's gaze flicked to me. Caleb stepped in front of me before I could storm into the living room.

"What the fuck was that?" I whisper-yelled, keeping my voice low so I wouldn't wake Claire.

"What?" Caleb's expression was all innocence. "I put a blanket on her."

"Don't patronize me. I'm not blind. Don't fucking do that. I told you—keep your hands off her and your fucking dick out of her."

"I was just—"

"I swear to God, if I find out you touched her—"

His smirk faded. "You need to relax, Reaper. Maybe take a nap."

I turned back to the files, fuming.

A box marked CONFIDENTIAL caught my attention. I'd never seen it before; it wasn't my scrawl across the label, not Caleb's either. I plucked off the top to see a USB drive and a decayed thing of red roses, each in their own evidence bag. There was a single, thin file and a manila envelope stamped *St. Vincent's Hospital – 2023.*

My breath caught. Why would there be a box from my stay at the hospital? What the hell was this? Why had I never seen this before?

I lifted the cover of the file folder and sifted through the first couple of pages. Medical reports, security logs. My stomach twisted as I read the next page:

CPD: Investigator Brooklyn Meeker was shot at close range by an unidentified suspect on 04/03/2023.

Surveillance footage in the hospital ward showed an unidentified man visiting Meeker while she was unconscious.

I looked at Caleb, my throat dry. "What is this?"

He exhaled sharply, his fingers raking through his hair. "Brooks." His voice was already defeated before he continued. "Please don't watch that." He eyed the bag with the USB in it.

I turned to my brother, a mix of strong feelings that I couldn't push down. "Plug in the USB," I ordered.

Brennan, either because he didn't feel like arguing with me or because he wanted to see the video himself, plugged the drive into the living room TV.

It was the hospital room. My hospital room. The grainy video flickered, its colour dulled in the dark room, the timestamp reading 11:51:43PM.

I was small in the hospital bed, unconscious and covered in IVs and tubes. This would have been shortly after I made it out of surgery.

The door creaks open, slowly flooding the room with a patch of light from the hallway before it shuts again. A large figure in a dark hood stepped inside, his movements fluid, practiced. A black-gloved hand emerged from the shadows, placing roses on my bedside table. Blood-red petals, stark against the sterile white sheets.

Then he turned toward me. I couldn't see his face, only the way he moved—like he belonged there, like this was routine. He reached out, took my hand. And held it.

For sixteen minutes.

He didn't move, didn't fidget. Just sat there, fingers curled around mine like he was waiting for something.

At 12:07, his free hand moved. Slowly, he unsheathed a knife— small, sharp, glinting in the dim light. The knife danced over my chest, covered by the sheets. My pulse pounded as he raised it, pressed the tip against my lips, dragging it just enough to break the skin. A single bead of blood bloomed.

Then he leaned in. And I swore he—

"Did he just—" Claire swallowed hard. "Did he taste your blood?"

The screen went dark.

And my hands wouldn't stop shaking.

"I think that's enough for the night," Jett announced with a finality that only I would dare protest against. But I didn't feel like protesting anymore. I felt like puking.

"Can you drive me home?" The sleepy and now startled Claire asked Caleb. He nodded, and I glared warningly at him.

Jett took my elbow, maybe a little bit more firmly than a normal person would, and started to guide me away from the files, out of my brother's house, and into his truck.

Jett drove in silence, his hands tight on the wheel, his jaw set. The quiet felt suffocating. I knew I should say something, but the words stuck in my throat. He hadn't said much since we left Brennan's, but I could feel the weight of his stare when he thought I wasn't looking.

I'd been avoiding him ever since the motel. Ever since, I have let things go too far.

I turned toward the window, watching the dark streets blur past. I'd barely had time to process the case, let alone what happened between us. My mind kept looping back to the way his hands felt on my skin, the way his breath had mixed with mine, the way I let myself get lost in him. It scared me—how easy it had been. How much I wanted more.

I knew Jett could feel the shift, too. He hadn't pushed, but he also wasn't letting me off the hook.

When he pulled up in front of my place, he finally spoke. "You gonna keep avoiding me, or are we gonna talk about it?"

I stiffened, my fingers curling around the long sleeves of Brennan's shirt I still had on. "I don't know what you're talking about."

Jett let out a humorless laugh, shaking his head. "Yeah, you do." He turned toward me, his expression unreadable. "Look, Brooks, I get it. You got spooked. But don't pretend it didn't happen."

"I'm not pretending anything," I snapped, then sighed, rubbing a hand over my face. "I just... I don't know how to deal with this right now."

He studied me for a long moment, then nodded. "Alright."

I blinked. "Alright?"

"Yeah." He exhaled sharply, glancing away. "You need time? Fine. But don't shut me out."

I hesitated. My instinct was to pull away, to push distance between us before things got even more complicated. But a part of me didn't want to. A part of me wanted to reach for him, to pull him back in.

Instead, I nodded. "Okay."

Jett didn't look convinced, but he didn't press. "Get some rest, Brooks."

I stepped out of the truck, feeling his eyes on me as I walked up the steps. When I reached the door, I glanced back. He was still there, still watching.

For a second, I thought about going back. Saying something, anything, to ease the tension between us. But I didn't.

Instead, I went inside, shutting the door behind me.

CHAPTER THIRTEEN

I was the first one on the scene this time.

For once, Brooks wasn't breathing down my neck, demanding details before I'd even finished taping off the area. Brennan and Skyla had a habit of calling her the second a body hit the ground, but I wasn't them. I wasn't about to risk her safety just because she had a sharp eye for a crime scene. If I could keep her at arm's length from this case, I would.

Didn't matter how many bodies I'd seen in my career—the smell of death never got easier. The way bodily fluids leaked, the way flesh soured and bloated—it all turned my stomach. And this guy, whoever he was, didn't just kill. He butchered.

The metallic sting of fresh blood clung to the damp morning air, thick and suffocating. The scent of copper and rot coated my tongue, threatening to drag up the coffee and eggs I'd managed to get down this morning.

The other officers weren't faring any better.

One of the new guys had already puked behind a patrol car. Another was bent over with his hands on his knees, taking slow, measured breaths. The crime scene tape had barely settled into place, and already, half of Brennan's department looked like they were reconsidering their career choices.

So, essentially, I was working this scene alone.

The weapon was obvious. An axe.

The head was destroyed, bludgeoned past the point of recognition. I hadn't been in this town long enough to have faces memorized, but even if I had, it wouldn't have helped. The victim had been reduced to an unrecognizable mess of splintered bone and pulverized tissue.

My hands clenched into fists inside my gloves.

A kill like this wasn't quick. It wasn't efficient. It was rage.

The quiet retching of another deputy snapped me out of my thoughts.

"Jesus fuck," a familiar voice snapped. "Get out of here if you're gonna be spewing."

Even without turning, I knew exactly who had just walked onto my crime scene.

Brooks.

That voice was both music to my ears and a pain in my ass.

She looked like she'd just rolled out of bed. The same mismatched sweatpants and hoodie I'd left her in a few hours ago, now rumpled and slept in, topped with an oversized corduroy jacket that swallowed her frame.

I scanned the area behind her. No Brennan. No Skyla. No sheriff-issued cruiser.

"How the hell did you find out about this so fast?" I muttered, still not looking away from the body.

She didn't answer me. Just adjusted a lens on her camera, snapped on a pair of gloves.

Good. She remembered to take her meds.

"It's not hard to find a crime scene in this town." Her voice was dry, but there was something else underneath it. Some unspoken weight.

She lifted her camera. "Hmm." That was all she said about the body before the first shutter clicked.

I let her do her job. What was the point in arguing?

She moved around the body, her lips moving almost imperceptibly.

She thought no one could hear her when she did this—muttering that quiet, rhythmic chant under her breath, the same one she used at every crime scene. I'd never figured out the words, but I knew the purpose. A ritual. A tether. Something to keep her grounded in the face of death.

I wasn't supposed to hear it. If she knew I could, she'd stop.

She lowered the camera after a few more shots, standing back to assess the carnage.

"Luke Harris." She glanced at me, expression unreadable. "This is his cabin. Went to prom with him. Greg on his way?"

I nodded. "Yeah."

"Who found the body?" She asked.

"Neighbor walking his dog. The dog bolted into the backyard and started barking his head off. Guy comes over to drag him away, sees this, calls it in."

Brooks frowned, tilting her head as she studied the body. "Why the axe?"

I exhaled sharply. "Same reason it's never the same weapon twice. The bastard likes variety."

She nodded slowly. "No hesitation wounds. He knew what he was doing."

"And took his time doing it." I gestured to the damage. "This wasn't one or two swings. He went at it like a goddamn machine."

She crouched closer, inspecting the blood spatter. "Where's the weapon?"

I shook my head. "Not here. He took it with him."

That wasn't what we wanted to hear. The killer didn't leave the weapons behind, which meant no prints, no trace evidence, nothing to tie him to it. He wasn't impulsive. He was controlled.

Brooks stood up, pressing the heel of her palm against her forehead. "Fuck," she muttered under her breath.

I didn't have to ask what she was thinking.

We were running out of time before he struck again.

Brooks

I parked a little haphazardly in front of Greg's office, hoping he'd have some useful information to offer me. If anyone knew something solid about the body found this morning, it was Greg. As useless as he was at a crime scene, his ability to get answers from a corpse on his table was uncanny.

But today, he didn't even let me get a full question out before he was shaking his head.

"Nope," Greg said, folding his arms across his chest. "I can't help you, Brooks. Orders."

I narrowed my eyes. "Orders? Since when do you take orders from anyone?"

Greg sighed. "Since Jett put me on strict instructions not to tell you anything about this case."

I opened my mouth, then snapped it shut, pressing my lips together so I didn't say something I'd regret. Instead, I turned on my heel and stormed out. If Jett thought he could control what I did, he had another thing coming.

Jett's house was exactly what I expected. Clean, tidy, practical—just like him. It had a distinct, almost impersonal kind of masculinity. Dark wood furniture, neatly arranged shelves, a few framed photos but nothing overly sentimental. The kind of place that looked lived in but not necessarily like a home.

I didn't bother knocking. I walked right in, the scent of something cooking hitting me immediately—garlic, maybe onions. Jett stood at the stove, stirring a pan, his back to me. He didn't look surprised when I slammed the door shut behind me.

"Breaking and entering, spitfire?" he said, not turning around.

"Don't leave your door unlocked if you don't want people barging in."

He sighed, shutting off the burner before finally facing me. His expression was unreadable, but his jaw was tight. He was bracing himself.

"Greg wouldn't tell me anything," I said, crossing my arms. "Because of you."

"That's right." He leaned against the counter, arms mirroring mine. "Because you need to stay out of it."

I laughed, short and humorless. "That's not your call to make."

"The hell it isn't," he snapped. "You're not a cop anymore, Brooks. You don't get to keep throwing yourself into the fire like this. You've got no badge, no weapon, no backup. You're asking to get hurt."

"This is what I do."

"Well, maybe you shouldn't."

Anger flared hot and sharp in my chest. "Oh, so what? I should just sit around and play good little girl while you handle everything?"

"Yes, Brooks!" he said a little too loudly. "I need you just to keep yourself safe so that I can do my fucking job."

"I am keeping myself safe. I'm still alive, aren't I? You're acting like you're the only person who knows how to investigate a case and follow leads. And you keep ruining things by getting in my way. Just like you did at the fucking motel."

Jett exhaled harshly and ran a hand through his hair like he was barely holding himself together. "Do you know why I went looking for you at your house that day? The day you took off to the motel?"

I scoffed, shaking my head. "Why? To check up on me? Make sure I was doing what I was told?"

"No," he bit out. "I was going to tell you how I feel about you."

That stopped me cold.

"I couldn't stop thinking about you. I couldn't stop thinking about holding you while we slept, being the person you called when you needed someone, knowing I made you feel safe."

For a second, neither of us spoke. I stared at him, my breath catching in my throat, and he stared right back like he was daring me to say something. But what the hell was I supposed to say to that?

So, I didn't say anything. I turned and walked out.

Claire showed up an hour later to my house with takeout, and I let her in without a word. Caleb was already here, sifting through case files on my chair while some news channel played in the background. He grabbed his food and disappeared into the other room when his phone rang, leaving Claire and me alone at the kitchen table.

She gave me a long, knowing look before digging into her noodles. "Okay," she said around a mouthful. "What happened?"

"Nothing."

She narrowed her eyes. "Liar."

I sighed, pushing my food around with my fork. "Jett said something."

"Something like?"

I hesitated, but Claire just waited, patient and expectant. I exhaled sharply. "He said he was going to tell me how he feels about me."

Claire froze mid-chew, then swallowed. "And?"

"And I left."

She stared at me, unimpressed. "You left."

"Yup."

She set her fork down with exaggerated patience. "Brooks. What the actual hell?"

"I don't know." I ran a hand through my hair, frustration bubbling under my skin. "It caught me off guard."

Claire rolled her eyes. "You've been dancing around this thing with Jett forever. And now, when he finally says something, you run away?"

"I didn't ask him to say it."

She gave me a deadpan look. "You didn't have to. He wanted to. You wanted him to."

I looked away, jaw tight. Claire sighed, softer this time. "Look, I love you, but you need to get your shit together. You can't keep acting like you don't care when you clearly do. Either let him in or let him go, but stop playing this game."

I swallowed hard, her words hitting too close.

"Listen, Brooks, you love pushing people away. I'm only here because I can be just as stubborn as you are. You don't have to walk through the world alone just to protect yourself. Now you have to stop being a coward about this."

"I don't know if I can," I admitted quietly.

Claire reached across the table, squeezing my hand. "Then figure it out before you lose him."

I paced my garage at midnight, unable to sleep, my arms locked tight across my chest, my sneakers scuffing against the concrete floor. The cool night air seeped in from the cracked door, but it wasn't enough to clear my head.

I tried to focus on the case. I ran through the facts in my mind, retraced the evidence we had, the pieces still missing. But every time I reached for logic, something else crashed through.

Jett. His words. His goddamn face when he said them.

"I was going to find you to tell you how I feel about you."

I scrubbed a hand down my face and let out a breath through clenched teeth. Feelings. I didn't know what to do with that. I didn't want to know what to do with that.

Commitment was messy. It was dangerous. I wasn't wired for it— not real, lasting, here's-my-heart kind of love. It required trust, and trust had never done me any favors. It only ever left me exposed. Vulnerable.

Jett was steady. Solid. The kind of man who didn't just dip his toe in—he dove headfirst, all or nothing. The kind of man who got married and settled down. And that scared the hell out of me.

Maybe I should stop this. Stop the tension, stop the flirting, stop letting myself get all wound up every time he was near. That would be the smart thing to do. Draw the line. Keep things clean.

But the second I thought about keeping my distance, all I could think about was him. The way he looked at me was like I was something he wanted to figure out. The way his voice dipped low when he was pissed, when we argued, when I challenged him, and he challenged me right back. The way his hands had felt on me—gripping, searching, sure.

A shiver rolled through me, though I wasn't cold.

I could stop this. I should stop this.

Instead, I was already moving.

Before I fully processed it, I was in my car. Then I was at his front door.

I lifted my fist and knocked, once, twice—firm, final.

It took a moment, but then the door swung open.

Jett stood there, half-asleep, hair mussed, body warm from bed, wearing nothing but dark boxer briefs that hung low on his hips.

His gaze swept over me, eyes heavy-lidded but sharp when they landed on my face. His brows pulled together. "Brooks?"

His voice was rough with sleep, with confusion.

I didn't answer. I couldn't.

My pulse pounded against my ribs, the fight still fresh between us, the lines of our boundaries blurred and crossed so many times they didn't exist anymore.

Something shifted in his expression, something sharp and knowing. His hand came up, fingers brushing my jaw, his thumb barely grazing the corner of my mouth.

"Tell me why you're here," he murmured.

I swallowed. My breath felt trapped in my chest. I could still walk away. I could turn around, drive home, and pretend I never came.

Instead, I stepped forward into his touch. Just enough.

That was all it took.

Jett grabbed me, yanking me inside, kicking the door shut behind me. His hands were on my face, my waist, pulling me in. And then his mouth crashed against mine, rough and urgent, stealing my breath, stealing my damn common sense.

I let him.

Jett kissed me like he had something to prove. Like he was trying to brand himself into me, make sure I felt him everywhere, even after this was over.

He was kissing me like he wanted to make sure I could never erase him from inside of me.

Heat uncurled low in my stomach as his hands slid down my back, fingers pressing into my hips, pulling me flush against him. He was warm, solid, *everywhere*, his body braced against mine like he was afraid I'd vanish if he let go.

I fisted my hands in his hair, pulling, and he groaned into my mouth, deep and low. His hands moved—one gripping the small of my back, the other slipping beneath the hem of my shirt, fingertips skimming over bare skin.

"Brooks," he murmured against my lips, his breath hot, his voice rough.

He didn't say anything else. He didn't have to.

I grabbed the back of his neck and kissed him harder, sinking into him, letting him pull me deeper. His hands grew more certain, more *hungry*. He broke away just long enough to tug my shirt up over my head, dropping it somewhere behind me.

His gaze dragged over my bare chest, dark and heavy, the kind of look that sent heat straight to my core.

I should've felt self-conscious. I should've been thinking about what this meant, about where this was going, about whether this was a mistake.

But I wasn't.

I was thinking about the way Jett touched me, how his fingers skimmed the edge of my waistband, his knuckles brushing my stomach as he took his time, as he unraveled me piece by piece.

"You gonna keep staring?" I teased, breathless.

His lips curved slightly, but his eyes stayed serious. "Maybe."

I rolled my eyes, but before I could come up with a snarky reply, he was kissing me again, walking me backward, guiding me down the hall.

We bumped into the wall once, then twice, but neither of us cared. My fingers slid over the ridges of his stomach, nails scraping lightly down his chest, and he hissed, the muscles flexing under my touch.

His mouth moved to my jaw, then lower, teeth dragging over the sensitive skin of my throat, his tongue following the path he'd just marked. I felt the scrape of his stubble, the heat of his breath, and my knees nearly buckled.

Jett caught me before I could stumble, his hands tightening on my waist. "I've got you," he murmured, his voice rough, wrecked.

And somehow, I believed him.

His hands moved again, undoing the button of my jeans, sliding the denim down my hips, his knuckles brushing bare skin as he went.

I inhaled sharply.

"Jett." His name barely made it out, breathless, wrecked.

He kissed me again, softer this time, dragging it out as if he was savoring every second.

By the time we reached his bedroom, I wasn't thinking at all.

Jett laid me out on his bed and stood above me, a look so hungry on his face that I was beginning to feel like a sacrifice. Jett hooked his thumbs into the waistband of his underwear and pulled them down. I followed the movement with my eyes, drinking in every inch of skin that he exposed.

Jett hovered over me, his body warm and solid, his breath brushing against my skin as he held himself above me.

His eyes devoured me, taking in every inch of exposed flesh, dark and heavy-lidded with want.

I swallowed hard, my pulse pounding in my ears.

He dragged his knuckles down my bare stomach, slow and deliberate, like he was savoring the feeling of me beneath his hands.

I should've been thinking about what this meant. About where this was going. About how I was handing myself over to him without hesitation.

But I wasn't thinking at all.

I reached for him, fingers skimming over his stomach, feeling the hard ridges of muscle flex beneath my touch.

Jett's breath hitched, his jaw tightening as my hands traveled lower, wrapping around him, feeling how thick and ready he was.

His head tipped forward, his forehead brushing mine, his breath warm and uneven.

"Brooks," he murmured, his voice so rough, so wrecked it sent a shiver through me.

His mouth found mine, slow at first—deep, thorough, like he was tasting me, like he was committing the moment to memory.

Then, his restraint snapped.

Jett kissed me harder, his body pressing flush against mine, his hands roaming—gripping my thighs, sliding down my hips, pulling me against him.

I moaned into his mouth, my fingers digging into his back, feeling his raw strength.

He ground against me, teasing, dragging himself along my slick heat, making my breath hitch, making my hips roll in search of more.

I was already shaking, already coming undone, and he hadn't even taken me yet.

Jett's lips trailed down my jaw, then lower, his tongue flicking against my pulse before he bit down—soft, sharp, just enough to make me whimper.

His hands gripped my thighs, spreading me open beneath him, fitting himself perfectly between my legs.

I was aching for him, my skin flushed, my body begging.

Jett leaned down, his lips hovering just above mine, his body pressing against me in all the right places.

"You ready for me?" he murmured, his voice thick, teasing, hungry.

I nodded frantically, my breath coming in shallow gasps.

I wanted him. Needed him.

Jett groaned, his fingers curling around my wrist, pinning it above my head, his other hand guiding himself between my thighs.

The first slow push inside me stole the air from my lungs.

I gasped, my body arching into him, my legs wrapping tight around his waist as he buried himself deeper.

"Fuck," Jett gritted out, his jaw clenching, his muscles tensing as he tried to give me a moment to adjust.

I was so full, so stretched, my body struggling to take him all in.

But it wasn't enough.

I rocked my hips against him, pushing him deeper, pulling him closer.

Jett groaned, his hands tightening on my waist, his control hanging by a thread.

"You feel so fucking good," he gritted out, his lips brushing mine, his breath hot and ragged.

I didn't have words—I just held onto him, my fingers dragging down his back, my body tightening around him.

Jett started to move, slow at first, deep and deliberate, each thrust sending a new wave of pleasure rolling through me.

I moaned, biting my lip, trying to keep quiet—but I couldn't. I was unraveling.

Jett must have sensed it because his hand shot up, covering my mouth, his eyes dark and knowing.

"Shhh," he whispered against my ear, his voice low, teasing.

I whimpered against his palm, my fingers fisting in the sheets, my body coiling, burning, desperate.

Jett chuckled, his control slipping, his pace picking up.

His thrusts grew rougher, deeper, each one pushing me further toward the edge.

I clawed at his back, my nails scraping down his spine, needing more, needing everything.

Jett groaned, his lips finding my throat, his teeth nipping, soothing, teasing.

"You gonna come for me?" he muttered, his breath hot, uneven.

I nodded frantically, my body tightening, trembling, the pressure building, unbearable.

Jett's hand slid between us, fingers finding me, pressing, circling, coaxing.

And then I broke.

I shattered beneath him, my body clenching, pulsing, a choked moan escaping past my lips.

Jett cursed, his grip bruising, his thrusts losing rhythm as he followed me over the edge.

He buried himself deep, groaning against my neck, his body trembling, spilling inside me.

We stayed like that, panting, tangled, completely wrecked.

Jett's forehead pressed to mine, his breath uneven, his lips brushing lazy kisses over my jaw.

I exhaled, boneless, spent, completely undone.

✝

Jett

The early morning light slipped through the blinds, throwing soft lines across the room. The sheets were tangled around our legs, the warmth of Brooks' naked body pressed against mine, grounding me in a way I didn't realize I needed.

I was sitting up against the headboard. She was curled up half in my lap, her head resting on my stomach, one arm draped lazily across my side. My fingers moved through her hair, slow and absent, the strands slipping between them like silk.

She was quiet. Still.

That was rare for Brooks.

I studied her face, the way her lashes skimmed her cheek, the way her fingers curled slightly against my skin like she didn't even realize she was holding on to me.

"Morning," I murmured.

She hummed, barely opening her eyes.

I smiled. "You good?"

Her lips pressed together for a beat before she spoke. "I'm scared."

I paused, fingers stilling in her hair. "Of what?"

Her exhale was shaky. I felt it more than I heard it.

"This." She shifted, lifting her head slightly to look at me. "You. Me." A pause. "Us."

I frowned, brushing my thumb along the curve of her temple. "Talk to me."

125

She sighed and let her head drop back down, like looking at me made it harder to say whatever was sitting heavy in her chest.

"I'm not a stable relationship person, Jett," she admitted, her voice quieter now. "You are."

My brows pulled together. "That's what you think?"

She let out a soft, humorless laugh. "It's what I know." She ran her fingers over my ribs absentmindedly. "You're steady. Dependable. You—" she hesitated, then pushed forward, "—you commit to things. People. I don't."

I kept my hand moving through her hair, slow and steady. "Brooks, it's not about what you've been. It's about what you want to be."

She scoffed lightly. "And what if I don't know what I want?"

I let that settle for a second before answering. "Then we figure it out."

She was quiet again, and when she finally spoke, her voice was almost hesitant. "You were already married once."

I blinked, not expecting her to bring that up. It wasn't something I hid, but it wasn't something I chose to bring up either, although I shouldn't be shocked that Brooks knew about it.

"That means something," she continued, lifting her head to look at me again. "It means you are that kind of person. You don't do half-measures."

I studied her face, the wariness in her eyes, the way she was bracing for something.

She was scared, really scared. Not of me. Not of what we'd done last night.

But of what it meant.

"You think that just because I was married before, I expect some perfect relationship out of this?"

She didn't say anything.

I exhaled, dragging my knuckles along her jaw. "Brooks, my marriage didn't work." I gave a small, wry smile. "Clearly, I'm not perfect at commitment either."

She frowned slightly, like she wasn't sure if she wanted to believe that.

I leaned in, pressing my lips to her forehead. "I don't want perfect. I don't want a version of you that you think you should be. I just want you."

Her fingers tightened on my side.

I shifted, moving so that she was on her back, my body hovering over hers. I searched her face, letting my hands map over her skin, slow, steady, deliberate.

"I'm not going anywhere," I murmured.

Her breath hitched as my lips brushed against the corner of her mouth.

"I don't expect you to have this figured out." I kissed along her jaw, the line of her throat, listening to the sharp little inhales she made when I hit the right spots. "But I need you to try."

She let out something between a sigh and a curse, her hands coming up to tangle in my hair, pulling me back down to her mouth.

And then she kissed me, deep and searching.

And I knew she was trying.

CHAPTER FOURTEEN

I wasn't used to this.

Waking up *with* someone.

Waking up with *him.*

Jett's arm was heavy around my waist, his breath warm against the back of my neck. The weight of him was solid, grounding, and *good.* I could feel the slow, steady rise and fall of his chest, the rhythmic drum of his heartbeat against my spine.

I should have felt trapped. Caged. Like I needed to get up and put distance between us before things got *too* real.

But I didn't.

I shifted slightly, testing the space between us, and his arm instinctively tightened, pulling me closer. His fingers skimmed over my stomach, barely there, but enough to make me shiver.

A slow inhale, then his voice, still thick with sleep.

"You awake?"

I turned my head slightly, just enough to see him out of the corner of my eye. His hair was a mess, his jaw dark with the start of stubble. He looked softer like this, less guarded.

"Mmm," I murmured.

His fingers flexed against my stomach, tracing the hem of his shirt—the one I had thrown on after last night, the one that still smelled like him.

"You okay?" he asked, voice low. The real question.

Because Jett *knew* me, he knew that waking up together, lingering in this moment, meant more than I probably wanted to admit.

I took a slow breath, pushing past the unease curling at the edges of my ribs. *I want this. I can try this.*

So I nodded. "Yeah," I said, and to my surprise, I meant it.

Something flickered across his face, something I couldn't quite read. His grip on me loosened slightly, giving me an out if I wanted it.

But I didn't take it.

Instead, I reached back and laced my fingers through his, keeping his hand against my stomach. His breath hitched—just barely—but then he exhaled, pressing a lazy kiss against my shoulder.

"Good," he murmured.

I smiled, small and barely there, but real.

For once, I didn't want to run.

The smell of coffee filled the air as I curled into the couch, Jett's shirt hanging loose around my thighs.

Jett stood in the kitchen, wearing nothing but his boxer briefs as he poured two mugs, looking way too comfortable in *my* home.

And the weird part?

I liked it.

He walked over, handing me a mug before settling onto the couch beside me. I tucked my feet under me, and without even thinking, I leaned into him, my head resting against his shoulder as he threw an arm across the back of the couch.

Caleb was already gone for the day. Good. One less interruption.

Jett took a slow sip of his coffee before speaking. "I've been thinking about something."

"Dangerous."

He huffed a quiet laugh, shaking his head. "Shut up."

I grinned against my mug.

He set his coffee down, turning slightly toward me. "I know you're not gonna stay out of this case."

"Correct."

"So." He ran a hand through his hair, sighing. "I'll keep you in, but under one condition."

I arched a brow. "Oh, this should be good."

Jett leveled me with a look. "You work *with* me. No running off on your own, no chasing leads solo. If we do this, we do it *together.*"

Something warm settled in my chest. Not just at the fact that he was keeping me on the case, but because of *why.*

"You're trying to keep me safe," I said.

Jett's jaw ticked. "Someone has to."

I swallowed, letting that sit for a second. I wasn't used to this—not just being looked after but *letting* someone look after me.

But if I was trying, *really trying*, then I had to meet him halfway.

So, I nodded. "Okay."

Jett blinked, clearly expecting a fight. "Wait—*okay?*"

I smirked. "Don't make me change my mind, Detective."

He exhaled a laugh, shaking his head. "Unbelievable."

I grinned, leaning back into him.

"Now." He picked up his coffee again, shifting gears. "I was gonna head to the Rusty Nail today. See if anyone there remembers Luke from the night before he was killed."

I hummed, thinking it over. "Not a bad idea."

Jett smirked. "I do have them occasionally."

I rolled my eyes, about to fire back—

And then the front door scratched open.

Claire walked in like she owned the place, her eyes already on her phone as she spoke. "Okay, first of all, *you* need to answer your texts because—"

She stopped dead.

I barely had time to register what she was staring at before she spoke again.

"Oh. My. God."

I followed her gaze—to me, curled up against Jett on the couch. *In his shirt.* Jett, very shirtless, very casual, drinking coffee like he belonged here.

Claire's mouth fell open. "No. Absolutely not. I cannot believe this. Did I manifest this or what?"

Jett sighed, rubbing his temple. "Morning, Claire."

She pointed an accusing finger at me. "You. Explain."

I groaned, shoving my face into Jett's shoulder. "I hate you."

She grinned. "No, you *don't.*"

"Give me a second to *wake up* before the interrogation," I muttered.

Claire dropped onto the chair across from us, arms crossed, looking way too pleased with herself. "Fine. I'll let you make yourselves decent. But then, I *want details.*"

Fifteen minutes later, after Jett had finally put on *pants* and I had changed into real clothes, we sat at the kitchen table while Claire sipped a fresh cup of coffee like she also *belonged* here.

"So," she said, grinning. "The bar, huh?"

I blinked. "How do you—?"

"Oh, please." She waved a hand. "I caught the tail end of your little pillow talk. You're going to the Rusty Nail?"

Jett shot me a look. *This is your fault.*

I sighed. "Yes."

"Great." Claire beamed. "I'm coming."

Jett looked entirely *done.* "No, you're not."

"Why not?"

"Because it's *work.*"

"It's a *bar.*"

I pinched the bridge of my nose. "Claire—"

"Nope. Not hearing it." She grabbed her coffee, standing up.

"Yes, you are hearing because you are not coming Claire. It's not safe for you to be snooping around with me."

Jett leaned in, lowering his voice. "You are such a little hypocrite, you know."

I groaned. "Yeah. Whatever."

Something was off about Claire.

She had been *too* casual all morning, like she was covering something up. Even though she was all bright and… pastel when she bound in this morning, something was bugging her. Something she was keeping from me.

I wasn't sure what tipped me off—maybe the way she avoided eye contact when Jett and I continued to talk about the Rusty Nail, or the slight hesitation when I asked casually if she'd been there before.

But something wasn't adding up.

And then, just as Jett and I were getting ready to head out the door, she made a passing comment. Completely irrelevant to the rest of our conversations.

"I mean, *some people* have no problem moving on quickly."

It wasn't directed at anyone. It wasn't even said with any weight. Just a casual throwaway line.

But my instincts locked onto it.

I studied her carefully. "What do you mean by that?"

Claire froze for half a second before laughing it off. "Nothing. Just talking in general."

But she wouldn't look at me.

And just like that, a quiet suspicion started curling in my gut.

Something had happened.

And I was about to find out *exactly* what.

✝

The Rusty Nail smelled like spilled beer, cigarette smoke, and poor decisions. The kind of place where the jukebox only worked half the time, and nobody asked too many questions.

Jett and I had been here long enough to hear the same stories twice, most of them useless. Luke Hollis had been here that night, he'd been drinking fast, he'd seemed stressed. *We already knew that.*

Jett pushed off the bar, scanning the room. "I already talked to Ed," he said, nodding toward the older man nursing a whiskey at the end of the counter. "Didn't get much."

I followed his gaze, eyeing Ed as he took a slow sip, his face unreadable. Weathered, lined, but sharp-eyed. A man who had never been in a hurry a day in his life. A man who *saw things.*

I scoffed, shaking my head. "That's because you're a cop. And an out-of-towner."

Jett smirked. "And you think you'll do better?"

I grabbed my drink, already making my way over. "I *know* I will."

Jett muttered something under his breath, but he followed, leaning against the bar a few feet away as I slid onto the stool next to Ed.

"Hey, Ed."

He barely glanced up, tilting his glass toward me in acknowledgment. "Brooks."

I let the silence stretch, giving him time to acknowledge me properly. When he finally looked up, I leaned in slightly, voice casual. "You hear about Luke?"

Ed exhaled through his nose. "Hard not to."

I nodded. "I know Jett asked you about it, but I also know you're not the type to talk freely to a badge." I lifted my drink, taking a slow sip. "So I'm asking."

Ed studied me for a second, then sighed. "Luke came in late that night. Jumpier than usual. Kept checking the door like someone was gonna walk in behind him."

I hummed. "That track with what you told the detective?"

Ed smirked slightly. "Didn't tell the detective much."

Jett exhaled sharply behind me. "Shocking."

I ignored him, keeping my focus on Ed. "Who was he looking for?"

Ed shrugged. "Dunno. But when I stepped outside for a smoke, I noticed something else." He lifted his drink, swirling the amber liquid. "A black SUV parked across the street. Engine running. Headlights off."

A slow weight settled in my chest.

Jett's voice came from behind me, clipped. "You're sure it was running?"

Ed gave him a look. "I ain't blind, son."

I bit back a smirk. "What else?"

Ed leaned back, rubbing his chin. "Didn't move while I was out there. But when Luke left? That thing pulled out right behind him. Didn't speed, didn't burn rubber. Just… eased out like it had all the time in the world."

I clenched my jaw. A slow, deliberate tail.

Jett stepped closer, his presence solid beside me. "You see the driver?"

Ed shook his head. "Windows were too dark."

Damn it.

I drummed my fingers against the bar. "What about the car itself? Anything stand out?"

Ed nodded. "Yeah. Back window had a crack in it. Looked like someone tried to break it once." He took another sip of whiskey before adding, "And one of the brake lights was out. Right side."

That was something.

Jett sat back, exhaling through his nose. I could practically hear the gears turning in his head.

I studied Ed, trying to get a read on him. "You ever seen that SUV before?"

He shook his head. "Not that I've noticed. But I'll keep my eyes open."

I nodded, sliding a twenty across the bar for his trouble. "Appreciate it, Ed."

He gave me a look. "I'd say 'be careful,' but I know you won't listen."

I smirked, finishing my drink. "Damn right."

Jett and I headed for the door, the weight of what we'd just learned settling between us.

Once we were outside, I exhaled, shoving my hands into my pockets. "This changes things."

Jett nodded. "We're not dealing with someone who just snapped."

"No." I glanced back toward the street, picturing the SUV sitting there, waiting in the dark. "This was planned."

Luke had known something. Or done something.

Either way, he had been marked.

And now, we had to figure out why.

By the time we pulled into my driveway, my head was still running through everything we had learned at the bar.

The black SUV. The cracked window. The busted brake light. The fact that whoever was driving had been waiting for Luke.

None of it sat right.

Jett shut off the engine, but neither of us moved to get out. The truck ticked in the silence, cooling from the drive. Outside, the wind carried the faint rustle of tree branches, the occasional distant hum of a car rolling down the highway.

I sighed, pressing my forehead against the window. "Luke didn't stand a chance, did he?"

Jett was quiet for a second. "No," he admitted. "I don't think he did."

I exhaled through my nose, fingers drumming against my thigh. "He knew something was off. He felt it." I shivered, knowing exactly what Luke would've felt.

Jett nodded. "And then he wound up killed."

Silence stretched between us, heavy and inevitable. I could feel the weight of it pressing down on both of us.

Then Jett shifted, his voice softer. "We'll figure this out, Brooks."

I turned my head, meeting his gaze in the dim glow of the dashboard lights. His expression was unreadable, but there was something steady in it. Something certain.

And, God help me, I needed that certainty right now.

So, I nodded. "Yeah. We will."

†

Getting inside without waking Caleb was an ordeal. Especially because I was having a hard time keeping my lips off of Jett as we made our way through the house.

I should've been focused on sneaking past the guest room, on avoiding waking my pain-in-the-ass houseguest. But instead, I was biting back a smile as Jett's hands gripped my waist, steady and possessive, guiding me toward my bedroom door.

The guest room door was cracked just enough that I could hear Caleb's snoring—deep and steady.

Jett shot me a look. *If he wakes up and sees me sneaking into your bedroom, this is on you.*

I rolled my eyes and tiptoed past, heart racing a little at how ridiculous this was. I was a grown woman, sneaking a man into my own damn bedroom.

What the hell was my life?

Jett shut the door quietly behind us, exhaling like he'd just cleared a minefield.

I smirked. "Relax, Detective."

His eyes darkened as I peeled off my shirt and tossed it aside, like I wasn't already testing every ounce of his patience.

His jaw clenched. "It's bad enough that Claire already knows, but I'd like a chance to break this news gently to Brennan myself. So, the fewer people that find out before him, the better."

I snorted and climbed into bed, stretching out against the cool sheets.

Jett kicked off his boots, then his jeans, settling in beside me like it was second nature.

And maybe—just maybe—I liked that it was.

I turned onto my side, propping my head on my hand. "So, what's our next move?"

Jett mirrored me, arm bent beneath his head. "Tomorrow, I'll see if we can pull traffic cam footage. A black SUV with a busted brake light shouldn't be hard to track if we know what time Luke left the bar."

I nodded. "I'll dig into Luke's background more. See if anything jumps out that might tell us why he was targeted."

Jett hummed in agreement. "Good."

The conversation should have kept going. Should have stayed focused on the case.

But then Jett's fingers brushed lightly against my arm, slow and absent. Not urgent, not expectant. Just there.

And suddenly, the air in the room shifted.

My throat went dry.

He was too close, his warmth pressing against my bare legs. The quiet between us suddenly felt louder.

Jett's voice dipped lower. "You really okay with this?"

I knew what he meant.

This. Us.

A part of me wanted to deflect, to throw up the usual walls, to push the moment away before it could settle into something too real.

But I didn't.

Instead, I reached for him, my fingers sliding over his wrist, feeling the steady pulse beneath his skin.

"Yeah," I said. "I think I am."

Something flickered in his expression—relief, maybe. Or something deeper than that.

"You're kinda cramping my style though." I told him. "Showing up to question people looking all… official." I smiled. "You scare people off."

He smirked slightly and then it gently faded from his face.

His hand drifted up, fingers brushing a loose strand of hair from my face, the touch lingering as his knuckles skimmed my cheek.

His thumb traced the line of my jaw, slow and reverent, like he was memorizing me.

"You're beautiful, you know that?"

I rolled my eyes, but my breath caught slightly at the warmth in his voice. "Don't start."

Jett smirked. "I'm serious." His fingers drifted down, trailing featherlight over my collarbone, along the inside of my wrist. "I don't just mean the way you look, either."

I raised a brow. "Oh, so you're saying I'm not pretty?"

He chuckled, shifting even closer, his bare skin brushing mine. "I'm saying you're ridiculous." His voice softened. "And strong. And sharp. And the most stubborn pain in my ass I've ever met."

I huffed a quiet laugh, but it came out softer than I meant it to.

Jett's hand drifted to my waist, his fingers skimming the hem of the t-shirt I stole from him earlier. He didn't push, didn't demand—just touched, slow and easy.

"I mean it, Brooks." His lips brushed my temple. "I see you."

My chest tightened.

I wasn't used to this kind of attention—the slow kind, the patient kind.

I wasn't used to someone looking at me like this.

Jett shifted, rolling me onto my back, his body settling between my legs, propping himself on his elbows.

His lips ghosted over mine. "Can I tell you something?"

I barely nodded.

He exhaled, his nose skimming mine. "I like this."

My fingers curled against his side, feeling the warmth of him. "This?" I whispered.

Jett hummed. "Being here. With you." His lips hovered over mine. "I like knowing you'll still be here when I wake up."

My throat went tight.

He kissed me then, soft and slow, like we had all the time in the world.

And when I kissed him back—needy and wanting—I knew there was no stopping this.

Jett's hands skimmed beneath my shirt, dragging the fabric up, exposing my bare stomach.

But then I heard it—a shift in the house.

A snore.

A creak.

Jett froze, his body tensing above mine.

I slapped a hand over my mouth, stifling my laugh.

Jett narrowed his eyes. "This isn't funny."

I giggled, my shoulders shaking, unable to stop myself.

Jett didn't look amused. He looked like a man seconds away from losing his patience in the best possible way.

He smirked, pressing a warning kiss to my throat, his lips barely brushing my skin. "If I have to be quiet," he murmured, his breath warm and teasing, "so do you."

I swallowed hard, biting my lip, my laughter fading as something thicker settled between us.

Jett's fingers hooked around the waistband of my underwear, his knuckles brushing the curve of my hip as he dragged them down, slow and teasing, his lips trailing down my body as he went.

I squirmed beneath him, heat pooling low in my stomach, my breath catching when he kissed the inside of my thigh—soft and deliberate.

"Jett—" I whispered, my fingers already curling into the sheets.

He looked up at me, his lips barely grazing the sensitive skin near my hip bone, grinning like a man who knew exactly what he was about to do to me.

His breath ghosted over my bare skin, and then—

Fuck.

I slapped a hand over my mouth, muffling the moan that tore out of me as his tongue found me, as he parted me with slow, languid strokes, taking his time like he had nowhere else to be.

My thighs tensed, my hips lifting off the bed as I struggled not to make a sound, but Jett just pinned me down, his hands gripping my waist, holding me exactly where he wanted me.

I whimpered into my palm.

Jett hummed against me, pleased with himself, his tongue flicking over me just right, sending another sharp pulse of heat through my core.

"Jett—" I gasped, desperate, overwhelmed, already trembling.

He just chuckled, the vibration sending shocks through me.

And then he sucked, slow and deep, his hands tightening on my hips as he kept me from escaping.

I bit down on my knuckles, my body coiling, my breath coming in short, shallow gasps.

"Jesus Christ," I hissed, arching into his mouth, my free hand fisting in his hair, tugging hard.

Jett groaned against me, and fuck, I felt it everywhere.

I tried so damn hard to keep quiet, but the moment he slipped a finger inside me, curling just right, a broken moan escaped past my lips.

Jett's hand shot up, covering my mouth, his other still working between my thighs.

He lifted his head, his lips wet, glistening, his pupils blown wide with hunger.

His voice was low, strained. "Told you to be quiet, sweetheart."

I shivered, the sound of his voice almost enough to push me over the edge.

But he wasn't done with me yet.

Jett pressed a final, lazy kiss to my thigh before moving up my body, his weight settling over me, his mouth finding mine in a slow, deep kiss.

I could taste myself on his tongue.

I whimpered into him, gripping his shoulders, feeling the heat of him pressing against my stomach, hard and ready.

I wanted him.

Needed him.

My fingers fumbled for his boxers, shoving them down, not caring where they landed, just needing to feel him, skin on skin, nothing between us.

He gritted his teeth, the muscles in his arms tensing as I wrapped a hand around him, stroking him slow, teasing, making him suffer the way he had just made me suffer.

"Brooks," he hissed, his forehead dropping to mine, his jaw clenched so tight I thought it might break.

I smirked, rolling my hips against him, coaxing him closer, teasing him with the slick heat between my thighs.

Jett groaned, his patience snapping.

In one swift motion, he lined himself up and pushed inside, burying himself to the hilt, stretching me in a way that made my head spin.

I gasped, my fingers digging into his back, my body arching into his.

Jesus.

His jaw tensed, his breath ragged, his body shaking as he tried to stay still, giving me a second to adjust.

"Fuck," Jett breathed against my neck, his voice wrecked. "You feel so goddamn good."

I bit down on his shoulder, needing something to hold onto, something to keep myself grounded.

He groaned, his hips twitching, like he was already on the edge of losing control.

I rocked my hips against his, coaxing him deeper, urging him to move.

"Jett," I whispered, desperate, needing more.

His hand slid over my mouth again, his eyes dark with something dangerous.

"Shhh," he murmured, teasing, controlling, pushing me to the brink.

I moaned against his palm, my nails scraping down his back as he finally started moving, slow at first, deep, dragging every inch of himself against me.

It wasn't enough.

I whimpered, rolling my hips to meet him, taking him deeper, harder.

His breathing broke, his control snapping.

Jett gritted his teeth, grabbed my thighs, and slammed into me, pulling a sharp gasp from my lips.

His hand stayed firm over my mouth, muffling the sounds I couldn't hold back as he thrust into me again, again, again—each stroke rougher, deeper, his pace quickening.

My fingers fisted in the sheets, my body coiling tighter, burning hotter.

I was so close.

Jett groaned, his forehead pressed against mine, his breath hot and ragged.

"You gonna come for me?" he murmured, his voice thick, teasing, coaxing.

I nodded frantically, my body trembling, my vision blurring.

And then he angled his hips just right—and I broke.

I shuddered beneath him, my body tightening like a vice, dragging him over the edge with me.

Jett gritted his teeth, his rhythm stuttering, his fingers digging into my hips as he spilled into me, a deep, wrecked groan tearing from his throat.

We stayed like that, panting, tangled, holding onto each other.

Jett's forehead pressed to mine, his breath uneven.

A long beat of silence.

Then—

"Think we got away with it?" he asked, smirking against my lips.

I snorted, running a hand through his damp hair, still trying to catch my breath. "Caleb sleeps like the dead."

Jett chuckled, brushing slow kisses over my cheek, my jaw, my collarbone. "Good."

I sighed, curling into him, letting him hold me.

And for the first time in a long, long time, I let myself believe that I was safe.

Jett was still inside me, still hard, still holding me close, and I wasn't ready for it to be over.

Neither was he.

I could feel it in the way his fingers trailed down my back, slow and possessive, his lips pressing lazy kisses against my throat, my shoulder, my collarbone.

I sighed into him, my body still humming, still sensitive, still wanting.

His hand slid over my hip, his thumb brushing slow, circling motions, grounding me, teasing me.

I tilted my head back, exposing my neck, my breath catching when he bit down—soft, sharp, just enough to make me shudder.

"Already ready for more?" he murmured against my skin, his lips smirking against my pulse.

I huffed a breathless laugh, my nails skimming down his spine, teasing.

"You're the one who hasn't moved," I whispered, rolling my hips slightly, feeling the way he was still thick, still pulsing inside me.

Jett groaned, low and wrecked, his hands tightening on my waist.

"You trying to kill me?"

I grinned against his jaw, my tongue flicking out to taste him, my fingers tangling in his hair, tugging.

Jett sucked in a sharp breath.

Then, without warning, he flipped me onto my stomach, his hands spreading me beneath him, pinning me down with his weight.

I gasped, my fingers gripping the sheets, my pulse racing.

"Jett—"

"Shhh," he murmured, kissing the back of my neck, down my spine, his voice thick, dark, teasing.

"Still gotta be quiet, sweetheart."

I swallowed hard, heat pooling low in my stomach again.

Jett shifted, pulling out just enough before thrusting back in, pushing me deeper into the mattress.

I bit down on the pillow, stifling the moan that threatened to give us away.

Jett groaned, one hand gripping my hip, the other trailing up my spine, his fingers wrapping around the back of my neck, holding me steady.

"Good girl," he muttered, his lips brushing my ear.

I shuddered, my body arching into him, my fingers scrambling for something to hold onto.

Jett's pace was slower this time, deeper, deliberate, dragging out every second, making sure I felt him everywhere.

It was intimate in a way I hadn't expected, hadn't prepared for.

Like he wasn't just fucking me.

Like he was memorizing me.

Like he was claiming me.

I turned my head, seeking his mouth, and he met me halfway, his kiss slow and thorough, his tongue sweeping against mine, matching the rhythm of his hips.

I moaned into his mouth, forgetting, just for a second, that we had to be quiet.

Jett's hand tightened on my waist, warning.

I bit his lip in retaliation, grinning when he groaned, when his control snapped.

He slammed into me, pushing me deeper into the mattress, harder, rougher now, his fingers digging into my skin.

I gasped, biting my own wrist to keep from crying out.

Jett smirked against my shoulder; his breath hot, uneven.

"You like that?" he murmured, his voice wrecked, teasing.

I nodded frantically, unable to form words, dizzy from the pleasure, from the way he filled me completely, perfectly.

Jett groaned, pressing his forehead to my shoulder, his hips stuttering as he angled just right, hitting that spot that sent me spiraling.

I fisted the sheets, my body tightening around him, my breath coming in short, ragged gasps.

I was right there, right on the edge—

Jett's hand slid between us, his fingers finding me, pressing slow, circling pressure, coaxing me over.

I bit down on the pillow, shaking, my body arching as the orgasm slammed into me, hard, fast, ripping me apart.

Jett cursed, his grip bruising, his thrusts becoming erratic as he followed me over the edge, burying himself deep, moaning against my skin.

We collapsed together, tangled, panting, our bodies still pulsing, still pressed tight.

Jett's lips ghosted over my shoulder, his breath warm against my skin, his fingers still trailing soft circles on my hip.

I exhaled shakily, my heart still hammering.

CHAPTER FIFTEEN

Caleb had weirdly and easily fit into a routine with Brennan and me. He was a little big city cop cocky, and it made me wonder if I had come to this town with the same air of superiority too. I still liked him though, he was really determined to keep Brooks safe, and that's all I really cared about. He was trying his best to transfer what he knew about the cases in Chicago to our fresh ones. But we were really still just going around and around in circles.

My mind was more and less focused on the case all at once. I drifted back to intimate tender moments with Brooks, and some not so tender but just as intimate moments. And for some reason, even though my brain was dizzy with her distractions it made me even more determined to find this bastard.

I was half-listening to Brennan and Caleb argue about something—probably the case, probably pointless—when the front door *slammed* open so hard it rattled the windows.

All three of us jerked our heads up as Brooks stormed in like a goddamn hurricane, eyes blazing, shoulders tight with barely contained fury.

"Oh, shit," Caleb muttered under his breath. "That's not a good face."

He was right. Brooks had a particular look when she was mad—dangerous, controlled rage. But this? This was nuclear.

She didn't even look at me or Brennan. Her eyes were locked on Caleb as she marched across the room.

"You *absolute piece of shit!*" she seethed.

Caleb blinked. "Okay, that's a strong opener."

Brooks didn't slow down. She *shoved* him, hard enough that he actually had to take a step back. "You slept with Claire?"

Caleb looked legitimately confused for half a second, then realization dawned. "Wait, what? No, I—"

Brooks *slapped* him. Hard. The crack echoed through the room.

I straightened. "Brooks—"

"*Don't,*" she snapped, pointing a sharp finger at me.

Caleb, to his credit, didn't retaliate. He just rubbed his jaw with a wince. "Jesus, Brooks."

She wasn't done. "I *warned* you. I *told* you—*explicitly*—not to mess with her. Claire is *innocent*. She's not some random girl you can screw around with and then leave in the morning like she meant *nothing*."

Caleb scoffed. "Oh, *come on*. Do you think so little of me that you actually believe I'd—"

"I *found her earrings* in the room you're staying in at *my house!*"

Caleb hesitated. "Oh."

"Oh? *Oh?!*" She swung at him again, but this time he caught her wrist before she could make contact.

"Brooks, *Jesus*, calm down—"

"*Do not* tell me to calm down, you smug, womanizing *prick*." She yanked her arm free.

Caleb held up his hands. "Look, Brooks, you're blowing this way out of proportion."

I could practically hear the snap of Brooks' restraint breaking.

"Out of proportion?" she echoed, her voice dangerously low. "Tell me, Caleb—what exactly is the right proportion for screwing around with my best friend when I explicitly told you not to?"

Caleb scoffed, rubbing his jaw where she'd slapped him. "It's not like that."

"Then what's it like?" Brooks demanded, stepping into his space again. "You wanna tell me you're serious about her? That this is some kind of real relationship and not just you adding another notch to your belt? Because I fucking know you haven't called her back. I can tell by how fucking sad she's been you asshole."

Caleb's expression flickered, like he hadn't considered the implications of what she was saying. "I didn't—"

Brooks cut him off. "Because I swear to God, Caleb, I told you if you used her, if you hurt her, I will personally make sure you regret it."

Caleb sighed, frustration bleeding into his expression. "Jesus, Brooks, do you really think I'm that much of an asshole?"

Brooks' eyes flashed. "Yes!"

He exhaled sharply, pinching the bridge of his nose. "This is ridiculous."

Brooks barked out a sharp, humorless laugh. "Oh, ridiculous? What's ridiculous, Caleb? That I care about my friend? That I don't want you treating her like one of your disposable flings? You think Claire's just some chick you can mess around with and then walk away from?"

Caleb's temper finally snapped.

"Oh, for fuck's sake, Brooks! You think you have the moral high ground here?" He gestured wildly between them. "You're acting like you don't have your own shit to answer for!"

Brooks narrowed her eyes. "Excuse me?"

Caleb let out a slow breath, rolling his shoulders like he was physically trying to shake off his frustration. Then he looked at her, sharp and knowing.

"Alright, fine," he said, voice edged with something almost smug. "If we're airing dirty laundry—"

I felt it coming a second before he said it.

"You wanna talk about screwing around? Why don't we ask Jett about what he's been doing? Or *who* he's been doing."

Silence.

A slow, creeping silence that felt like a countdown to an explosion.

Brennan's head snapped toward me. "What the fuck is he talking about?"

I shot Caleb a look so murderous that he actually took half a step back. "*Don't.*"

Caleb smirked, rubbing his jaw. "What? You two really thought you could keep it a secret? You think I *wouldn't* hear you sneaking around?"

Brooks' face paled. "Caleb, *shut up.*"

He didn't. "Come on, Bren, your *little sister* and your *best friend* have been—" He made a gesture with his hands.

Brennan turned on me, his expression darkening. "Tell me he's lying."

I didn't say anything.

"Tell me he's lying, Jett."

I exhaled, running a hand down my face. "Brennan—"

That was all it took.

Brennan *lunged.*

I barely had time to brace before his fist *slammed* into my jaw, snapping my head to the side. Pain exploded across my face, sharp and immediate.

"Jesus *Christ*," Caleb muttered.

I staggered back, jaw throbbing, but I didn't hit back. I *couldn't.* This was Brennan. My best friend. And the second I raised a hand to him, there was no coming back from it.

"Brennan, *stop!*" Brooks shoved herself between us, hands against his chest.

But Brennan wasn't backing down. His chest heaved, eyes burning with something dangerously close to betrayal.

"How long?" he spat; his voice tight with fury.

I exhaled through my nose, tasting copper. "Brennan—"

"How long, Jett?"

Brooks' back was against my chest now, physically keeping us apart. I could feel the tension radiating off her, her breath uneven.

"Awhile," I admitted, because what was the fucking point of lying?

Brennan's jaw *clenched.* His hands balled into fists again, but he didn't swing. Not yet.

"You *son of a bitch*," he breathed. "You were supposed to *have her back*, not—not get her on her back!" He ran a hand through his hair, his breathing rough. "Christ, *you* of all people, Jett."

"I didn't plan for this to happen," I said, voice low. "It just *did.*"

"Bullshit."

I clenched my jaw. "You think I don't know she's your sister? You think I don't know what that *means*? I didn't go looking for this, Bren. But I'm *not* sorry."

The room went deathly silent.

Brooks tensed against me.

Brennan's eyes flashed. "You're *not sorry*?"

"No." I squared my shoulders, meeting his glare. "I'm not."

His breath came in sharp, uneven bursts, hands still shaking with the need to throw another punch. But then his gaze flickered—to Brooks, to where she was still standing between us, not moving away from me.

Something in his expression cracked.

"You're really with *him*?" he asked her, voice quieter now. Not less angry. Just…less sure.

Brooks hesitated.

And then, instead of answering, she reached back, her fingers brushing over mine. Just a light touch. But it was enough.

Brennan saw it.

His mouth pressed into a hard, unyielding line.

"Get out," he said.

I lifted my chin. "Bren—"

"I *said get out*."

Brooks turned to me, her eyes filled with something complicated. But before she could speak, I nodded once.

I wasn't going to fight him on this. Not now.

So, I wiped the blood from my lip, shot Caleb a look that promised *retribution*, and walked out the door.

Brooks

The second the door slammed behind Jett; I turned on *Brennan*.

"You *asshole*," I snapped. "Was that really necessary?"

He scoffed. "Was *what* necessary? Finding out my best friend has been *screwing* my little sister behind my back?"

I threw my hands up. "Oh my God, Brennan, I'm a grown woman. I don't need your permission to sleep with whoever the hell I want."

His face twisted in disgust. "I *don't* want to hear that."

"Then maybe you should *stop acting like my father*," I shot back. "Jesus, Brennan, you're my *brother*, not my keeper."

His jaw tightened. "I'm just trying to look out for you."

"I don't need looking after," I said, voice sharp. "I can take care of myself."

We glared at each other, neither of us willing to back down. The tension was suffocating, thick with unspoken things—his protectiveness, my resentment, Jett's absence like an open wound between us.

But I wasn't here to fight with Brennan. *Not about this.*

I inhaled sharply, forcing myself to refocus.

And then I turned to *Caleb*.

Because *he* was the reason I stormed in here in the first place.

Caleb, who was lounging against the kitchen counter with his arms crossed, watching this whole mess unfold with that same lazy smirk he always wore. Like this was all some *big joke*.

I stalked toward him, my blood still simmering. "*You*."

His brows lifted, like he hadn't expected me to circle back to him. Like he thought Brennan and I would be too distracted by our screaming match to *remember* why I was here.

I *shoved* him in the chest. "What the *fuck*, Caleb?"

He barely budged, still smirking. "Gonna have to be more specific, sweetheart."

I slapped him.

Not hard enough to really hurt, but hard enough to make my point.

His smirk faltered.

"You *slept* with Claire?" I seethed. "Claire, who has never had a one-night stand in her *life*? Claire, who bakes cookies for her *mailman*? *That* Claire?"

Caleb exhaled, rubbing his jaw. "It's not that deep, Brooks."

"Oh, *fuck you*," I snapped. "You are *exactly* what she doesn't need. And I *told* you to stay away from her."

He gave me a lazy grin, eyes dancing with amusement. "Yeah, well. She didn't seem to mind."

I slapped him again.

"*Jesus*, Brooks," Caleb muttered, catching my wrist before I could do it a *third* time.

"*Enough*," Brennan barked.

We both turned to him, still breathing hard.

Brennan pinched the bridge of his nose. "Caleb, you're a fucking idiot," he muttered.

Caleb just shrugged.

Brennan turned to me, exhaling through his nose. "Look, Brooks, I get why you're pissed. But Claire's a grown woman. If she wanted to sleep with Caleb, that's *her* decision."

I glared at him. "You're seriously defending *him*?"

"I'm saying it's not your job to control who she sleeps with."

I crossed my arms, still furious.

But damn it. *He wasn't wrong.* "Can you see how fucking hypocritical you're being right now? You just fucking decked your best friend because I chose to have sex with him. And now you're saying I should just let Claire get run through by the biggest manwhore I know, because *she's* an adult. Christ, Brennan."

I clenched my jaw, inhaled sharply, and *pivoted*.

"If Claire gets hurt because of you," I warned Caleb, voice low, "I *will* make your life a living hell."

His smirk was back. "I'd expect nothing less."

I scowled at him one last time before turning back to Brennan.

"And for the record," I added, "my sex life is none of your business."

His eye twitched.

And with that, I grabbed my keys off the counter and *stormed out.*

Jett

I found Brennan exactly where I figured he'd be—out back behind his house, a beer in one hand, shoulders stiff as he stared out at the setting sun.

I hesitated in the doorway, gripping the frame. If it were anyone else, I'd have let this ride, given it space. But this wasn't just anyone. This was Brennan—my best friend, my boss, the guy who'd had my back since I landed in this town. And right now, he was pissed at me for something I couldn't, and wouldn't, take back.

I sighed, stepping onto the porch. The screen door creaked behind me. Brennan didn't look over, just took a slow sip of his beer.

"You gonna ignore me all night?" I asked.

He let out a short, humorless laugh. "Thinking about it."

I sat on the step beside him, stretching my legs out. "Look, man. I know you're pissed."

Brennan turned his head then, his eyes flashing. "*Pissed?*" He scoffed. "You fucked my sister, Jett." Then his eyes flicked briefly to the purple bruise blooming on my jaw, and the split in my lip. Regretted flashed across his features momentarily.

I winced. No point denying it. "Yeah. That part's… undeniable."

"No shit."

Silence stretched between us. I could hear the wind moving through the trees, the distant sound of a car rolling down the highway. It felt like we were stuck in a stand-off, neither of us willing to be the first to drop our guard.

I exhaled, bracing my arms on my knees. "I didn't mean for it to happen like that."

Brennan let out a dry laugh. "Oh? And what way *did* you mean for it to happen?"

I rubbed the back of my neck, choosing my words carefully. "I don't know, man. I just—" I sighed. "It's not just some random thing, okay? I know that doesn't make it better, but it's not like that."

Brennan stared at me for a long moment, then shook his head. "You could've told me."

I huffed a laugh. "Yeah, that would've gone great. 'Hey Brennan, just a heads-up, I want to sleep with your sister, hope that's cool.'"

His scowl deepened, but something in his posture eased.

I ran a hand over my face. "Look, I get it. You're protective. You should be. But Brooks isn't some kid you need to shield from the world. She's smart, she's tough, and if I screw this up? She'll make me regret it long before you ever get the chance."

Brennan let out a deep sigh, rubbing his temple. "That's true."

A beat passed.

Then, finally, he turned his head and looked at me. "You serious about her?"

I didn't hesitate. "Yeah."

Brennan exhaled sharply, shaking his head. "Fucking hell."

I smirked. "That an acceptance?"

"It's a reluctant 'I won't kill you in your sleep.'"

I clapped him on the back. "I'll take it."

Brennan rolled his eyes, muttering under his breath before taking another swig of his beer. But the tension between us had shifted, just enough.

"Don't make me regret it," he said after a moment.

I looked out at the dark, at the quiet stretch of land that felt more like home than any place I'd ever been.

"I won't."

"She treating you well?"

I breathed out a laugh. He knew his sister so well. "She's trying."

"That's something I guess."

We sat in silence for a while, the sky darkening around us.

Then Brennan let out a slow breath, rubbing a hand over his face. His fingers flexed against the bottle in his grip, knuckles turning white before he finally set it down beside him.

"Sorry I was such a dick today," he muttered. "Too much stress lately. Too much."

I turned my head toward him, waiting.

He cleared his throat, shifted uncomfortably, then buried his face in both hands. When he spoke again, it was muffled against his fingers.

"I got Skyla pregnant."

I blinked. "You what?"

Brennan groaned and dragged his hands down his face. "Yeah. That."

I stared at him, the words slowly sinking in. My best friend. The same guy who'd sworn up and down that his whole thing with Skyla was *casual*, that it was nothing serious, that neither of them wanted more.

Jesus.

I scrubbed a hand over my jaw, my busted lip throbbing slightly. *Probably not the time to look exasperated.*

"You guys okay?" I asked instead, not really sure what the appropriate response was here.

Brennan huffed out a laugh, but there was no humor in it. "I'm not sure." He picked up his beer again, rolling the bottle between his palms. "Apparently, asking your long-time friend-with-benefits to marry you just because you got her pregnant is *not* the response she was hoping for."

I winced. "Yeah, uh… probably not."

"Yeah, well. Would've been nice if she *said that* before laughing in my face."

I couldn't help it. My lips twitched. "She *laughed*?"

Brennan scowled at me. "Glad you're enjoying this."

I raised my hands in surrender. "Not enjoying it. Just… trying to picture it."

He groaned again, tipping his head back against the railing. "She thought I was joking, Jett. Then when she realized I wasn't, she got *pissed.* Said she wasn't about to marry someone just because of a baby." He sighed, shaking his head. "Told me if that was the only reason I asked, I needed to *think* before I spoke again."

That sounded like Skyla.

"She's not wrong," I said carefully.

Brennan shot me a glare. "Yeah, yeah, I know. But Christ, I wasn't trying to be an asshole. I just—" He exhaled sharply, rubbing a hand over his jaw. "I don't want to do this *wrong.*"

I nodded slowly. "What do you *want*?"

His grip tightened around the bottle. "I don't know." A pause. "I mean, yeah. I *care* about her. More than I ever admitted before this. But I don't know what the hell I'm supposed to do now."

I studied him for a second, then smirked. "So, you're saying you want to be with her, but you fucked up the delivery?"

Brennan let out a frustrated growl. "Yes, Jett, that is *exactly* what I'm saying."

I chuckled, shaking my head. "Then tell her that."

He frowned.

I shrugged. "She doesn't want you proposing out of obligation. Fair. But if you actually *want* her, and not just because of the baby, maybe *say that.*"

Brennan muttered something under his breath, rubbing his temple.

I clapped him on the shoulder. "Hey. You love making my life hell— think of this as karma."

He shot me a look, then sighed, rolling his beer bottle between his hands again.

"Guess I've got some groveling to do."

"Yeah," I smirked. "Big time."

CHAPTER SIXTEEN

The feeling started before I opened my eyes.

That slow, creeping unease. Like something was just off.

I rolled onto my side, staring at the dim glow of my alarm clock. 2:47 AM.

Jett wasn't here. I knew that already. He was on duty tonight, and I had told myself I didn't need him here anyway. Told myself I was fine.

But I wasn't sleeping.

And the feeling in my gut wasn't going away.

I shifted, listening.

The house was still. No voices, no movement Caleb.

I should've woken him up. At least he had a gun. But I was still too pissed at him to ask for help. And more than that? I didn't want him telling me I was imagining things.

I wasn't.

There was something wrong.

I threw back the covers, heart knocking against my ribs as I moved to the window. The yard was too dark. The trees stood still in the humid night air, the edge of the woods a jagged black mass against the sky.

And yet…

I wasn't alone.

I swallowed, pressing my fingers to the windowpane. I was being watched.

I knew the feeling well.

I took a slow step back, my pulse thrumming hard against my skin. I could wake Caleb. I could call Jett.

But I didn't.

Instead, I grabbed the flashlight from my nightstand and reached for my pocketknife before slipping out the back door.

The air outside was thick and quiet, the kind of silence that felt unnatural. I hesitated for only a second before stepping onto the grass, aiming my flashlight toward the treeline.

A breeze picked up, rustling through the trees, and for a split second, I thought I saw something move.

I went still.

No sound. No footsteps. But I swore, swore, something had just been there.

The flashlight's beam wobbled slightly as I took another step forward. I gritted my teeth, forcing my hands steady.

I should have woken Caleb up.

I should turn around.

I didn't.

I pushed forward, past the first layer of trees, moving slow, eyes darting over the forest floor. My flashlight flickered over something nestled at the base of a tree.

A plastic container.

A normal person might have left it alone. Might have turned back, locked their doors, called for backup.

But I wasn't normal.

I crouched, flipping my knife open just in case. The container was about the size of a shoebox, dirt streaked along the edges like it had been placed here recently. Deliberately.

The unease in my gut curdled.

I pressed my lips together and popped the lid off.

I wished I hadn't.

Polaroids. Dozens of them.

I pulled one out, my stomach dropping like a lead weight.

A body.

No—pieces of a body. Flayed open, arranged like some grotesque piece of art.

The blood looked almost fresh in the flash of my light, though I knew that wasn't possible. I shuffled through the rest, my fingers going numb as the images blurred together. More bodies. More carnage. Some from the cases I'd worked, some I hadn't even seen before.

And then—one that hit too close.

The Darby's body, Luke's, Wilson's.

My breath hitched.

This wasn't just some sick trophy collection.

This was meant for me.

A gift.

Something inside my chest cracked. A familiar feeling crawled up the back of my skull, squeezing like a vice—the flashes.

The ground beneath me wasn't real anymore. I was somewhere else, somewhere colder. The smell of blood hit my nose, the snap of a camera shutter echoing in my ears—

No. No no no.

I pressed my palm against the dirt, forcing in a slow, steady breath.

I wasn't at a crime scene. I wasn't there. I was here. Here.

I gritted my teeth and clenched my trembling fists, nails digging into my palms, riding out the storm behind my eyes. Don't spiral. Don't lose it. Not now.

After what felt like forever, my pulse slowed enough for me to move again. I gathered up the Polaroids, shoving them back in the container with shaking hands. I snapped the lid shut and stood, legs unsteady, my breath uneven.

And then, finally, I turned back to the house.

I threw open Caleb's door.

He jolted up, his hand already reaching for something under his pillow. I barely gave him a second to shake the sleep from his eyes before I shoved the container onto the bed.

"Get your gun," I snapped. "Now."

Caleb blinked, rubbing a hand over his face. "Brooks, what the hell—?"

"Now, Caleb!"

Something in my voice must've gotten through to him because he muttered a curse and grabbed his weapon from the nightstand, checking the magazine before sliding it into place.

He didn't ask questions until we were in his rented SUV, the engine roaring to life as he peeled out of the driveway, gravel kicking up behind us.

"Alright," he said, gripping the steering wheel tight. "Now tell me what the fuck is going on."

I held the container against my lap like it was a live grenade. "Someone left this for me. Outside. In the woods."

Caleb's face darkened. "And you went out there alone? Jesus, Brooks."

I ignored him, my head still buzzing, my body still too wired from what I'd found. "I think it's from the killer. It has photos. Polaroids. From the crime scenes." My voice wavered slightly, but I forced it steady. "Some of them—some of them haven't been released."

Caleb sucked in a breath.

That meant one thing.

The killer had access to these crime scenes. Had been there. Had been watching.

Had been watching me.

I clenched my jaw.

Caleb gunned it through a red light. "We're taking it to Brennan."

"No." I turned to him, my voice sharp. "We're taking it to Jett."

Caleb side-eyed me but didn't argue. He just pressed harder on the gas.

Fifteen minutes later, we pulled up to the sheriff's office. The lot was half-empty, the streetlights buzzing overhead. I barely waited for Caleb to throw the car in park before I was out the door, moving toward the entrance with single-minded purpose.

Jett was inside.

And he needed to see this now.

The second I pushed through the doors of the sheriff's office, Jett's head snapped up from behind his desk. His brows pulled together in a sharp, instinctive furrow, his entire body tensing the moment he saw me.

I must've looked like hell—hair tangled, face pale, dirt streaking my clothes. But it wasn't just my appearance that had him on edge. It was something else.

Me.

The way I stood there, shaking and breathless, clutching that fucking box like it was the only thing keeping me upright.

"Brooks?" Jett's voice was sharper than I'd ever heard it. He was already halfway out of his chair, his concern flashing into something almost panicked. "What happened?"

I tried to answer.

I really did.

But the moment my eyes locked on his, something inside me cracked.

Before I even knew what I was doing, I crossed the space between us and collapsed into him, the container dropping to the floor with a dull thud.

Jett caught me instantly, his arms snapping around me, holding me against his chest like he might lose me if he didn't grip me tight enough.

"Hey, hey, hey," he murmured, voice low and steady as one hand cradled the back of my head. "I've got you. Just breathe."

I did.

I don't know how long we stayed like that, my face pressed into his shoulder, my fingers tangling in the fabric of his shirt, but eventually, the tremors in my hands dulled enough for me to step back, blinking up at him through blurry eyes.

Jett's hands lingered on my arms, steadying me. His eyes swept over my face, cataloging every detail, every mark of distress. His jaw clenched, like he already knew he wasn't going to like what I had to say.

Caleb bent down, kicking the container toward the desk. "That's what happened," he muttered. "Go ahead. Open it."

Jett exhaled sharply and crouched down, lifting the lid—

And froze.

His fingers twitched around the plastic edge, knuckles going white as he stared at the Polaroids inside.

One slid loose, landing face-up on the desk.

Luke's crime scene.

Jett didn't move.

Caleb glanced at it, his face darkening. "That's the backyard, isn't it? The one behind Luke's house?"

It was. The blood-soaked grass, the outline where Luke had been found, the violent splatter that had painted the damp earth.

But that wasn't what made the breath stall in my lungs.

It was me.

I was in the photo.

Kneeling beside the blood, my camera in hand, examining the ground.

Jett picked it up slowly, his body so rigid I thought he might snap the damn thing in half.

"He was there," I whispered, my voice barely audible. "He was there, watching me."

Jett didn't respond. He was flipping through the rest of the stack, his movements sharp, methodical. More bodies. More crime scenes. More evidence that the killer had been there, just out of sight.

And then—another photo of me.

This one was closer.

My face was more visible, my focus entirely on my work. In the background, blurred but unmistakable, was Jett.

Jett stiffened beside me. His breathing slowed, controlled, but I could feel the fury radiating off him.

Caleb ran a hand down his face. "This sick fuck isn't just watching the scenes." He gestured at the Polaroids. "He's watching you."

My stomach lurched.

Jett set the stack down carefully—too carefully—before he gripped the edge of the desk like he was trying to hold himself together.

"This isn't just a message," he said, his voice dangerously even. "This is a goddamn taunt."

I swallowed hard, nausea creeping in. "He wanted me to see this."

Jett's head snapped up.

"No." His voice was sharp, final. "He wanted you to know."

A heavy silence fell over the room.

I pressed a hand against my stomach, trying to will away the churning unease.

"I didn't feel him," I admitted. The words felt wrong in my mouth, like something I should've been able to stop. "I didn't see him."

Jett turned away, running a hand through his hair, his chest rising and falling with controlled breaths.

Then he pivoted back toward me, his dark eyes blazing.

"You're not going back to that house."

I opened my mouth to argue, but Jett wasn't asking.

"You can stay with me," he said, his voice clipped, edged with something bordering on desperation. "Or Brennan. Hell, Skyla. But you're not staying there alone."

I hesitated, my pride bristling—but then my gaze drifted back to the Polaroids, and I felt it all over again.

That feeling.

The one I had in my house tonight. The one I had at the crime scenes. The one I had in the woods at the Halloween fest. The one I had right now.

The feeling of being watched.

I exhaled slowly, rubbing a hand over my face. "Fine."

Jett stepped closer, his fingers curling into fists at his sides like he wanted to grab me again, like he wanted to pull me back into his arms and keep me there. Instead, he said, "We'll catch him."

I wanted to believe him.

I really did.

But all I could think about was the photo of me at Luke's crime scene.

And the fact that I hadn't seen him.

Hadn't felt him.

How close had he been?

And how much closer was he willing to get?

CHAPTER SEVENTEEN

The second my shift ended; I was out the door.

I should've stayed longer. Should've kept going over the photos, should've checked in with Brennan, should've done something.

But the only thing I could think about was Brooks.

By the time I pulled into my driveway, the tension in my chest had tightened into something nearly unbearable. Caleb had dropped her off earlier, heading back to her place to keep watch for anything suspicious. I'd texted her once, told her I wouldn't be long, but she never responded.

Now, standing on my porch, keys in hand, I hesitated. For the first time in a long time, my house wasn't empty.

I exhaled slowly and pushed open the door.

The sight that greeted me knocked the breath from my lungs.

Brooks was curled up on my couch, fast asleep.

She was wrapped in one of my old sweatshirts, the sleeves swallowing her hands, the fabric bunched under her cheek where she'd used it as a pillow. One bare leg was hooked over the armrest, her body loose and relaxed in a way I wasn't used to seeing. She was safe.

For the first time in hours, the knot in my chest eased.

I set my keys down quietly, toeing off my boots before making my way toward her. I should let her sleep She probably hadn't gotten much rest after what happened tonight.

But I needed to touch her.

I sank onto the edge of the couch, letting my fingers trail lightly over the curve of her knee, up her thigh, slow and careful. Her breath hitched, but she didn't wake.

I leaned in, brushing my lips over her temple, then the delicate skin beneath her ear. Soft. Slow.

"Brooks," I murmured, my voice rough from hours of tension.

She stirred, her lashes fluttering before she blinked up at me, eyes still hazy with sleep.

For a second, she didn't say anything—just stared at me like she was trying to remember where she was.

Then, slowly, her fingers reached for me, pressing against my chest, as if she needed to make sure I was real.

That was all the invitation I needed.

I kissed her.

It started slow—just the press of lips, the quiet warmth of here, you're safe, I've got you.

But then she sighed into me, her hands sliding up my chest, fingers curling into my shirt, and I was gone.

I deepened the kiss, tilting her head back, slipping my hand beneath the sweatshirt she was wearing—my sweatshirt—fingertips skimming bare skin.

Brooks let out a quiet, needy sound against my mouth, and fuck—I needed her closer.

I lifted her, pulling her into my lap. She straddled me easily, her body warm and soft against mine, her lips parting as I kissed her deeper, harder.

Her fingers tangled in my hair, tugging slightly, and my breath hitched as heat coiled low in my stomach.

I needed her.

Not just wanted.

Needed.

I reached for the hem of my shirt—the one she stole, the one she was drowning in—but before I could get it off her, she was already yanking my own shirt over my head, tossing it aside like it was the least important thing in the world.

And then her hands were on me—skimming over my shoulders, dragging down my back, claiming.

I groaned, dipping my head to press open-mouthed kisses along her collarbone, then lower, sucking a bruise against the delicate skin just above her breast.

Brooks arched against my mouth, breathless. "Jett—"

"Shhh," I murmured, my lips trailing lower. "I've got you."

Her only response was a soft moan as I lifted her hips, shifting so I could press her exactly where I wanted her. I licked her, tasted her like she was a meal, and I was a starving man. She tried to settle against the pressure of my tongue, but her hips kept bucking against me. I wrapped a strong hand around her waist holding her to me.

Everything after that blurred into heat and need and desperation.

The living room was too hot, too small, too much. But it didn't matter.

She was here.

I was here.

And for the first time since finding that fucking container, the rest of the world didn't exist.

I finished undressing, needing to be inside her, needing to be consumed by her body as she sought her pleasure from me. I sat back against the couch guiding her on top of me. Normally I preferred being on top, so she had nowhere to go, except to arch into me as I fucked her. But I was too desperate, we weren't making it to the bed and I just needed to be inside her.

She guided me inside of her, bare nothing between, never anything between us, and *fuck*, she had me wrapped around her.

She rocked her hips, gliding along my length, and I watched with hooded eyes, as the beautiful woman on top of me took her time extracting her pleasure from my body. I watched like it was my perfect, private show, I watch until I couldn't restrain myself any longer. Until I had to grab her hips and meet her thrusts, pushing up into her from below.

Brooks made a sound, somewhere between a cry and a moan, and her nails scratched up my body and into my hair where she tugged me closer, burying my face in her breasts, where I sucked her nipple into my mouth running my tongue over the bud. Brooks was digging her nails into my back, grasping as she chased her orgasm.

"That's it. Good girl." I growled, coaxing her through it as I chased my own release, spilling into her and filling her up.

Afterward, we lay tangled together on the couch, my arm draped over her waist, my fingers trailing lazy circles against her hip. She had redressed in my sweater, but it was bunched up to her waist. Her head rested against my chest, her breath slow and even.

I hadn't meant for it to happen like this—on my couch, in the middle of my living room—but I couldn't help myself and I wasn't complaining.

Brooks shifted slightly, her fingers brushing over my ribs. "You're quiet."

I hummed, tilting my head down to press a kiss against her forehead. "Just thinking."

She made a soft, unimpressed noise, then turned her head slightly, her eyes finally flicking over my face.

Her brows furrowed.

I sighed. "Here we go."

Brooks reached up, her fingers gently tracing the bruise on my jaw, then the split in my lip. "It's worse than it looked earlier."

I smirked, but it faded when she frowned.

"It's not that bad," I assured her, brushing my knuckles along her arm. "Your brother just got a lucky shot."

Brooks rolled her eyes. "Please. You let him hit you."

I didn't deny it.

Her fingers lingered on my jaw, softer this time, like she was memorizing the shape of it.

Her voice was quieter when she spoke again. "Does it hurt?"

I turned my head, pressing a kiss to her palm. "Not anymore."

Her lips parted slightly, something unreadable flickering in her expression.

I knew this was new for her—this intimacy. The way we touched, the way we existed together. She didn't say things like be careful or don't get hurt, but I saw it.

I felt it.

I kissed her again, slow and deep, until she sighed into me, her body melting against mine like she belonged there.

Like she was safe.

Like she was home.

And fuck me if I didn't want to be her home.

I knew I couldn't tell her that yet.

We had to move at her pace. Timid wasn't a word anyone would ever use to describe Brooks, but when it came to this—us—she was cautious. Like she was standing at the edge of something terrifying, deciding whether or not to take the leap.

So, I didn't push.

But I also didn't stop myself when my fingers slipped beneath the hem of my sweatshirt—the one she was wearing—brushing along the soft skin of her stomach.

Her breath hitched.

I let my hands wander, slow and unchallenging, dragging over her waist, up her ribs, feeling the way she shivered under my touch.

Her thighs tightened around me, her fingers still resting lightly on my jaw.

"Again?" she whispered, like she already knew the answer.

A deep, low sound rumbled in my chest, my hands gripping her hips, feeling her already hot and slick against me.

She knew the answer.

I pushed her back against the couch, caging her beneath me, drinking in the sight of her—her swollen lips, her flushed skin, the way her pupils were blown wide with something needy.

She looked like she wanted to devour me.

Or maybe she was waiting for me to devour her.

I wasn't going to make her wait long.

Brooks reached for me, fingers sliding into my hair, tugging.

God, I loved when she did that.

I groaned, dropping my head to her throat, dragging my lips down the length of her exposed, perfect skin. I sucked at her pulse point, letting my teeth scrape lightly over her collarbone, satisfied when I felt her shudder beneath me.

I wanted to hear her.

I wanted to make her come apart again, to ruin her in the best way possible.

I shifted lower, my mouth trailing downward as I slowly, deliberately peeled my sweatshirt off of her, watching the fabric drag over her bare skin.

She lifted her arms, letting me pull it away, exposing her.

I groaned, taking a moment just to look.

Fucking perfect.

She squirmed beneath my stare, and I smirked, running my hands over her ribs, memorizing every inch of her.

"You're beautiful," I murmured against her skin, pressing kisses down the valley between her breasts, moving lower.

Her breath caught.

I smirked against her stomach, pressing one more slow kiss to the sensitive skin there before gripping her thighs and spreading them apart.

And then I went to work.

Brooks was wrecked by the time I moved back over her, pressing her deep into the couch cushions, dragging my lips along the column of her throat.

She was breathless, ruined, mine.

I positioned myself between her thighs, teasing her, feeling her arch into me, demanding more.

Her hands fisted in my hair.

I lined myself up, holding myself just at her entrance, teasing her with the tip.

She growled—a real, frustrated, impatient growl.

"Jett—"

I didn't let her finish.

I thrust into her in one smooth motion, burying myself deep.

Her head fell back against the couch, a gasp spilling from her lips, her nails digging into my shoulders.

"Fuck," I groaned, my forehead dropping to hers.

She fit me. Took me. Welcomed me like she was made for it.

We moved together, slow at first—lazy rolls of her hips, deep dragging thrusts that made her gasp into my mouth.

But then she tightened around me, her nails scratching down my back, and I lost all patience.

I slammed into her, pushing her deeper into the couch, holding her right where I wanted her.

Brooks let out a sharp, breathless moan, wrapping her legs around me, letting me take everything from her.

"Good girl," I murmured against her lips, driving her higher, coaxing her toward the edge.

She whimpered, her body tightening, trembling, giving in.

I kissed her deep as she came apart beneath me, my own release chasing hers, my body pulsing as I buried myself to the hilt, filling her up for the second time tonight.

We stayed like that, tangled together, our bodies still pressed close.

I pressed slow kisses to her jaw, her cheek, her temple.

Brooks let out a deep, satisfied sigh, her arms curling loosely around my neck.

I stayed inside her, not wanting to pull away yet.

Not ready to let her go.

Not ready to lose this perfect fucking moment.

Eventually, I shifted, rolling onto my back, taking her with me so she was sprawled across my chest.

Her fingers traced light, lazy patterns over my stomach, her body still warm and soft against mine.

I smirked at the ceiling.

"So, uh," I murmured, tightening my arms around her waist. "Living room sex is apparently a thing we do now."

Brooks snorted against my chest.

"Not opposed," she murmured sleepily. "But your couch is kind of uncomfortable."

I grinned, tipping her chin up so I could steal another slow, lingering kiss.

"Then let's move to the bedroom."

Her lips twitched, her fingers trailing lower again.

"You trying to kill me?" I asked, my voice already roughing out again.

She smirked, her teeth grazing my jaw. "Don't act like you wouldn't die happy."

And fuck—she was right.

Because I'd give her anything she wanted.

Even if it killed me.

CHAPTER EIGHTEEN

The first thing I noticed when I woke up was the silence.

No creaky footsteps from Caleb pacing outside my bedroom. No muffled sounds of the TV playing some late-night crime documentary.

No Jett.

I blinked against the early morning light filtering through the blinds, the bed beneath me too big to be mine. And then I realized that I was in Jett's bed.

I stretched, my body aching in the best way, the evidence of last night lingering on my skin. The rough grip of his hands. The scrape of his stubble. The bruises he left with his mouth.

I shifted, the sheets sliding down my bare body, and I exhaled slowly, pressing my fingers to my lips. Jesus.

Last night happened. Both the good sex and the horror of finding those photos.

A faint noise from the kitchen pulled me from my thoughts, and I reached for the oversized sweatshirt I'd stolen from him the night before, tugging it on over my naked body as I padded toward the door.

The smell of coffee and something warm and buttery met me before I even stepped into the kitchen.

Jett was standing at the counter, his back to me, bare-chested, a coffee mug in one hand, flipping something in a pan with the other.

My gaze dragged over him, taking in the muscles flexing beneath his tanned skin, the faint red lines scratched across his back.

My scratches.

Heat flushed through me, memories flashing behind my eyes—the way I'd clawed at him, desperate and wild, while he fucked me into the into the couch twice. And then once more into the mattress.

Jett must have felt me staring because he glanced over his shoulder, a smirk tugging at the corner of his sinfully kissable mouth.

"Morning, sweetheart." His voice was low, gravelly, still rough from sleep.

I folded my arms, leaning against the doorway, trying not to look as affected as I felt. "You're cooking?"

Jett turned back to the stove, lifting a plate with toast and eggs. "Figured you'd wake up hungry. Caleb dropped off a bag for you earlier—pills, clothes, whatever else you might need." He nodded toward the kitchen table, where a small duffel sat beside a stack of Polaroids.

My stomach turned.

The photos.

I crossed the room, my bare feet cool against the hardwood, and sank into a chair, pulling the bag toward me while my eyes unintentionally landed on the Polaroids spread out across the table.

Luke's body.

Blood splattered across the ground.

And then—the next photo—me.

Taking crime scene photos of Luke's body.

My breath hitched, and my fingers curled into my sweatshirt.

Jett must have noticed, because he set my coffee down in front of me before crouching beside my chair, his hand warm against my thigh.

"Hey," he murmured, his gaze sharp, searching. "You good?"

I swallowed hard, my eyes still locked on the chilling evidence of how bold this bastard had become.

He wasn't just watching his victims anymore.

He was watching me. And he was telling me that he was doing it.

"This is getting worse," I muttered, forcing myself to look at the Polaroids again, even though my stomach was twisting into knots.

Jett grunted, his fingers tightening around my thigh. Agreement. Frustration. Restraint.

He didn't have to say it. We both knew it.

"This guy's getting bold," I continued, pushing the photos around, my fingertips hovering just above them like they were something toxic. "He's watching the crime scenes. Watching me. And now he's leaving souvenirs."

Jett exhaled through his nose, pushing to his feet as he reached for his coffee. "Brennan's coming here," he said. "Wants to see the photos for himself. Figure out our next move."

I nodded, rubbing at my temple, feeling the early press of a headache creeping in.

Jett set a plate of food in front of me, a mug of coffee beside it, and my pill bottle just within reach. "Eat."

I didn't argue.

We ate in silence, the weight of the morning sitting heavy between us.

I could feel Jett watching me between bites, his gaze flicking between my face and my hands every time I lifted my fork.

I didn't comment on it.

When I was finished, I stood to take my plate to the sink. But as I passed the table, my eyes caught on a particular Polaroid, something about the angle, the lighting, the way the blood pooled and glistened in the flash of the camera—

The room tilted.

A familiar suffocating pressure wrapped around my chest.

I squeezed my eyes shut for half a second—

Too long.

Flashes.

Flashes of blood, of hands trembling over crime scene tape, of the smell of copper thick in the air—

A gasping, gurgling breath—

A gunshot.

A sharp, tearing pain in my back—

I yanked myself out of it violently, sucking in air like I'd just surfaced from deep water. My pulse hammered, my hands were shaking, and I had to grip the edge of the counter to steady myself.

Jett noticed.

Of course he did.

He was on me in seconds, his hand curling around my wrist, grounding, anchoring. "Brooks," he murmured. Not a question. Not a demand. Just my name.

And it was enough.

I exhaled shakily, blinking hard, forcing the flashes back down.

I hated this.

Hated how fragile it made me feel.

Hated how, for one split second, I was there again.

I let out another breath, steadying myself, my eyes locked onto his.

And suddenly, the space between us felt too big.

I didn't think.

Didn't hesitate.

I just climbed into his lap, straddling him where he sat, my knees pressing into the chair on either side of his thighs.

Jett stilled.

"Brooks—"

But I didn't let him talk.

I kissed him.

Hard.

His hesitation lasted half a second, before his arms came around me, one hand gripping my waist, the other tangling into my hair.

It was desperation, it was need, it was the only thing that could pull me back to the present.

His mouth was hot and demanding, his tongue teasing against mine, coaxing me deeper. His fingers pressed into my skin, holding me there, keeping me close.

Keeping me here.

He knew exactly what I needed.

I whimpered against his mouth, grinding against him, feeling him hard beneath me, and that was all it took.

Jett groaned, his hands gripping my thighs, standing in one smooth motion, lifting me.

My legs locked around his waist as he carried me to the counter, setting me on top of it before pushing at the hem of his sweatshirt, sliding his hands underneath.

I shivered as his fingers explored, tracing the line of my stomach, teasing higher, pushing the fabric up, exposing my bare skin.

"Christ, Brooks," he muttered, his mouth trailing down my throat, along my collarbone, lower—

I arched against him, fingers tangled in his hair, tilting my head back, a quiet moan slipping past my lips as he—

The front door slammed open.

Jett yanked back like I'd electrocuted him.

Brennan's voice boomed through the house.

"Oh, what the fuck?"

I froze, still half-straddling Jett, my sweatshirt pushed up, my bare thighs on display as my brother stood in the doorway, his face rapidly cycling between shock, disgust, and impending homicide.

Jett's hands were still on me, still gripping my waist, still holding me in place.

I could actually hear the exact moment his soul left his body.

"Fucking—Christ," Brennan swore, spinning on his heel like he could rewind time if he just turned around fast enough. "I knew you two were screwing around, but did I need to fucking see it? No. No, I did not."

Jett exhaled, pinching the bridge of his nose. "Yeah, well, this isn't exactly how I planned it either."

Brennan's hands flew into the air as he whirled back around. "Planned it? PLANNED IT? Jesus Christ, Jett, I was barely holding it together before this! Now I have actual, visual proof burned into my fucking brain!"

I sighed, finally pulling my sweatshirt back down, hopping off the counter before my brother dropped dead from premature cardiac arrest.

Brennan pointed at Jett, then at me, then back at Jett.

Then he groaned, rubbing both hands down his face. "I knew. I fucking knew. But knowing it and seeing it—" He shook his head violently. "I can't fucking unsee it."

I rolled my eyes. "Oh, calm down. It's not like you walked in on us actually having sex."

Brennan's face twisted in horror.

Jett let out a strangled cough.

I blinked.

Oh.

Oh.

Brennan squeezed his eyes shut, exhaling through his nose like he was physically restraining himself from homicide. Then he pointed at me, then at Jett, then at the fucking counter.

"You know what? No. I don't need details. I don't need visuals. I sure as hell don't need to know how many goddamn surfaces in this house you two have defiled."

Jett dragged a hand over his face. "Bren—"

"Nope!" Brennan cut him off, shaking his head violently. "Not another word. I'm barely holding on as it is."

I snorted, crossing my arms. "Bit dramatic, don't you think?"

Brennan glared at me. "Dramatic? Dramatic? Brooks, I was content ignoring the reality of my best friend plowing my sister—"

"Jesus Christ," Jett muttered.

"—but now? Now I have an actual, physical memory of this moment that will haunt me forever."

I smirked. "We could give you worse memories."

Jett shot me a warning look. "Not helping."

Brennan groaned into his hands. "I hate everything."

Jett exhaled slowly, finally, mercifully, redirecting the conversation. "You're here for the photos."

Brennan grunted. "Yeah. And to bleach my fucking brain."

Jett and Brennan were still glowering at each other, but the focus had shifted.

The Polaroids were spread across Jett's table, each one another piece of the puzzle we were desperately trying to fit together.

I tapped one of them, the one where I was crouched over Luke's body, the flash of my camera reflecting off the blood. My stomach twisted, but I forced myself to ignore it.

"This angle," I said, dragging my finger over the image, then glancing at another where I was standing over the victim from last week. "Whoever took these, they had to be positioned just outside the crime scene. Close enough to see everything, but not too close to be noticed."

Jett exhaled sharply, crossing his arms. "Which means he's either blending in, or he's getting into position before we even show up."

Brennan ran a hand through his hair. "So, what's the play? We sit around and wait for him to send another batch of these?"

"No." I shook my head, already feeling the itch of needing to move, needing to do something. "I want to go back to the crime scenes. Retrace my steps. See if I can pinpoint where he was standing when he took these."

Jett's jaw ticked, his eyes narrowing. "No."

I arched a brow. "I wasn't asking."

"Brooks—"

"I won't go alone," I interrupted, already anticipating the argument. "Caleb will go with me."

Jett let out a dry, humorless laugh. "Oh, great. That's so much better."

Brennan cut in. "I hate to say it, but she's got a point. We need to figure out how close this guy is getting. If she can find his vantage point, we might be able to work backward from there."

Jett still didn't look happy, but he ran a hand over his jaw, his irritation evident.

I pressed my advantage. "I promise, we'll be careful. And Caleb has a gun."

Jett looked conflicted, jaw ticking.

"Relax, Jett. I'll come back in one piece."

Jett muttered something under his breath that sounded a lot like, a string of curses, but he finally gave a curt nod.

"Fine. But you check in regularly."

I grinned, satisfied. "Scout's honor."

†

Caleb and I drove in tense silence for the first few minutes, the SUV bouncing along the uneven roads leading toward Luke's last known location.

I kept my eyes on the passing scenery, mapping out the potential spots where our killer might have set up his twisted vantage point.

After a beat, Caleb sighed. "So... are we gonna pretend like you didn't slap the shit out of me the other day?"

I smirked. "You deserved it."

He chuckled. "Fair."

A pause.

"Look," Caleb finally said, his usual cocky edge softened. "About Claire—"

I cut him off. "I don't want to talk about it."

"Well, too bad."

I rolled my eyes, but he kept going.

"I didn't mean to hurt her. And if I did, that wasn't the plan." He tapped his fingers against the steering wheel. "You warned me, and I ignored you. That's on me. But it's not some bullshit one-night thing. I actually... I don't know." He exhaled sharply, like it physically pained him to admit it. "I actually like her. I know I fucked it up but I'm trying to fix it okay? We're starting again. As friends."

I turned my head to study him, searching for any trace of his usual bullshit.

He looked... serious.

I sighed, leaning back in my seat. "Fine."

Caleb glanced at me. "Fine?"

I shrugged. "I'll back off."

He scoffed. "Just like that?"

I smirked. "Well, if you do screw this up, I reserve the right to slap you again."

He chuckled. "Fair."

"And if you really fuck up, hurt her again, I'll kill you."

"I'd expect nothing less."

It wasn't a peace treaty, but it was close enough.

The wind had picked up since we arrived.

It whistled through the trees, rustling the dead leaves and undergrowth, making it impossible to ignore just how exposed this place was.

I pulled my jacket tighter around me, scanning the scene like I wasn't being watched.

Even though I knew I had been.

The Polaroids were clutched in my hand, edges bent from how tightly I'd been gripping them.

Caleb stood a few feet away, hands stuffed in his pockets, his usual smirk long gone. He was watching me carefully, letting me lead this, but I could feel his eyes flicking over the tree line every few seconds.

Like he had the same unnerving feeling that I did.

I took a steadying breath and forced myself to focus on the photos.

Luke's crime scene was the most chilling.

The shot was perfectly framed—the blood pooling in the dirt, my own crouched form in the background, camera in hand.

I'd been examining the splatter pattern, completely unaware that someone else had been examining me.

My throat felt tight.

I turned, slowly, holding the photo up, lining it up with the scene.

It was like stepping back into a nightmare.

The shot had been taken from a higher elevation. Not far—just slightly above where I had been.

A small incline.

My eyes lifted, tracking the only place the killer could've been standing.

The ridge.

My stomach twisted violently.

I swallowed hard. "He was right there."

Caleb followed my gaze, then nodded slowly. "Looks like it."

The ridge wasn't deep in the trees. It was right there.

A mere thirty feet from where I'd been kneeling in the dirt.

Close enough to see every detail of my face.

Close enough that I should have felt him.

I inhaled sharply, the cold air burning my lungs. "He wasn't hiding."

Caleb's jaw ticked. "No."

"He wanted to be close," I murmured. "Close enough to see me working. To see my reactions. To—"

To study me.

A sharp chill slid down my spine.

Caleb exhaled sharply, scanning the tree line again. "He had to have known the patrols would be combing this place." He looked at me. "He wasn't worried about getting caught."

No.

He wasn't.

I turned back to the ridge, staring at the exact spot where he had stood, watching me.

It was so close.

The Polaroids in my hand suddenly felt heavier.

I moved slowly, walking toward the incline, Caleb's footsteps crunching behind me as he followed.

When I reached the top, my stomach dropped.

Because from here, the view was clear.

The killer had been able to see everything.

Luke's ruined body.

The blood seeps into the dirt.

And me.

My movements. My expressions.

He had been documenting me as much as he had been documenting the crime itself.

I crouched, pressing my palm against the dirt. It was cold, damp from last night's frost.

But I wasn't thinking about the ground.

I was thinking about what it must have felt like to stand here.

To watch, unseen.

To have complete control.

Caleb was silent for a long moment. Then he sighed, running a hand through his hair. "This is fucked."

I nodded absently, my pulse loud in my ears.

I could almost feel him here.

The weight of his gaze.

The way he had probably stood with his camera raised, waiting, breathing, soaking in every little move I made.

I stood abruptly, wiping my hands on my jeans. "We should check the others."

Caleb gave me a look. "You sure?"

No.

But I didn't hesitate.

I had to know.

Our second location wasn't any better.

Darby's crime scene was older now, nature starting to reclaim the space, but I could still see it.

The body had been positioned between two trees, the blood soaking into the earth, sticky and black when I took the last pictures of Darby.

I had been standing right here.

And the killer…

I turned slowly, scanning the trail.

The trees were tall, but there were too many thick clumps to hide in.

I circled around, trying to line up the vantage point, the Polaroid clenched tight in my fingers.

Caleb was close behind me, staying quiet, letting me work through the thoughts spinning like sharp knives in my head, giving me an endless headache.

I tilted the photo, lining it up.

My stomach turned.

"He was up there."

Caleb squinted, following my gaze up to the small bank, towards dense roots and foliage. "You sure?"

I nodded, swallowing hard.

It was the only place he could've been.

This one was further away. Not as close as the last.

But it was still precise. Still deliberate.

Caleb exhaled, shifting on his feet. "This isn't just about the kills anymore, is it?"

"Was it ever?"

I didn't answer right away.

Because I knew the truth.

And so did he.

It had never been just about the victims.

Not for this guy.

I looked down at the Polaroids again, flicking through them with increasing unease.

One after another.

Images of me.

Taken by him.

I sucked in a slow breath.

"He's obsessed with me."

Caleb mutters a curse under his breath, rubbing his hands over his face. "Fucking Christ, Brooks."

I shook my head. "He's been following me. Tracking my movements. He doesn't just want to show me the bodies. He wants me to see him."

The realization settled like lead in my gut.

"He's not just killing for the sake of it." My voice was quiet. "He's killing for me. Always for me."

Caleb's head snapped toward me, his expression going from wary to dead serious.

"You mean—"

I swallowed hard, my pulse pounding.

"He's performing for me." I flipped to the last Polaroid. The most recent crime scene. "This is about us. Him and me."

A long, heavy silence stretched between us.

Then, softly, Caleb said, "…Shit."

I nodded because yeah.

Shit.

The air felt thinner now, and for the first time in a long time, I felt something I hadn't let myself feel in years.

Not just anger.

Not just determination.

Fear.

For the first time, I wasn't just hunting a killer.

For the first time, I realized—

He was hunting me, too.

CHAPTER NINETEEN

The precinct was quiet when we got back, the usual buzz of activity dimmed by the late hour.

Skyla was at Jett's desk, organizing notes, while Jett stood beside her, arms crossed, focused on something on the screen in front of him.

Brennan was flipping through files nearby.

I set my bag on the desk, perching on the edge. "Find anything?"

Jett glanced up. "Traffic cam footage outside The Rusty Nail is a bust. The SUV never stopped long enough for a clean ID. Fucking cameras in this town are so old, everything's blurry."

Caleb cursed under his breath, dropping into the chair beside me.

"We're missing something," Skyla murmured, tapping her pen against her lip.

Before any of us could respond, Jett's desk phone rang.

The shrill sound cut through the silence.

The room froze the second the phone rang.

It was late, too late for a normal call.

Jett reached for it, hesitation flickering across his face before he finally pressed the button for the speakerphone.

"Jett."

For a second, there was nothing. Then—

A low, muffled voice came through the line.

Distorted. Calculated.

"Enjoying my presents, Brooks?"

A sick, cold weight settled in my stomach.

Jett's entire body went rigid, his grip on the edge of the desk tightening until his knuckles turned white.

"Who is this?" he demanded.

A soft chuckle.

The sound of static, like whoever was on the other end was adjusting something.

"You already know, Detective."

Skyla's pen slipped from her fingers, clattering onto the desk.

Brennan was already moving, silent but sharp, signaling for Skyla to trace the call.

I swallowed, forcing my voice to stay steady. "Why me?"

The voice hummed, almost pleased.

"Because you see them."

A pause.

"You understand them. The way they die. The way they fall. You don't just look at them, Brooks. You study them. I know you can replay their death over and over just by closing your eyes."

A slow, suffocating dread curled around my spine.

Jett's muscles coiled so tight I thought he might snap.

"What do you want?" he gritted out.

Another chuckle, softer this time. Like a lover's sigh.

"I'm already getting what I want."

A beat.

Then, his voice dipped lower. Mockingly intimate.

"You were beautiful last night, Brooks."

The room dropped ten degrees.

My heart stopped.

I barely registered the way Jett stiffened beside me, the way Brennan's entire posture snapped to attention.

I could feel Caleb's eyes on me now, his gaze sharp, confused, but I couldn't look away from the phone.

The killer sighed, almost wistful.

"The way you scratched him up like that…"

The oxygen left the room.

Jett's hand slammed down on the desk. "Where the fuck are you?"

The killer ignored him, his attention locked onto me through the invisible tether of the phone line.

"Did he fuck you the way you like, Brooks?"

I gasped, my stomach turning violently, my body locking up so tight I thought I might be sick.

Caleb cursed under his breath, but Brennan was already moving, seething, grabbing for the phone like he might be able to strangle the voice through the receiver.

The killer laughed again, breathier this time, like he was enjoying himself.

"Tell me, my sweet Brooks," he purred, "did he hurt you? Did you leave those pretty little marks on him because he fucked you too rough? Or because you wanted to keep a piece of him?"

I squeezed my eyes shut, a sharp, suffocating horror crawling over my skin.

"I wonder," the voice mused, "if he left marks on you too. Did you like it? Do you like it rough, hard?"

Jett's control snapped. "I swear to God, if you come near her—"

The killer cut him off with a snarl, the first real crack in his composure.

"She was already mine before you touched her, Detective."

The sound of distorted breathing filled the room, labored, ragged with something ugly.

"You think you've claimed her, but you haven't. I've been watching her for a long time. I know her. I know how she works, how she thinks, how she bleeds. You? You're just a cop in her bed. I'm the one inside her head, in her heart, Detective."

The room was dead silent.

Jett's hands clenched so tight on the desk that I thought the wood might splinter beneath his grip.

Brennan looked murderous, his face dark and taut with rage, his eyes flicking between me and Jett like he was barely restraining himself from tearing the office apart.

Skyla was pale, her hands hovering over the keyboard where she was trying to track the call.

But all I could do was stare at the phone, heart pounding, feeling sick, exposed, completely fucking trapped.

The killer's breathing evened out, his tone dropping back to something smooth, calculated.

"It's alright, Brooks," he crooned. "I don't mind sharing. For now. But when I do come for you, you'll be only mine."

The line went dead.

The silence was deafening.

Jett reached for the phone, slamming it back onto the receiver so hard the entire desk rattled.

Brennan exhaled sharply through his nose, looking like he was on the verge of putting his fist through a wall.

Caleb let out a slow, low whistle, shaking his head. "Well. That was...fucking horrifying."

Jett turned to Skyla, sharp as a blade. "Did we get it?"

She shook her head. Tense. Angry. "He bounced the call. The best I can do is narrow it down to somewhere in the county."

"We knew that. We already knew he was in the fucking county Skyla." Jett spat. He took a deep breath. "Sorry, it's not your fault."

Jett's jaw ticked, his hands still braced on the desk, body coiled tight with fury.

My stomach lurched.

I suddenly felt too exposed, too raw.

His words were still crawling through my brain. She was already mine before you touched her.

I shoved back from the desk, pacing toward the corner of the room, trying to breathe, trying to shake the feeling of invisible eyes on me.

Jett was on me in seconds, one hand pressing against my lower back, grounding me. Holding me steady.

"Hey," he murmured, his voice rough, urgent. "You're okay."

I forced in a breath, then another. Focused on him.

I wasn't okay.

But right now, I needed to pretend I was.

Brennan's voice cut through the quiet.

"We need to lock this town down." His tone was pure steel. "Whoever the fuck he is, he's getting bolder. We're running out of time before he does more than just watch."

Jett's grip on me tightened, his fingers pressing into my hip like he was silently agreeing with my brother.

I nodded once, swallowing hard, forcing down the lingering tremors in my chest.

I turned back to the desk. To the photos. To the case files.

To the evidence of what he had already done.

"He's not going to stop," I said quietly.

Jett's jaw flexed, his expression dark. "No."

I exhaled slowly.

Then I met his gaze, steady, resolute.

"Then neither do we."

The silence in the room was suffocating.

The call had ended, but the words still hung in the air, contaminating everything.

"She was already mine before you touched her."

"I don't mind sharing. For now."

I stared at the dead phone on the desk, my fingers curling into shaky fists so hard my knuckles ached.

Something wasn't right.

Something wasn't clicking.

I exhaled, my pulse hammering in my throat. My skin itched, my body vibrating with an emotion I couldn't quite name.

Jett and Brennan were still talking, strategizing, their voices a low buzz in my ears.

I barely heard them.

Because the longer I stood there, the more I felt it.

That feeling.

The one I'd had in the woods. At the crime scenes. Everywhere.

The prickle at the back of my neck.

The sensation of being watched.

I lifted my head slowly.

Caleb noticed the change in my expression first. "Brooks?"

I didn't answer.

Instead, I turned toward the front windows, the ones that looked out onto the street, onto the parking lot, onto the dark beyond the glow of the streetlights.

I felt him.

Out there.

Waiting.

Watching.

He wasn't far away. He wasn't hiding in some remote location, playing games from a distance.

He was here.

My breath caught in my throat, rage coiling tight in my chest, drowning out the fear.

The Polaroids. The calls. The stalking.

I was done.

My body moved before my brain could catch up.

I stormed toward the front doors, my hands shaking with the adrenaline crash of too many realizations happening all at once.

"Brooks—"

I barely heard Jett.

Barely heard Brennan curse.

Barely felt Caleb's fingers brush my sleeve before I was pushing the doors open and stepping into the night.

Cold air hit my skin, sharp and immediate, but I barely noticed.

Because my focus was on the dark.

On the parking lot.

On the space just beyond the streetlights, where the shadows were deep and wide and full of possibilities.

I scanned the area, chest heaving, my breath coming too fast, too shallow.

I could feel him.

He was out here.

And I was fucking done playing his games.

"You want me?" I shouted into the night, my voice sharp, reckless, laced with fury.

Brennan and Jett's shouts from behind me barely registered.

"Then fucking TAKE me!"

I stepped further into the lot, my hands clenched into fists.

"You think you own me?" My voice shook with the weight of everything he'd stolen from me. "You think I'm yours? Then stop fucking hiding!"

A breeze kicked up, rustling the trees.

But no response came.

No sound.

No movement.

Nothing.

Just silence.

The kind of silence that felt like it was waiting.

I felt my heartbeat in my ears, my vision narrowing, my breath ragged as my rage peaked.

I wasn't thinking anymore.

I was daring him.

Daring him to do it.

To come out. To face me. To stop toying with me like I was something to be collected, to be admired from the dark.

But then—

Arms wrapped around me.

Not his.

Jett.

I jerked in surprise, but his hold was ironclad, his arms locking around my waist as he yanked me back toward the station.

"Let me go—" I snarled, struggling, but another set of hands grabbed me.

Brennan.

"Enough, Brooks!" His voice was sharp, livid.

Caleb was there too, all three of them forcing me backward, dragging me toward the doors.

"Jesus Christ," Caleb muttered. "Have you lost your damn mind?"

I fought them, but I was outnumbered.

My boots scraped against the pavement; my body pulled back against Jett's chest.

"Get the fuck inside, now." Jett's voice was low and lethal, spoken right against my ear.

I shook with fury, but I let them drag me in.

The moment the doors slammed shut behind us, Brennan whirled on me, shoving me back against the wall.

"What the fuck was that?!"

I was panting, my body still buzzing with rage, my hands still shaking from the adrenaline.

"He's out there," I spat, my voice ragged.

"We know," Brennan snapped, his face red with fury. "And you just went and gave him a fucking invitation?"

I opened my mouth—

But Jett was already in my space, his eyes wild, his jaw locked.

"Do you have any idea what could've happened just now?" His voice was low, but there was no missing the edge of fear beneath the anger.

"He wasn't going to do anything," I said, my voice shaking now.

Jett's hand slammed against the wall beside my head.

"You don't know that," he growled.

The air between us was thick, unbearable.

I was pushing too hard.

I knew that.

But I didn't care.

Because what was worse?

Screaming into the dark?

Or waiting for the dark to swallow me whole?

Caleb exhaled sharply, dragging a hand down his face. "Jesus fucking Christ, Brooks," he muttered. "You're really trying to speedrun a murder, huh?"

I shot him a glare, but the fight had already drained out of me.

Jett's chest was still rising and falling too fast, his fingers still twitching like he wanted to shake some goddamn sense into me.

Brennan stepped back, pinching the bridge of his nose.

A long, tense silence stretched.

Then, finally, Jett spoke, his voice quieter now.

"Promise me you won't do that again."

I swallowed, shoving down the last of my reckless anger.

"I promise."

Jett searched my face like he didn't quite believe me.

But eventually, he sighed, stepping back.

Brennan muttered something under his breath before moving toward Skyla's desk, shoving his hands through his hair.

Caleb shook his head, still eyeing me like I was an idiot.

I let out a slow, shaky breath and turned back toward the window.

The parking lot was still.

The streetlights hummed.

The shadows stretched long and deep.

And somewhere, just beyond them—

I knew he was still watching.

CHAPTER TWENTY

The first real snow of the season was falling.

I only knew because the weatherman said so.

I hadn't actually seen it.

Every single blind and curtain was shut, the windows locked, the doors deadbolted. There was no peeking outside, no standing on the porch with a hot cup of coffee, no watching the slow drift of flakes under the glow of the streetlights.

It was late November. Normally, I would have noticed the way the air smelled like winter, the way the frost clung to the edges of car windows before the first snowfall.

Instead, I only had the news broadcast in the background, telling me what I was missing.

Because I wasn't going outside.

Not until we found him.

Not until I knew that if I stepped past the front door, I wouldn't be stepping into his hands.

Jett, Brennan, Skyla, and Caleb had all agreed to take shifts watching me.

Jett's house had become a safe house.

Or a cage.

Depends on how you looked at it.

I shifted under the weight of the warm blanket draped over me, stretching my toes out toward the fireplace, letting the heat lick at my skin.

Jett's arms tightened around me, his breath steady and warm against my shoulder.

His heartbeat was slow, solid.

I counted them sometimes. The beats.

When I couldn't sleep.

When the shadows felt too deep.

When the weight of being watched—even in my hiding place—was too much.

Jett grounded me.

I sighed, burrowing further into the heat of his chest, feeling his fingers trace absent patterns against my ribs beneath the oversized hoodie I had stolen from his dresser.

Neither of us spoke.

There wasn't much left to say.

I closed my eyes, feeling the slow rise and fall of his breathing, the scent of his skin—soap, cedar, and something undeniably him.

"You warm enough?" His voice was low, rough from sleep.

"Yeah."

He kissed the top of my head, his fingers slipping beneath the hem of my hoodie, tracing the bare skin at my waist.

For the first time in days, I felt the tension in my body ease.

I wasn't sure how long we had been curled up here, but time had stopped meaning anything.

Claire had come by a few times, mostly to check on me, always staying longer than she meant to. She and Caleb would sit on the couch across from Jett and me, talking quietly while I let my mind drift, trying not to feel trapped.

Claire was worried, but she tried to act normal.

Like this was just some long winter weekend, like we were hunkered down because of the snow.

Not because of him.

Not because every time I so much as stood by a window, Jett would tense like he was ready to throw himself in front of me.

Like the glass wasn't just a window anymore.

Like it was a target.

The fire crackled, the warmth pressing against my skin, but it didn't melt the ice in my veins.

Jett must have felt it—the shift in my breathing, the way my body stiffened against him.

His arms tightened, his lips pressing against my temple.

"I've got you," he murmured.

The words were so simple.

But I clung to them.

Because as much as I hated it, I needed them.

I needed him.

Jett had to leave soon.

I wasn't ready for it.

I curled closer to him, pressing my forehead into the warm skin of his collarbone, inhaling deeply. He smelled like coffee and wood smoke, like home, and I wasn't ready to let that go just yet.

His shift at the sheriff's office started in less than an hour, which meant Caleb would be taking his place, keeping watch over me like I was some fragile thing that needed guarding.

I hated it.

Hated the way they were tiptoeing around me, treating me like I might shatter.

But at the same time, I didn't want to be alone.

I hated that even more.

Jett sighed, his fingers still idly tracing circles against my hip beneath the blanket. He hadn't moved much in the last hour, like he knew I needed this—to be held, to be steady.

"Caleb will be here soon," he murmured, like he could hear my thoughts.

I nodded against him, my fingers fisting into the fabric of his shirt, holding him there.

"He's bringing Claire, hopefully." His voice was softer now, like he knew I needed something to look forward to. "She said she'd try to convince him."

I nodded again, this time with a little more relief. Claire had been here a lot lately, keeping me company, pretending things were normal. I needed that, even if it was a lie.

Jett shifted, his hand skimming down my thigh before squeezing lightly. "And if Caleb shows up without her?"

I sighed. "Then you better let me come with you. Ten hours of Caleb alone would kill me."

He chuckled, but it was low, tired. "Not happening, Brooks."

I knew it wouldn't.

Didn't mean I wouldn't try.

"Just stay here," he murmured, pressing a slow kiss to the top of my head. "Stay warm. Stay safe."

I exhaled, my body still reluctant to let him go.

He knew it, too.

Because Jett never rushed me when it was time for him to leave.

He just held me a little tighter, kissed me a little longer, and let me have every last second of this before he had to step back into the real world.

Before I had to watch him go.

Jett shifted beneath me, tilting his head down so his lips brushed against my temple. "I'll be home as soon as I can."

I huffed. "Not soon enough."

He chuckled, his breath warm against my skin. "I'll bring takeout. You pick."

I lifted my head slightly, peering up at him. "Are you bribing me with food?"

"Yup." He grinned, his thumb brushing slow circles against my hip. "And when I get back, we can have an actual date."

I blinked. "A date?"

"Yeah." He smirked, tilting his head. "You know, those things people go on when they're in relationships?"

I narrowed my eyes. "Isn't that for… couples?"

Jett's lips twitched, his grip on my waist tightening slightly. "Brooks."

"Jett."

His gaze dropped to my mouth for a second before flicking back up. His voice dipped lower, smoother. "Whether you like it or not, we are a couple."

I sucked in a slow breath, my heart giving one sharp, traitorous thump.

It wasn't like we hadn't been inching toward this for weeks, maybe even longer, but hearing him say it so plainly—so surely—made something inside me twist.

I licked my lips. "You're awfully confident for someone who just declared us a couple without asking me."

His smirk deepened, fingers sliding just a little higher beneath the hem of my sweatshirt. "Did I say something inaccurate?"

I opened my mouth to respond—probably with something sarcastic—but nothing came out.

Because he wasn't wrong.

And he knew it.

Jett leaned in, brushing his nose against mine, his lips hovering just close enough to tease. "Say the word, Brooks. If you don't want this, tell me now."

I swallowed, staring at him, memorizing the certainty in his eyes.

I could've pushed back. Could've denied it, could've found some way to keep a little distance.

But I didn't.

Because the truth was, I wanted this, too.

I just didn't know how to say it.

So, instead, I grabbed his collar and pulled him down into a kiss that said it for me.

He groaned against my mouth, his arms tightening around me, pulling me closer, sealing me to him.

And just like that, I stopped thinking.

For now, I wasn't worried about the killer outside.

I wasn't worried about the dark.

I wasn't worried about what this meant.

Because Jett was right here.

And whether I liked it or not—

We were a couple.

A sharp knock at the door pulled me and Jett apart.

His grip on my waist lingered, his thumb brushing just beneath the hem of my sweatshirt before he let out a slow, reluctant exhale. He rested his forehead against mine for a brief second, like he didn't want to let go just yet.

Then, with one last quick kiss, he pushed himself up and moved toward the door.

He checked the peephole first—because, of course, he did—before unlocking it and pulling it open.

Claire and Caleb stood on the other side, the cold night air swirling in behind them.

Jett barely gave them a second to step inside before he locked the door again, flipping the deadbolt and checking it twice.

Caleb raised a brow. "Gee, thanks for the warm welcome."

Jett ignored him, his focus flicking to Claire instead. "Good thing you're here. She's getting sick of one-on-one Caleb time."

Claire nodded, unwinding her scarf. "I figured." She shot me a look. "Figured Brooks could use some normal company."

Caleb smirked. "Good luck finding any in this house."

I scoffed. "Rude."

Jett ignored the exchange, his attention snapping back to me.

"I gotta go," he said, voice lower, meant only for me.

I nodded, but the words still sent a cold prickle down my spine. I hated it when he had to leave. Even though I was surrounded by people, he was the only one who made me feel safe.

He must've seen the hesitation on my face because his hand found mine, fingers squeezing once, firm and reassuring.

"I'll be back soon," he promised, kissing my forehead.

I swallowed, nodding again, forcing my grip to loosen so he could step away.

Jett turned toward Caleb, his jaw tightening slightly. "Don't let her do anything stupid."

Caleb grinned. "No promises."

Jett shot him a deadpan glare before turning back to me one last time. He lifted his knuckles, brushing them lightly against my jaw, then dropped his hand and moved toward the door.

"Lock it behind me," he said.

Caleb sighed. "Paranoid much?"

Jett just shot him a look, then pulled the door open, slipped outside, and was gone.

I exhaled slowly, my fingers tightening around the edge of the blanket still wrapped around me.

Claire plopped onto the couch beside me, kicking her feet up onto the coffee table. "Sooo." She dragged the word out, giving me a knowing look.

I raised a brow. "So?"

She gestured vaguely between me and the now-closed door. "You and Jett, how's it going?"

I rolled my eyes. "Oh, shut up."

Claire smirked, clearly enjoying this way too much.

"Should we get popcorn?" Caleb asked, flopping onto the opposite couch. "Because I feel like this is about to be entertaining."

I shot him a glare.

Claire ignored both of us, tugging her sleeves over her hands as she leaned back against the cushions. "So, what's the plan for tonight?"

I shrugged. "I was gonna mope and count how many times Jett texts me to check in."

Caleb snorted. "The texts will be two minutes apart, max."

Claire smirked. "Sounds about right."

I sighed, curling deeper into the warmth of the couch. "You guys are insufferable."

Caleb grinned. "That's why you love us."

I didn't respond.

But maybe, just maybe, he wasn't wrong.

CHAPTER TWENTY-ONE

The house was quiet when I pulled into the driveway.

For the first time in what felt like days, there was no tension coiled tight in my chest, no lingering paranoia creeping up my spine. I was home. And she was here.

The digital clock on my dash read 2:07 AM as I killed the engine and stepped out into the cold November air. My boots crunched against the thin layer of snow coating the driveway, the air crisp and biting, but I barely felt it. My head was too full of her.

Brooks.

I found Caleb and Claire in the kitchen, leaning against the counter, half-empty mugs of coffee in their hands. They looked comfortable, like they had been talking for a while, the last of the evening's energy fading into quiet exhaustion.

Caleb noticed me first, lifting his mug in mock salute. "Look who finally decided to show up."

I grunted, setting the bag of takeout down on the counter. "Long night?"

Claire smirked, eyes flicking toward the living room. "For her, yeah."

I turned, my chest tightening at the sight of Brooks curled up on the couch, tangled in the same blanket I had left her in. One arm was tucked beneath her cheek, her breathing deep and even.

I let out a breath I didn't even realize I was holding.

"Figured you wouldn't want us to wake her up for a debrief," Caleb said, setting his mug down. "So, I'll take off. Gotta drop Claire off, anyway."

I nodded, clapping him on the shoulder as he passed. Claire shot me one last knowing smile before following him out the door.

The lock clicked behind them, sealing the house in silence once more.

I turned back toward the couch.

Toward her.

For a second, I just stood there, taking her in—the way the soft glow from the fireplace flickered across her sleep-flushed face, the way her fingers curled loosely into the blanket, the way her chest rose and fell in steady, quiet breaths.

It was rare to see her this still.

I crouched down beside the couch, brushing a few loose strands of hair from her forehead, my fingers lingering against her skin.

"Brooks," I murmured, my voice low, coaxing.

She stirred slightly, her nose scrunching the way it always did when she was on the edge of waking up.

I leaned in, pressing a soft kiss to her temple.

"Time to wake up, sweetheart."

She made a soft, reluctant noise, burying her face deeper into the pillow. "Mmm…no."

I smirked. "You gotta eat."

She cracked one eye open, squinting at me like I had personally offended her.

"I brought takeout," I added, grinning.

Brooks huffed but slowly sat up, rubbing the sleep from her face. "Fine."

I helped her to her feet, watching the way she leaned into me, still half-asleep, and guided her toward the kitchen. She sat at the table while I pulled out the containers, passing her one before grabbing my own.

For a while, we ate in comfortable silence, the only sound the occasional scrape of plastic against cardboard. She was still a little sleepy, blinking slowly, but she ate—which was good.

I let myself just watch her for a moment, memorizing the way she curled her fingers around her fork, the way she sighed contentedly after the first bite, the way she was here, safe, in my kitchen.

Eventually, she looked up, her expression shifting into something more thoughtful.

"You were right earlier."

I raised a brow. "About what?"

She set her chopsticks down, fiddling with the edge of her napkin. "About us."

Something in my chest tightened.

She inhaled, exhaled, then finally met my gaze.

"I'm okay with admitting it." She swallowed, her voice quieter now, more certain. "We're a couple."

A slow, satisfied grin spread across my face.

"Yeah?"

She rolled her eyes, but there was no heat behind it. "Yeah." She exhaled, like she was stepping into something new, like she was settling into it.

I leaned across the table, brushing my knuckles against her jaw. "Took you long enough."

Brooks snorted, but she didn't pull away.

"You're making it… less scary," she admitted, her voice softer.

My chest ached in a way I wasn't used to.

I ran my fingers over her cheek, my touch slow, deliberate.

"That's the goal," I murmured.

She tilted her head into my touch, her eyes half-lidded, her fingers curling around my wrist.

And just like that, the need to touch her, to have her, became unbearable.

I didn't even wait for her to finish her food.

The second I saw the way she was looking at me, the way her lips were parted, her breath coming just a little quicker, I needed her.

I stood, pulled her up with me, and kissed her hard.

Brooks barely had time to react before I had her pressed against the table, my hands gripping her waist, her ass, pulling her against me. She let out a sharp, breathless gasp against my mouth, but she didn't push me away.

She pulled me closer.

Her hands fisted in my shirt, tugging me forward, her body already melting into mine like she had been waiting for this, too.

Fuck, I would never get enough of her.

I slid my hands under her thighs, lifting her onto the edge of the table, spreading her wide, pressing my hips between her legs. I could already feel her heat, the way her body responded to me so easily.

Her nails dug into my shoulders, dragging over my skin, making me groan into her mouth.

"I barely got to finish my food," she whispered, teasing against my lips.

I smirked, nipping at her lower lip. "I'll make it up to you."

She opened her mouth to reply, but I didn't give her the chance.

I grabbed her thighs, dragged her to the very edge of the table, and rolled my hips forward, pressing my hard length against her, making sure she felt every inch of me through our clothes. Making sure she knew what she did to me.

Her head fell back, a quiet, breathless moan escaping her lips.

That sound.

Fuck, I needed to hear it again.

I tore my shirt over my head, then reached for hers, pushing it up, dragging my hands along the warm skin of her stomach as I pulled it off her. The moment she was bare, I palmed her breasts, rolling her tight nipples between my fingers, and she shuddered beneath me.

"Jett," she breathed, her back arching, pushing her chest further into my hands.

I took one peaked nipple into my mouth, swirling my tongue over it, sucking until she gasped, her fingers yanking at my hair like she couldn't handle it.

I groaned, letting my teeth graze her, feeling the way she tensed, shuddered, melted.

Her hips bucked forward, searching for friction, and fuck, I was already hard as stone, barely hanging on to my control.

I hooked my fingers around the waistband of her leggings, dragging them down, taking her underwear with them. She lifted her hips, letting me strip them away, leaving her completely bare beneath me.

I stood back for just a second, letting my gaze rake over her, drinking in the sight of her flushed and breathless, naked and spread out on my kitchen table, like a meal.

"You're gonna kill me," I muttered, my voice rough, wrecked.

She smirked, but it faltered when I pressed my palm between her thighs, feeling how fucking wet she was.

"For me?" I murmured, teasing, dragging my fingers through her slick heat.

Brooks bit her lip, but I caught the way her body trembled, the way she was already clenching around nothing.

"Shut up and do something," she muttered.

I smirked. "That's more like it."

And then I dropped to my knees.

I hooked her legs over my shoulders, spread her open, and devoured her.

She cried out, her hands flying to the edge of the table, gripping tight, her thighs trembling as my tongue licked a long, slow stripe through her slick heat.

Fuck, she tasted so good.

I sucked her clit into my mouth, flicking my tongue against her, feeling the way she gasped, jerked, tried to close her thighs around my head.

I held her open, tightening my grip, pushing my fingers inside her, curling them just right, pressing against the spot that had her moaning my name.

She was already so close, her body shaking, tightening.

"Jett—" her voice cracked, her nails digging into the table, her head tipping back.

"Let go," I murmured against her, my tongue working her exactly how she needed.

And then she shattered.

She gasped, her body locking up, thighs trembling, back arching as she came hard, soaking my fingers, my mouth, everything.

I didn't stop until she was whimpering, sensitive, pushing at my head.

I finally pulled back, grinning as I licked the taste of her from my lips.

Brooks was wrecked, her body still loose and boneless, her chest rising and falling in sharp breaths.

I stood between her legs, undoing my belt, shoving my jeans and boxers down in one movement.

She barely had time to recover before I was lining myself up, rubbing the head of my cock against her soaked entrance.

She whimpered, lifting her hips instinctively, reaching for me, pulling me in.

I groaned, pressing in just enough, teasing her.

"No waiting this time," she warned, her fingers gripping my shoulders.

I smirked, grabbing her thighs, and then I slammed into her in one hard thrust.

Brooks gasped, arching off the table, her nails digging into my back.

"Fuck—" she choked out.

I held still, buried deep inside her, letting her feel every inch.

"Goddamn, Brooks," I growled, voice strained, fighting the urge to pound into her.

She was tight, hot, fucking perfect.

I drew back, then slammed into her again, setting a rough, relentless pace, driving into her over and over until all she could do was moan, gasp, and cling to me.

Her thighs squeezed around me, her body clenching down, pulling me deeper, and fuck, I was already close.

I reached between us, circling her clit, wanting her to come with me.

Her breath hitched, her body tightening, her moans growing desperate.

"That's it," I muttered, gritting my teeth, feeling her on the edge.

She fell apart around me, her body milking me, pulling me over the edge with her.

I groaned, burying myself deep, spilling inside her, pressing my forehead to hers, riding out every last wave of pleasure.

We stayed like that for a moment, breathing hard, tangled together, her body still clenching around me.

And then, finally, I kissed her.

It was slow this time, languid, our bodies still pressed together, still humming from what we'd just done.

Eventually, I pulled back, my voice low and rough. "I think we just defiled my kitchen table."

Brooks snorted, still breathless, completely fucked-out, and satisfied.

"Yeah," she murmured, grinning up at me. "We really did."

I laughed, pressing one last lazy kiss to her lips.

Then, without even bothering to dress, I picked her up, carrying her toward the bedroom.

Because as much as I loved this—

I wasn't fucking done with her yet.

Brooks was still catching her breath when I lifted her off the table, her body warm, loose, and completely wrecked in my arms.

Her legs tightened around my waist, her arms draped over my shoulders, her fingertips ghosting over the back of my neck.

She was so damn beautiful like this—flushed, breathless, sated but still wanting.

I pressed my lips to her temple, murmuring, "You okay?"

She hummed, fingers threading into my hair, tugging slightly in a way that sent a hot pulse straight through me.

Fuck.

I wasn't done with her.

Not even close.

I carried her to the bedroom, my grip tight, secure, unwilling to let go. I liked the way she clung to me, the way she just let me take care of her.

I barely registered setting her down on the bed, my focus entirely on the way she looked beneath me—spread out, waiting, trusting.

I let my gaze trace every inch of her, memorizing the rise and fall of her chest, the soft flush of her skin, the way she was already reaching for me again.

Fuck, she had me wrapped around her.

I kissed her, slow and deep, lingering, tasting her, letting her feel exactly how badly I needed her.

Brooks melted into it, her nails raking gently down my chest, over my ribs, her fingers exploring, mapping me out, just as desperate to commit me to memory.

I groaned against her lips, my hand trailing down her side, gripping her thigh, pulling her against me.

Her body fit so perfectly against mine, like she was made to be here.

"Jett," she whispered, her voice softer than usual.

I hummed, kissing down her jaw, down the column of her throat, feeling the way her pulse fluttered beneath my lips.

"Hmm?"

Her fingers dragged down my back, her nails catching just enough to make me shudder.

"I want you inside me again," she murmured.

Fuck.

My body went tight, my grip hardening on her hip.

She wasn't hesitant.

She wasn't scared.

She just wanted me.

Just as badly as I wanted her.

I lifted my head, searching her gaze, needing to make sure.

"You do?" I asked, teasing, running my hand between her legs, finding her hot, slick, and still ready.

Brooks bit her lip, nodding, her breath shaky. "Yeah."

I kissed her slowly, lingering, before pressing my forehead to hers.

"Fuck, sweetheart," I murmured, barely holding on.

I reached between us, lining myself up, feeling the heavy heat of her against me, and then—

Jesus Christ.

I exhaled sharply, my grip bruising on her hips as I pushed in—slow, deep, bare.

Brooks gasped, her fingers tightening on my shoulders, her back arching into me as I stretched her open, filling her completely.

Fucking perfect.

I stilled, buried deep, letting her adjust, letting myself feel every inch of her.

"Goddamn, Brooks," I growled, voice strained, my control hanging by a thread.

She was tight, hot, so slick from our spent mixing together inside her, fucking unreal.

I drew back, then slammed into her again, setting a slow, measured pace, making sure she felt every thrust, every inch.

Brooks moaned softly, her body tightening around me, pulling me even deeper.

"Jett," she breathed, her nails digging into my skin.

I kissed her slowly, swallowing every sound, letting her feel how much this meant to me.

"You're so fucking perfect," I murmured, pressing my lips to her cheek, to her jaw, to the curve of her throat.

Brooks shivered, her fingers dragging down my back, gripping tight.

I rolled my hips, grinding against her, finding that perfect angle that made her whimper, her legs tightening around me.

"Yeah, baby," I whispered, my lips brushing hers. "Just like that."

She matched my rhythm, moving with me, her body pulling me deeper, harder.

I could feel her getting close, the way her breath hitched, her thighs clenching around my waist, her walls fluttering around me.

"You feel so good," I murmured, dragging my lips over her skin. "So fucking good."

She moaned, arching into me, her fingers tangling in my hair.

"I love watching you like this," I whispered, kissing her jaw, her cheek, the corner of her mouth.

Brooks exhaled a shaky laugh, matching my energy now.

"Then don't stop," she murmured, her breath hot against my lips.

Fuck.

I growled low in my throat, thrusting harder, deeper, dragging her over the edge.

She came with a gasp, her body clenching around me, pulling me under with her.

I groaned, burying myself deep, spilling inside her for the second time tonight, pressing my forehead to hers, riding out every last pulse of pleasure.

We stayed tangled together, our bodies still connected, still pulsing.

I kissed her temple, her cheek, her jaw, whispering soft praises as we slowly came down.

"You're mine," I murmured against her skin, my voice soft but certain.

Brooks was quiet, her chest still rising and falling in uneven breaths.

Then—

She swallowed, her hands sliding up my back, holding me closer.

"Yeah," she whispered, her voice barely there. "I think I am."

My heart fucking stopped.

I lifted my head, staring at her, my own breath stolen.

She just looked at me, her fingers tracing lazy circles against my skin, her expression soft, open, real.

I didn't even think.

I kissed her.

Not hard.

Not hungry.

Just slow, deep, consuming—like I could pull her into me, hold her there forever.

Brooks melted into it, letting me have her.

And just for tonight, we forgot about everything else.

I didn't want to move.

Didn't want to let go of her.

Brooks was still pressed against me, our bodies tangled together, our breaths slowly evening out. I ran my fingers over the soft skin of her back, feeling the way she still shivered, still trembled from everything we'd just done.

She was warm, soft, and perfect.

And she was mine.

I pressed my lips to the top of her head, inhaling the scent of her skin, the heat of her still wrapped around me.

Brooks sighed, curling into my chest, her fingers tracing lazy circles over my ribs.

For a long time, neither of us spoke.

The world outside this moment felt so fucking far away.

Eventually, I felt her shift, her body stretching slightly beneath me.

I brushed my knuckles along her jaw. "You good?"

She hummed, eyes still closed, voice soft, sleepy. "Mmm. I don't think I can move."

I smirked, kissing her forehead. "I'll carry you to the shower if you want."

She snorted, her breath warm against my chest. "Romantic."

"Always." I grinned, rolling us so she was sprawled half on top of me, her cheek resting against my chest.

After a second, she sighed, pushing up onto her elbows. "Fine. Shower."

I forced myself to let go of her, ignoring the way my body already missed the weight of her pressed against me.

Brooks slid out of bed first, and I let my gaze trail down her body— her bare skin flushed from my touch, the marks I'd left along her hips, her thighs, the gentle curve of her neck.

Mine.

She glanced over her shoulder, catching me staring, and rolled her eyes. "Come on, lover boy."

I chuckled, following her into the bathroom, letting the steam from the running shower wrap around us as she stepped under the warm spray.

For a moment, I just watched her.

She didn't try to hide.

Didn't shrink away.

She just let me look at her.

That trust?

It wrecked me.

I stepped in behind her, wrapping my arms around her waist, pulling her back against my chest.

She let out a quiet sigh, her head tipping back against my shoulder.

I pressed a slow, lingering kiss to the side of her neck, the curve of her shoulder, my lips following the path of water droplets sliding over her skin.

Brooks reached for the shampoo, twisting off the cap, then hesitated.

She turned, looking up at me, something almost shy flickering in her expression.

"Can I?" she murmured.

I raised a brow, amused. "You wanna wash my hair, sweetheart?"

She shrugged, squeezing some of the shampoo into her palm. "Maybe."

I smirked, lowering my head so she could reach. "Knock yourself out."

The second her fingers slid into my hair, my breath caught.

She was gentle, her nails scraping lightly over my scalp, massaging slow circles, dragging the shampoo through my hair in slow, methodical strokes.

I closed my eyes, a low hum of appreciation slipping from my lips.

Brooks laughed softly, pressing a kiss to my jaw. "Enjoying yourself?"

"Way more than I should be," I muttered.

She chuckled, her fingers continuing their slow, soothing work, the tension I hadn't even realized I was carrying melting under her touch.

Fuck.

This was dangerous.

Not the sex.

Not the fighting.

This.

The softness.

The quiet.

The way she touched me like she wanted to take care of me.

She tilted my head slightly, rinsing the shampoo out, her fingers trailing down my neck, my shoulders, my chest, and back up again, cupping my jaw.

Her touch wasn't sexual.

Just curious.

Just comfortable.

"I like this," she whispered, running her fingers over my stubble. Here, I thought I needed a shave.

I kissed her palm and trailed my eyes over her perfect body.

She caught me watching her again and rolled her eyes, nudging my ribs. "You're being weird."

I smirked, grabbing her wrist, pulling her back against me. "You love it."

Brooks huffed a soft laugh, then pressed her lips to my collarbone. "Maybe."

I wrapped my arms around her, holding her close, just standing there, feeling the warmth of her against me, letting the water wash over both of us.

I could've stayed like this forever.

But eventually, she pulled back, tipping her head up at me.

"Bed?" she murmured.

I nodded. "Bed."

And with that, I turned off the water, wrapped a towel around her, and carried her back to my room.

CHAPTER TWENTY-TWO

I was getting nowhere.

Hours spent staring at the same crime scene photos, the same surveillance footage, the same dead-end reports—and I still wasn't any closer to catching this bastard.

I ran a hand through my hair, exhaling sharply, frustration pressing against my ribs like a vice. The clock on the wall read 12:47 PM, but it felt like I'd been here for days.

It wasn't just about the case anymore.

It was about Brooks.

Every dead end meant I was no closer to making sure she was safe. No closer to ending the sick fucking game the killer was playing with her.

I rolled my neck, trying to ease the tension in my shoulders. Left her with Caleb this morning. At least I knew she was safe for now. Caleb might be an ass, but he wouldn't let anything happen to her.

I just needed to focus.

Needed a break in the case.

Something. Anything.

The front door to the station slammed.

I barely glanced up before recognizing the heavy footsteps down the hall—Brennan.

He didn't say a word to anyone, didn't stop at my desk. He just walked straight into his office, shut the door, and locked it.

I frowned.

Brennan wasn't the kind of guy to lock himself away unless something was seriously wrong.

I heard his chair scrape across the floor, then nothing.

Just silence.

That was weird.

I forced myself to keep working, flipping through another set of crime scene photos, but my focus was shot.

Fifteen minutes passed. Then twenty. Then thirty.

Brennan still hadn't moved.

I glanced toward his office again. The blinds were drawn, but I could picture him sitting there, unmoving.

Finally, I pushed back from my desk and knocked. "Brennan?"

Nothing.

I tried the handle. Still locked.

"Bren," I called again, this time firmer.

A few seconds later, the lock clicked, and the door swung open just enough for me to let myself in.

Brennan was at his desk, head in his hands.

He didn't even look up when I stepped inside.

I shut the door behind me, studying him. His shoulders were tense, his fingers gripping his hair.

Not anger.

Not exhaustion.

Something else.

Something I hadn't seen in him before.

Panic.

I didn't say anything right away.

I just walked over, standing near his desk, waiting for him to talk.

He still didn't look at me.

Instead, he reached into the top drawer of his desk, pulled out a small black-and-white printout, and slid it across the table without a word.

I stared at it for a second before realizing what it was.

An ultrasound.

Shit.

I picked up the ultrasound, staring at the grainy image, the tiny baby taking shape on the screen.

Brennan exhaled sharply, dragging a hand down his face. "I know we already knew," he muttered. "But… fuck, man. Seeing it? That's different."

I nodded slowly, setting the ultrasound back on his desk. "Yeah," I said. "It's real now."

Brennan let out a short, humorless laugh. "Yeah. Real. As in, I'm about to be a fucking dad." He scrubbed his hands over his face. "I thought I had time to wrap my head around it, but now? There's a goddamn photo of my kid sitting in front of me."

I leaned back against the desk, arms crossed. "And that's bad?"

He shook his head. "No. It's just… a lot."

I didn't push. Just let him talk.

Brennan tapped his fingers against the desk, staring at the ultrasound like it was a fucking puzzle he couldn't solve.

"I keep thinking about all the shit I've seen," he admitted, voice tight. "The cases we've been working on. The families we've had to knock on doors for." His jaw flexed. "What kind of world am I bringing a kid into, Jett?"

I knew that feeling.

Knew the weight of the job, the knowledge of how fucking dark the world could be.

I exhaled, running a hand over my jaw. "The kind of world where you'll be there to protect them."

Brennan scoffed. "You say that like I'll know what the hell I'm doing."

I smirked. "You didn't know what the hell you were doing when you became sheriff either, but here you are."

Brennan let out a short laugh, shaking his head. "Christ." He tilted his head back, staring at the ceiling. "I don't even have a nursery. Fucksakes… I'm going to need a crib."

I chuckled. "That's what baby stores are for."

He shot me a look. "When the hell have you ever been inside a baby store?"

"Never," I admitted, smirking. "But I'd pay good money to watch you walk into one."

Brennan snorted, shaking his head, but something in his posture eased just slightly.

Then his expression sobered again.

"I keep wondering if I'm gonna screw this up," he muttered. "If I'm even built for this."

I exhaled slowly.

"I think that's what makes you ready for it," I said. "The fact that you're scared of fucking it up means you care."

He let that sit for a second.

Then, finally, he nodded.

Still unsure.

Still figuring it out.

But getting there.

I smirked. "Better start practicing your dad voice. The one you've been trying to use on Brooks wasn't working."

Brennan groaned. "God help me if this kid ends up anything like their aunt."

I left Brennan in his office, still staring at that ultrasound like it held all the answers he needed.

Back at my desk, I tried to refocus.

Tried to drown myself in case files, in blood spatter patterns, surveillance footage, timelines, anything that would get me closer to catching the son of a bitch who was taunting Brooks.

But my brain was elsewhere.

I caught myself staring at my screen without really seeing it, my mind stuck on Brennan's words.

I'm about to be a fucking dad.

It had knocked him sideways. Made it real.

And now, for some reason, I couldn't stop thinking about it either.

Would I be a dad someday?

Would I hold a photo like that in my hands, feeling the weight of it sink in?

The thought should've freaked me the fuck out. But it didn't.

I tried to focus. Tried like hell.

But my mind was somewhere else.

Somewhere dangerous.

I leaned back in my chair, dragging a hand over my jaw, over the stubble I left there for my girl, my fingers absently tapping against the desk.

Because now?

Now, I couldn't stop thinking about Brooks.

Couldn't stop thinking about her body beneath mine, her thighs wrapped tight around me, her breathless moans in my ear as I fucked her deep, slow, claiming her, filling her.

Couldn't stop thinking about what it would feel like to keep going, to spill inside her, to push her past the edge over and over until my come was dripping down her thighs. Knowing that we were fucking for more than just pleasure.

To pump her full of me until she had no choice but to take, take, take—

Until she had no choice but to get pregnant with our kid.

Fuck.

A slow burn ignited low in my stomach, spreading through my veins like gasoline catching a spark.

I gritted my teeth, gripping my pen tight as hell, because if I didn't, I might actually lose it right here at my damn desk.

I imagined Brooks, weeks later, standing in front of our bathroom mirror, her stomach still flat but knowing.

Knowing what we did.

Knowing she was carrying a product of *us* inside her.

I imagined her months later, her belly rounding out beneath my hands, my mouth pressed to her skin, whispering dirty things about how I was the one who put her in this state, how I'd do it again and again.

She'd glare at me, try to act annoyed—but she'd love it.

I'd tease her, palm her swollen breasts, feel her body change, stretch, take up space, all because I fucked her raw and made her mine.

Mine.

The thought wrecked me.

I wanted it.

I fucking wanted it.

I wanted to watch her get bigger, softer, heavier with my kid.

I wanted to see her full, round, swollen with the proof of what I did to her, what we had done together.

I wanted to fuck her through it, too—slow and deep when she got tired, rough and desperate when she needed it, until she was gasping my name, until she was begging me to give her more.

And when she finally had that baby?

I'd watch her hold them, see the life we created, see Brooks—my wild, reckless, untouchable girl—become a mother.

My chest tightened, my dick already aching, my body so wired with the thought of her round and heavy and mine that I almost forgot where the fuck I was.

Then, just as fast as the fantasy had hit me, reality came crashing back.

Because none of that could happen.

Not yet.

Maybe not ever.

Because Brooks was barely willing to admit we were a couple.

Because I still had a fucking killer to catch.

Because until I found the sick fuck hunting her, I had no right thinking about owning her like that.

I gritted my teeth, exhaling sharply.

If I wanted any chance at keeping her, coaxing her into a future where she wouldn't feel trapped, where she wouldn't bolt—

I had to get my shit together.

Had to end this.

Had to hunt down the motherfucker who thought he had any claim on her.

Because Brooks was mine.

And if I ever got the chance to really make her mine, to fill her up, to watch her carry my kid?

No one— not a single fucking person on this earth— was going to take that away from me.

CHAPTER TWENTY-THREE

Brooks sat cross-legged on my bed, tugging at the hem of my T-shirt—one of mine because she barely had any of her own clothes left. Her hair was still damp from the shower, loose waves curling over her shoulders. She looked comfortable here, despite everything. Too comfortable.

And I knew what was coming before she even opened her mouth.

"I need to go home for a bit."

My body went tense immediately.

She said it carefully, like she was trying not to spook me, but she knew better.

"I need more clothes, Jett. I can't keep living out of your damn closet."

I exhaled, rubbing the back of my neck. "Brooks, you know it's not safe."

Her jaw tightened. "It's the middle of the day. I'll have Caleb with me. We'll go straight there and back—no detours, no trouble."

"You are trouble," I muttered, but she heard, her lips twitching in something that almost resembled amusement. But this wasn't funny.

She was asking me to let her out of my sight, even for a short time, and I wasn't sure I was capable of that anymore.

"Jett." Her voice softened, her eyes locking onto mine, trying to soothe the tension already coiling inside me. "I need this. I feel like a prisoner. Just let me breathe for an hour."

I hesitated, fingers tightening around my belt buckle as I got ready for work. Every instinct told me to shut this down, to keep her where I knew she was safe. But she had a point—she'd been cooped up in my house for too long.

And if I didn't give her this, she'd find a way to do it on her own.

I sighed. "Straight there and back. You stay in the car while Caleb clears the house. You don't step inside unless he says it's clear. And if anything feels off, you leave."

She nodded too quickly. "Got it."

I didn't trust that response. "Swear it."

She rolled her eyes but held up two fingers. "Scout's honor."

"You were never a scout, sweetheart."

She waved me off. "Details."

Caleb showed up ten minutes later, leaning against the doorframe with his usual cocky smirk. I regretted entrusting him with a key. "Babysitter is here, Reaper."

I ignored him, eyes on Brooks. "Phone on. Answer when I call."

She saluted me. "Yes, sir."

I gritted my teeth but let it go.

Before I left, I stepped closer, cupping her face in my hands.

"Be careful," I murmured against her lips before pressing a slow, lingering kiss there—reluctant to let go.

Her fingers curled lightly in my shirt, like she wasn't ready to let go either.

I kissed her once more, harder this time, before stepping back. "I mean it."

She gave me a small, reassuring smile. "I will."

I didn't watch them pull out of the driveway. Didn't let myself second-guess this decision. I really wanted to be the one driving her over there, but if I was being realistic, Caleb could keep her just as safe as I could. That's why he was entrusted with a key and, as he loves to put it, *babysitting duties.*

I should have doubted my choice more.

I was halfway through my second cup of coffee at the station when my phone rang.

The number was blocked.

I almost didn't answer.

"Jett." My voice was distracted, scanning over a case report.

The voice on the other end made my blood run cold.

"She screams so pretty."

I stood up so fast my chair scraped against the floor.

"Who the fuck is this?"

A chuckle. Slow. Amused. "You really shouldn't have let her leave the house, Detective. That was a mistake."

My grip tightened around the phone. "Where is she?"

"That's up to you. Come alone, and maybe I won't gut her." A pause, then the voice turned teasing, almost affectionate. "She looked real nice in that black shirt and ripped jeans. Is this your shirt, Detective?"

A cold sweat broke out along my spine.

He'd seen her leave.

And now he has her.

I shot to my feet, already heading for the door. "If you touch her—"

"Ah, ah. You're not really in the position to be making threats. I'll send you the address. No backup, Detective. No warnings. No calls. Just you. Or I start carving."

The line went dead.

I called Brooks. Straight to voicemail.

Caleb. No answer.

My heart slammed against my ribs. This was my fault.

I ran for my truck.

†

The drive was a blur, and every muscle in my body was coiled with tension. My grip on the wheel was white-knuckled, jaw locked so tight it ached. My mind ran through worst-case scenarios at a sickening pace, images of Brooks hurt, broken, bleeding.

I let her go. I had kissed her goodbye, let her walk out that door, and now she could be—

No. I couldn't think like that. I had to focus. Had to get to her.

I pressed the gas harder, the engine growling as the speedometer climbed. My pulse pounded in my ears.

"Come on, Brooks," I muttered. "Pick up. Pick up."

Nothing.

The warehouse loomed ahead, dark and silent. My gut twisted. I yanked the truck into park and bolted out, gun drawn, heart hammering against my ribs.

"Brooks?" My voice echoed through the space.

Nothing.

Just the faint scent of cigarette smoke, the remnants of a sleeping bag shoved into the corner, stacks of newspaper clippings about the murders pinned haphazardly to the wall.

Someone had been living here.

A slow realization settled over me, sharp and cruel.

There was no Brooks.

I'd been set up.

The blow came from behind. Hard and fast. My knees buckled before I even registered the impact, my vision darkening at the edges.

The last thing I heard before slipping into unconsciousness was a voice, soft and pleased. "Gotcha."

Pain.

My head throbbed, a deep, pulsing ache radiating through my skull. My body felt heavy, sluggish. Something rough and cold pressed against my wrists and ankles.

I forced my eyes open.

Dim lighting. Concrete walls. The scent of rust and mildew was thick in the air.

I was tied to a chair.

I was down to nothing but my underwear. Nothing else. My skin was chilled from the damp air, but the burn in my ribs told me I'd been worked over pretty good while I was out.

A figure stood in front of me, just out of reach of the flickering light. He was average height, wiry but strong, with shaggy brown hair and an unsettling smile. I didn't recognize him.

"Who the fuck are you?" My voice was hoarse, my throat dry.

The man tilted his head, eyes gleaming with something that made my stomach turn. "You don't know me, Detective. But I know you. And I know Brooks."

My stomach twisted.

Oh, fuck.

He took a step closer, and without warning, a fist crashed into my ribs. Pain flared hot and sharp, stealing my breath. I barely had time to recover before another blow struck my cheek, snapping my head to the side.

"She doesn't belong to you," he hissed. "She never did. She's mine. And you're in the way."

I forced a breath through my teeth. "She doesn't belong to anyone."

He sneered, driving his knee into my gut. "She belongs with me. I've waited long enough. You're nothing but an obstacle. And I'm going to remove you." He spat at me like he was trying to expel the anger inside of him "But she needs to detach from you. I can't have her mourning your death while I'm trying to love her."

The knife was in his hand before I could process it, pressing just below my ribs, slowly, slowly breaking the skin. "You don't break her heart; I'll break her body. Gradually. Creatively. I'll make her suffer in ways you can't imagine."

A sick smile stretched his lips. "And when she's too broken to fight me anymore, I'll pick up the pieces. I'll be the only thing she has left."

Rage and fear warred inside me, but the steel inside my skin was real. Brooks was real. And he wasn't bluffing.

He pressed my phone into my hand. "Call her. Tell her it's over. Make her believe it. Or she dies screaming."

I swallowed hard, staring at the phone, knowing there was only one way to keep her safe.

I had to do what he said.

"Go on, Detective," he whispered. "Break her heart."

I had to break her heart to save her.

CHAPTER TWENTY-FOUR

I stepped out of Jett's shower, steam curling around me in the dim light of the bathroom. The warm water still clung to my skin, droplets tracing paths down my arms and back. I grabbed a towel from the rack and ran it over myself absentmindedly, my mind far from the simple task at hand.

Something was off.

The house was too quiet.

Even with Caleb snoring from the couch in the other room, a heavy, sinking feeling settled in my gut, like a weight pressing down on my chest.

Then, my phone buzzed.

I turned, startled by the sudden sound slicing through the quiet. Two missed calls from Jett. One voicemail.

A pit formed in my stomach.

He always checked in. But if I missed a call, he never left voicemails.

I reached for my phone, my fingers already trembling as I hesitated for a second before pressing play.

Jett's voice came through, strained, broken—like it physically hurt him to speak.

"Brooks... I need you to listen to me. This... this isn't working. I can't do this anymore."

My heart stopped.

"I don't want you anymore."

It felt like someone had just kicked me in the chest. Like all the air had been sucked out of the room.

"You were right all along. We were never going to work. You're not... you're not the type of person I need. You're not—" He hesitated, and for a split second, it almost sounded like he couldn't get the words out.

"You're not relationship material."

The words hit me like a physical blow.

"I should've known this from the start, but I ignored it. I ignored all the signs. You'll never be able to give me what I need, and that's my fault for thinking you could."

I stood there, frozen, my chest caving in as the voicemail kept playing.

"Just... move on, Brooks. Please. Don't call me. Don't come looking for me. It's over. I can't keep doing this."

The line clicked dead.

Silence.

Then, all at once, the reality of what I had just heard slammed into me.

My knees gave out.

I collapsed onto the bed, my phone still clutched in my hands, my breathing sharp and ragged. My heart pounded so violently that I thought I might be sick. I couldn't breathe.

Jett... left me.

He left me.

A sound clawed its way out of my throat—a broken, painful thing that barely resembled a sob. He said it was over. He said I wasn't enough, that I never would be. The words cut deeper than any wound, burned hotter than any scar.

I curled into myself, my entire body shaking. How could he do this?

How could he just... walk away? After everything? After all the times he pulled me closer, whispered promises against my skin, made me believe I was safe?

I was drowning in disbelief, lost in the pain of it.

And then, I did something stupid.

I hit replay.

I closed my eyes, forcing myself to listen again, to hear every word, every nuance, every breath.

This time, I focused on the way he said it—not the words themselves, but everything underneath them.

The way his breath hitched.

The way his voice shook.

The a small pause before he said, "not relationship material," like it physically hurt him to say it.

And then—

A sound.

The tiniest, almost inaudible clink.

Chains. Metal scraping together in the background.

My breath hitched.

I knew that sound.

I knew it because I had heard it a hundred times before.

The warehouse. The old industrial warehouse on the outskirts of town. When I was younger, we used to go drinking there. Those chains hung from the ceiling, swaying with the wind, clinking like oversized windchimes.

Jett wasn't breaking up with me.

Jett was in trouble.

And he had just left me the only clue I needed to find him.

I shot to my feet, my pulse hammering in my ears.

Jett was being held at the warehouse.

I didn't even hesitate.

I grabbed the closest clothes I could find—a fresh t-shirt from home, my jeans from earlier, my boots, my corduroy jacket—and I bolted.

Caleb was still asleep on the couch, completely oblivious.

If I woke him, he'd never let me leave. He'd call Brennan, they'd lock me down, and by the time we made a plan, it might be too late.

So, I didn't wake him.

I slipped out the front door without a sound.

By the time I was in Caleb's rented SUV, my hands were shaking so badly I could barely get the keys in the ignition.

I wasn't thinking. I didn't need to.

Jett needed me.

And I wasn't going to sit around waiting for someone else to save him.

I slammed my foot down on the gas, the engine roaring as I sped through the darkened streets, the tires biting into the pavement. My hands gripped the steering wheel so tightly that my knuckles were white. My pulse pounded in my ears, a steady drumbeat of panic and resolve. I could feel the weight of the situation pressing down on me—Jett was in trouble, and I had to get to him, no matter what.

Once I was far enough from the house, I called Brennan. My voice came out sharp, steady, but beneath it was a thread of desperation that I couldn't hide.

"I know where he is. I'm heading there now."

"What? Brooks, where—"

"The killer, he has Jett. The old warehouse near the industrial district. Pick up Caleb on your way. I'll be there first."

"Brooks, wait for us—"

I hung up before he could finish.

I wasn't going to wait. Not when I knew something was wrong. Not when Jett might be out there, suffering, and I was the only one who could get to him.

Because waiting could mean the difference between Jett being alive or not.

†

The warehouse loomed ahead, hulking and ominous against the night sky. A skeleton of rusted steel and shattered windows, abandoned and forgotten—except by whoever was waiting inside.

Dread wrapped around my throat, squeezing tighter with every passing second.

I parked a block away, killing the engine, my fingers gripping the steering wheel so hard my knuckles turned white.

I could still turn back.

I could still wait for Brennan and Caleb.

But I knew, deep in my bones, that waiting wasn't an option.

Jett was in there.

And if I wasted time, I might never get him out.

I shoved open the door and stepped into the cold night air, my breath coming in fast, uneven bursts. The streets were empty, lined with cracked pavement and abandoned buildings. Shadows stretched long under the flickering glow of a distant streetlamp. The world felt deserted.

Like I was already too late.

I popped open the glove compartment, grabbed a flashlight, and slipped into the darkness, moving fast, keeping low.

Every footstep echoed against the broken concrete, swallowed by the suffocating silence. It was too quiet. The kind of quiet that made your skin crawl.

And then I saw it.

The front door—ajar.

Just slightly.

Like someone had been expecting company.

Or worse—like someone had left it open just for me.

My stomach twisted.

I swallowed my fear, stepped inside.

The air hit me like a slap.

Rust.

Mildew.

And blood.

The scent was faint, but it was there—metallic, sharp, unmistakable.

My pulse hammered in my ears as I crept forward, the beam of my flashlight cutting through the darkness.

Something was wrong.

Terribly, terribly wrong.

Then, the light landed on him.

Jett.

Tied to a chair. Slumped forward. Shirtless. Bruised. Bleeding.

I stopped breathing.

Bruises bloomed along his ribs, dark and vicious. Blood was matted in his hair, trickling from a gash on his temple. His chest rose and fell—shallow, too shallow.

My stomach dropped.

The sight of him like that—beaten, vulnerable, hurting—made something snap inside me.

I took a step forward, my voice barely above a whisper.

"Jett."

His head lifted, just slightly. His eyes found mine.

For one brief, flickering second, I saw relief.

And then—

A slow, mocking clap echoed through the room.

I froze.

Every muscle in my body went rigid.

My grip on the flashlight tightened.

I wasn't alone.

A figure stepped from the shadows.

Tall. Menacing. A predator closing in.

His movements were deliberate, measured, like he was savoring the moment.

Enjoying this.

A sick, twisted smile stretched across his lips.

"Took you long enough," he drawled, voice thick with amusement.

My heart slammed against my ribs.

And then—I saw his face.

The air ripped from my lungs.

My mind screamed at me to run.

To wake up.

To do anything but stand here frozen as recognition crashed into me like a freight train.

Joseph.

The name slammed into my brain like a bullet, knocking the breath from my lungs.

The man who'd been so close to us. Watching. Lurking in the background.

The man I should've seen sooner.

Should've known.

But now, standing in front of me, his eyes alight with something dark, something twisted, something triumphant—

I knew.

And I was exactly where he wanted me.

CHAPTER TWENTY-FIVE

The silence of the warehouse was oppressive, thick with tension and the sound of my heart hammering in my chest. My hands trembled, but I couldn't let Joseph see it. Not now.

He smiled at me, but it wasn't a smile of pleasure. It was something colder, darker. A victory that hadn't fully sunk in for him yet.

He stepped forward and motioned to Jett, still slumped against the chair, his eyes shut tight. "Let's wake him up," Joseph said, his voice dripping with malicious glee.

I froze, but Joseph's eyes never left mine. "I want him to see this. He deserves to see it."

The words twisted something inside me. He wanted Jett to witness me play into his sick little game. He wanted Jett to see me admit that I was his. He wanted to watch Jett's face as I whispered the words that would shatter him.

Joseph knelt beside Jett, his hand roughly shaking him awake. The groan that escaped Jett's lips sent a jolt of panic through me, but I forced myself to stay still, to hold my ground.

"Wake up," Joseph mocked softly, running his hand across Jett's face. "You need to see this, Jett. You need to see Brooks finally admit it."

Jett's eyes fluttered open, blurry at first, but then they sharpened, looking up at Joseph and then to me. The confusion in his eyes was almost enough to make me lose it.

He tried to speak, but all that came out was a hoarse whisper. "Brooks..."

"Shhh," Joseph crooned, his voice smug. "Watch her. Watch your beloved Brooks admit her feelings for her true love."

My throat felt dry. But I wasn't going to back down now. If I didn't play into his twisted fantasy, he would kill us both.

I turned toward Joseph, forcing the words to come. "It's true, Joseph," I said, my voice soft, careful. "I've always known we were meant to be. That's why I came here tonight. I couldn't stop thinking about you."

Joseph's smile widened as he leaned in, his voice low and sweet, as though trying to seduce me into his twisted world. "You see now, don't you?" His voice was a slow drawl, dripping with self-satisfaction. "You've always known, in the back of your mind, that you and I were meant to be. You've always known that what we have—what I've done for you—it's all for you."

I felt a surge of disgust, but I held it back, forcing myself to play along. "Yes," I said softly, taking a small step toward him, letting my voice be a breath of quiet desire. "I see now. I see what you've done for me."

Joseph's eyes sparkled with something dark, his smile turning into something far more sinister. "You know," he said, his voice turning almost whispery, "I noticed how you reacted when we had those photos in class. When you saw them—" He paused for a moment, watching me with a glint of triumph in his eyes. "You couldn't look away, could you? The bodies. The blood. You couldn't stop thinking about them."

My stomach lurched, and I had to fight not to recoil. It wasn't just the thought of the bodies that made my skin crawl—it was the sickening knowledge that he had been watching me all along, studying me, tracking my every move.

"You could see them," Joseph continued, his voice thick with satisfaction. "You could close your eyes, and they'd be there. You could watch them die, every single one of them, in your mind. That's what I wanted, Brooks. That's why I killed them for you. So you could feel them. So you could see them die. Just for you."

I froze, sickened by the realization that this whole nightmare had been orchestrated by him for me. His obsession was deeper, more twisted than I could ever have imagined. My breath caught in my throat as I tried to force the bile down.

His eyes never left mine as he asked, his voice a velvet whisper, "Did you like it? Did you like watching them die?"

I wanted to say no. I wanted to scream at him, to tell him he was insane. But I knew, deep down, that if I didn't play along—if I didn't feed into this sick fantasy—he'd kill me, or worse, he'd kill Jett.

I closed my eyes for a moment, swallowing hard, and then I whispered, "Yes."

Joseph's smile widened at my words, and I could see the satisfaction flooding his features, like a man who had just won the ultimate prize.

But then, in a flash, his hand shot out, grabbing me by the throat, pulling me back into him. His breath was hot against my ear as he hissed, "I've waited for this. I've waited for you to finally admit it."

I felt the cold metal of a knife against my lips, its pressure sharp and unyielding. Every inch of my body screamed to fight back, to pull away, but I knew I couldn't. Not yet.

Then, I heard it—the sound of footsteps crashing through the door. Brennan and Caleb.

"Brooks!" Brennan's voice rang out, sharp with panic.

"Stay back!" Joseph snapped, spinning around and pulling me closer, the knife now digging into the skin of my neck. His voice was furious, dangerous. He twisted my arm behind my back; I felt the pain shoot through my arm."I'll kill her if you come any closer! You understand me?!"

I looked at Brennan and Caleb, who stood frozen, their eyes wide, their hands hovering over their weapons. I saw their hesitation, the confusion, the sheer shock of seeing me here, in this situation.

But I couldn't let them make a move. Not yet.

I leaned into Joseph's painful grip, my voice a calm, almost soothing whisper as I spoke to the men. "Put your weapons down," I told them, not breaking my gaze from Joseph. "He isn't going to hurt me. He loves me; he won't hurt me."

Joseph's grip tightened, and I could feel the heat of his breath on my skin, but I pushed the fear down. I needed him to believe this. I needed him to stay in his delusion long enough for Brennan and Caleb to get close enough.

I turned my face to Joseph, my words soft but full of intent. "Joseph," I whispered, letting my voice drip with a twisted kind of affection. "You love me. You love me so much you'd bleed for me, wouldn't you?"

He froze for a moment, and I could see the flicker of confusion in his eyes—his mind reeling at the suggestion. But then, slowly, that twisted smile returned. He seemed to grow more excited by the prospect, more consumed by his own fantasy.

"Yes," he said, his voice low and almost reverent. "I would. I would do anything for you."

"Then show me and show them, so they know I'm safe with you," I breathed, not breaking eye contact. "Show me how you bleed, Joseph. Show me just how far you'd go for me."

His hands shook slightly, a mixture of excitement and madness flickering across his face. He lifted the knife, positioning it against his own neck.

Joseph's eyes flicked around my face, and in an instant, his grip on me tightened even more, the knife now pressed harder against my throat. "Don't come any closer!" he shouted, his voice thick with panic, addressing the men behind me. "I'll kill her! Do you hear me?! I will!"

I could see it in his eyes. The madness, the obsession, the utter certainty that I was his, that I always had been. At that moment, I knew I had him. He would do anything to keep me in his twisted fantasy.

With one last look at me, he pushed the blade against his skin, his face contorting with pain as he drew it lightly across his throat, just barely drawing blood.

The blood welled up, and for just a moment, his guard was down.

I didn't waste a second.

My hand was on his, pressing the blade into his neck, deep. His mouth opened in a soundless scream as he collapsed to the floor, the life draining from his eyes.

"You're right, Joseph. The sound of someone drowning in their own blood is more satisfying than a plastic bag over their head."

I stood over him, chest heaving, my hands slick with his blood. But I didn't feel relief. Not yet.

I rushed to Jett, my hands trembling as I frantically worked to untie the ropes that bound him. My fingers were clumsy, my heart pounding in my chest, but I couldn't stop. I had to get him free.

Finally, the rope slipped off his wrist, and the instant it did, he reached out, his hand gripping mine with a desperation that stole my breath. His touch was like a lifeline, and I felt it all the way to my bones. He pulled me close, his other hand moving to my back, his fingers digging into my skin, as if he was afraid I would vanish if he let go.

"Will," I gasped, my voice breaking as I buried my face against him. His body was weak, trembling, but the warmth of his arms around me felt like home. "You're going to be okay. I won't let you go. I promise."

His eyes fluttered open, his gaze unfocused, but when they found mine, the vulnerability in his eyes broke something deep inside me. He opened his mouth, but his voice was strained, barely a whisper. "I'm sorry... I thought I was keeping you safe... I never meant to—"

"Shh," I interrupted, pressing a finger to his lips, the tears welling in my eyes. "I know," I whispered through the lump in my throat. "I know you were trying to protect me. I understand." My hands trembled as I cupped his battered face, wiping away the blood and sweat that clung to him. "You love me, Jett. I know you do."

His eyes softened, and something between us shifted—something that had always been there, but now it was undeniable. His hand, shaky and weak, reached up to touch my cheek, as if making sure I was real.

"I love you," he whispered, his voice hoarse but full of so much emotion it broke me. "I never stopped loving you. I thought I was doing the right thing, but I—"

I couldn't listen to him apologize again. I couldn't. Not now, not after everything we'd been through. "Don't," I breathed, my chest tight as I kissed him—soft at first, tentative, like we were both afraid of the fragility of the moment. But then it was no longer soft; it was desperate. It was hungry.

I kissed him like it was the last chance I would ever have to taste him, like I needed to prove to myself that we were still here, still alive, still fighting. His lips moved against mine, just as eager, just as desperate. His fingers gripped the back of my head, pulling me closer as if he never wanted to let me go again.

"I love you," I gasped between kisses, "I love you so much, Will."

"I'm sorry... for everything," he whispered against my lips, his voice rough with emotion. "I thought... I thought I could protect you. But I failed you."

"Don't," I said again, the words coming out almost like a plea. "You didn't fail me. You saved me. You saved us." My hand went to his chest, pressing down against the blood that still flowed, the sight of it only making me want to hold him tighter, to keep him safe, never to let anything tear us apart again.

"I don't care what happened, Jett," I murmured, my voice shaking as I kissed him again. "I only care that you're here. That you're alive."

His hand moved to my waist, pulling me closer, his body trembling with the effort of staying awake, staying alive long enough for me to say the words we both needed to hear. His lips moved over mine, more urgently now, as if he were trying to make up for lost time, for all the moments we'd spent apart, all the things unsaid between us.

"Don't leave me, Brooks. Don't ever leave me," he pleaded, his eyes locked on mine with an intensity that made my heart ache.

"I'm right here, Will," I whispered fiercely, my hands trembling as I held him. "I'm never leaving you again. I'm not going anywhere."

He exhaled, and the relief in his breath was almost too much. He leaned into me, his forehead resting against mine, and for a moment, it felt like the world had paused, like everything outside of this small, fragile bubble we'd created didn't matter.

But then the reality of the situation slammed into me again, the blood on his chest. "Get an ambulance," I shouted at my brother over my shoulder. He and Caleb had been making sure Joseph was truly dead.

I pushed back slightly, looking down at the wound in his side, my breath catching in my throat. "Jett, stay with me. Please. I need you to stay with me."

His eyes fluttered closed, his body trembling as I worked to apply pressure to his wounds. "I'm here, Brooks. I'm not going anywhere."

"I won't let you go," I promised, my voice raw as I held him tighter, my hands pressed against the bleeding wound, desperate to stop the flow.

"They're on their way," Brennan said to me. Then he added to Jett, "They're coming, man, just hang in there for us okay?"

I didn't look away from Jett's face, from the way his eyes were soft with love and fear all at once. "You're going to be okay," I whispered fiercely. "We're going to be okay."

And even though everything around us was still spinning out of control, I believed it because we had each other now. And that was all that mattered.

CHAPTER TWENTY-SIX

The low hum of the hospital machines filled the space between me and Brennan as we sat in my room, talking shop to keep ourselves from spiraling.

We were both running on adrenaline and exhaustion, but we weren't the type to sit around and process things like normal people. We needed distractions.

So, we did what we knew best. We worked.

"I keep replaying the sequence," Brennan muttered, arms crossed tight over his chest, eyes flickering toward the door every so often, like he expected more bad news to walk through it. "The fact that Joseph was in plain sight this whole time... We should've seen it. I should've seen it."

I shook my head, wincing at the pull in my ribs. "He was careful. Calculated. A narcissist with a martyr complex. The perfect fucking storm."

Brennan let out a slow breath, running a hand through his hair. "We're still sifting through his warehouse. Full-on shrine to Brooks. Newspaper clippings, more fucking Polaroids. Years' worth of obsessions."

My jaw locked. I didn't need to hear it to know how deep Joseph's sickness ran. I'd felt it. Lived it.

And Brooks had been at the center of it all.

Before I could respond, the familiar sound of stomping and an argument from the hallway caught my attention.

Brooks.

"I swear to God, Caleb, if you don't get your hands off me, I will break your goddamn nose!"

"Brooks, would you just—Jesus!—for once, just listen? The doctor said—"

"Yeah, Sherry can shove her fucking opinions up her ass! It isn't fucking broken Caleb, I told you."

I closed my eyes, exhaling.

Of course, she was causing a scene.

Brennan let out a snort. "Oh, we should've known she wouldn't go quietly."

The argument escalated, the sound of a door slamming open following seconds later.

Then, there she was.

Disheveled hospital gown, wild hair, and eyes full of determination and fire.

And all I could think was: She's here. She's okay.

Her gaze locked on mine instantly, and I saw it—the way her entire body softened, but her mouth was still set in that defiant smirk.

"I'm not staying in my room," she announced, planting herself at my bedside like she'd just won a battle. "You're gonna have to deal with it."

I sighed. "Brooks—"

"Don't start." She crossed her arms, daring me to argue.

I glanced at Brennan, who only shook his head, smirking. "She's your problem now, man."

Before I could say another word, the door swung open again, and Sherry stepped in, looking thoroughly pissed off.

"Brooks," Sherry snapped, crossing her arms. "I told you to stay in your room. We need to get your X-ray results. And Jett needs to rest."

Brooks waved her off without even looking at her. "I'm fine."

Sherry shot me a glare like it was my fault she was a nightmare patient.

Brennan and Caleb both muttered something under their breaths, probably betting on how long it would take before Sherry sedated Brooks just to get some peace.

I finally spoke up, gripping Brooks' hand gently. "Babe. Just go get the results."

She frowned, eyes narrowing. "Jett, I swear if you're trying to—"

"I'm trying to get you to stop arguing for five minutes so you don't give this poor woman an aneurysm," I cut in.

Sherry's lips twitched, almost like she wanted to thank me.

Brooks muttered something under her breath but squeezed my hand before reluctantly standing.

"This isn't over," she warned.

I smirked. "Didn't think it was."

Sherry gave me a grateful nod before dragging Brooks out.

Brennan let out a long breath, shaking his head. "You got your hands full, man."

I just grinned.

Yeah. And I wouldn't have it any other way.

I must've dozed off at some point because I woke to the sound of low voices in my room.

Brennan. Skyla.

And then—Brooks.

I blinked the exhaustion away, watching as she walked in with Claire, both of them carrying coffee.

Brooks's eyes found mine instantly. And just like that, the tightness in my chest eased.

She was here. She always came back.

I gave her a small smile as she handed me a cup. "X-ray clear?"

She nodded. "Sprained. Not broken."

I exhaled, relieved.

She nudged my knee lightly. "Told you I was fine."

Before I could reply, Sherry walked in, glancing at Brennan and Skyla. "Will you both be at the ultrasound on Monday?"

I barely caught the sharp inhale from Brooks.

Her head snapped toward Brennan. "Ultrasound?"

Brennan tensed.

Skyla just smiled knowingly, resting a hand on her stomach.

Brooks gaped. "You knocked her up?"

Brennan groaned, dragging a hand down his face.

Skyla grinned. "You really thought you'd get out of this conversation, didn't you?"

Brooks turned to me, blinking. "Did you know?"

I fought the smirk creeping onto my lips. "Yeah."

Her mouth opened. Closed. Then she smacked Brennan's arm. "How the hell was I the last to know?"

Brennan just sighed. "Because you were kind of busy being stalked, Brooks."

Fair point.

By the time everyone left, it was just me and Brooks.

The room was quiet, but the weight of everything still lingered.

She crawled onto the bed, carefully pressing against my uninjured side.

Her fingers traced absent patterns against my arm. "So."

I turned my head slightly, watching her. "So?"

She inhaled slowly. "I love you."

My chest tightened, but in the best way.

I shifted, wincing slightly, but I needed to face her.

My fingers curled into her shirt, tugging her closer. "Say it again."

She smiled softly.

"I love you, Will."

I exhaled, pressing my forehead against hers.

"I love you too, Brooks."

I felt her relax against me.

Her hand slid up, cupping my jaw, thumb brushing over the bruise there.

"I thought I was gonna lose you," she whispered.

I closed my eyes.

"You won't," I promised. "Not now. Not ever."

She let out a slow breath.

"I don't know what comes next," she admitted.

I kissed her forehead. "We figure it out together."

She smirked. "That sounds disgustingly domestic of us."

I chuckled, wincing at the movement. "Shut up."

She grinned, then settled against me.

The world outside was still chaotic. Still uncertain.

But for now—

We had each other.

And that was enough.

EPILOGUE

I'd always hated hospitals.

The smell of antiseptic, the too-bright fluorescent lights, the endless waiting rooms filled with the sounds of people coughing and babies crying—it all set my teeth on edge. But as I sat on the exam table in Sherry's office, my fingers lightly flexing around the stress ball she'd handed me to test my grip strength, I realized that—for once—I didn't mind being here.

Because this wasn't about bullet wounds or concussions or broken ribs.

This was just a check-up.

Normal. Routine. The kind of thing normal people did after they got out of life-threatening situations.

It had been a year. A year since we took down Joseph.

Sherry glanced up from my chart. "Hand looks good. Strength's coming back, mobility's improving—been doing your exercises?"

I nodded. "Every damn day."

She smirked. "Good girl."

I rolled my eyes.

She scribbled something down and then, without looking up, asked casually, "And the meds?"

I exhaled, bracing for the lecture I thought was coming. But I didn't need one.

"Yes," I answered truthfully. "I've been taking them."

Sherry finally looked up, searching my face like she didn't quite believe me. But I held her gaze, steady and firm.

Because I wasn't lying.

I wasn't great at remembering things, but Jett was. He always checked my nightstand before bed, always grabbed me a glass of water, and always made sure I took care of myself even when I wanted to pretend I didn't need to.

And even on the nights he wasn't there, I still took them.

For me.

For him.

For us.

Sherry nodded approvingly. "Good. That's good, Brooks. I'm sure Brennan will be just thrilled to have you cleared to work for him."

I didn't say anything because I knew my brother was equally relieved that my hands were getting better enough that I was being cleared to go back to work, as he was aggravated that I'd decided to stay and work for him. But someone had to replace Skyla while she stayed home with the baby.

I slid off the table, stretching my fingers once more before reaching for my jacket. "So, I'm good to go?"

"Yup," she said, jotting down a few last notes before closing my file. "Everything's looking solid. But keep up with your check-ins, okay? Otherwise, I'll revoke my clearance."

I nodded, already halfway out the door, when—

I hesitated.

My hand froze on the doorknob.

And before I could think better of it, before I could talk myself out of asking, the words slipped out.

"Hey, um…" I cleared my throat, hating how weird I suddenly felt. Why was I nervous? "Is it okay to, uh… you know, get pregnant on these meds?"

Sherry blinked. Then her lips twitched, like she was trying not to smirk. "No issues at all. Completely safe."

"Oh."

I should have left it there. Should have nodded and walked out like a normal human being.

But of course, I didn't.

Because then Sherry asked, "Are you and Jett trying?"

And I panicked.

"What? No! Oh my God, no. We haven't even talked about that." I let out a weird, slightly manic laugh. "I was just wondering. You know. Curious."

Sherry hummed like she didn't believe a damn word I was saying.

I backed toward the door. "Okay, thanks, gotta go, bye."

And then I practically sprinted out of the office.

Jett had just finished his shower when I walked in.

His hair was wet, curling at the ends, a towel slung low on his hips, droplets of water still trailing down his chest.

I should have had more self-control.

But I never did when it came to Jett.

He barely had time to react before I was pushing him against the wall, kissing him hard, deep, needy. His stubble scraped my face, the stubble I knew he only kept for me.

"Jesus, Brooks," he muttered against my lips, his grip tightening on my waist, dragging me flush against him.

I could feel him, hard and hot against my stomach, and it only made me wilder.

I tore at his towel, letting it fall to the floor, and then he was lifting me, hands under my thighs, walking us backward toward the bed.

We barely made it.

He laid me down, his body pressing over mine, his weight pinning me in the best way. I wrapped my legs around his hips, dragging him closer, desperate to feel all of him.

"Jett," I gasped as he sank inside me, slow but deep, stretching me open, filling me.

His forehead dropped to mine, his breath ragged.

"I love you," he whispered, his voice wrecked, raw.

I arched into him, gripping his shoulders. "I love you too."

His movements grew harder, rougher, deeper, but his lips on mine were soft, reverent like he was worshipping me. Like he was making sure I knew exactly what I meant to him.

I came fast and hard, his name a breathless prayer on my lips.

Jett followed right after, his body shuddering against mine, burying himself deep as he came, pressing a kiss to my throat.

He didn't move for a long time. Just stayed inside me, holding me close, our breathing evening out together.

And for once, the world felt quiet.

†

We were arguing over breakfast.

"You can't possibly like that coffee better than my place," I scoffed, watching as Jett took a sip from his new favorite spot that had opened up down the road.

He smirked, setting his cup down. "What, you mad your coffee shop isn't the best in town anymore?"

"Yes," I said immediately.

Jett chuckled, shaking his head. "You're impossible."

"And yet, you keep me around."

He hummed, eyes twinkling with something I didn't quite catch. Then he pulled something from his pocket and set it on the table between us.

A small black box.

I froze.

My heart stuttered.

Jett just shrugged, completely unfazed, like he hadn't just casually pulled out a fucking engagement ring.

"You wanna marry me?" he asked, just like that.

No speech. No grand romantic moment. Just Jett being Jett.

I blinked at him. "Are you serious?"

He raised a brow. "I literally just put a ring on the table, Brooks. What do you think?"

I stared at the box. Then back at him. Then at the fucking ring again.

And then—I laughed.

Because, of course, this was how he proposed. No big production. No bullshit. Just us.

I reached for the ring, turning it over in my fingers, my stomach doing something stupid and fluttery, just gold and a small stone.

"You sure about this?" I teased. "You're asking a lot. I'm kind of a menace."

Jett smirked. "Yeah, well, so am I."

I tilted my head, watching him. "What if I say no?"

His eyes darkened, and he leaned forward. "Then I'll just keep asking until you say yes."

I exhaled, shaking my head with a grin.

And then I slid the ring onto my finger.

Jett's lips quirked. "That a yes?"

I leaned in, kissing him hard, my fingers gripping the front of his shirt.

"Yeah," I murmured against his mouth. "That's a yes."

Jett barely gave me a second to breathe after I said yes.

One moment, we were at the table, the weight of the ring still settling on my finger. The next, I was in his lap, straddling him in the booth, my hands threading into his hair as he kissed me like he owned me.

His grip was firm, possessive, his hands sliding under my sweater, palms hot against my bare skin.

"Brooks," he murmured, voice wrecked, hoarse, full of something deeper than lust.

I pressed my forehead to his, breathless, my fingers tugging at the hem of his shirt. "We need to go home."

Jett's grin was pure sin.

"Yeah," he agreed. "We really do."

We barely made it inside.

The second the door slammed shut, he had me against it, his hands gripping my ass, lifting me, his mouth hungry, desperate, wrecking me.

I gasped as he sank his teeth into my throat, sucking hard, marking me, claiming me.

"Mine," he growled against my skin.

Heat coiled low in my stomach, my body arching against him, friction, heat, need, all of it unbearable.

I tugged at his belt, desperate to get his jeans off, to feel him, skin to skin, no barriers.

Jett smirked against my mouth, palming me between my legs, feeling how wet I was for him, groaning at the way I rocked into his hand.

"You're dripping for me, sweetheart," he muttered, slipping his fingers past the waistband of my jeans, dragging them through my slick folds. "So ready. So fucking perfect."

I moaned into his mouth, my fingers fumbling with his belt, pulling it open, shoving at his jeans until I could finally get my hands on him.

I wrapped my fingers around his cock, stroking him slow, teasing, making him hiss, making his control slip.

His head dropped to my shoulder, his breath ragged, his hips jerking into my touch.

"Fuck, Brooks—"

I smirked, dragging my thumb over the tip, feeling the precome slick against my skin.

"I need you," I whispered, my voice wrecked, my thighs tightening around his waist.

"You have me."

Then, Jett grabbed me, spun me, and carried me to the bedroom.

We didn't take our time.

We ripped off clothes, gasping, touching, devouring.

Jett shoved me onto the bed, climbing over me, kissing down my body, sucking bruises into my skin as I writhed beneath him.

"I love you," he murmured against my stomach. "I love you so fucking much."

Then he spread my thighs wide, settled between them, and licked me like he was starving.

I arched off the bed, gasping, moaning, clawing at the sheets as he worked me over with his tongue, his fingers, his mouth—devouring, worshiping, breaking me apart.

I was already so close, so wound tight, and he knew it.

"Come for me," he murmured against me, his voice rough, wrecked, filled with love and possession. "Give it to me, Brooks."

And then I was falling apart, shattering beneath him, his name a desperate, breathless moan on my lips.

But Jett wasn't done.

Before I could even catch my breath, he was kissing up my body, positioning himself between my thighs, and then—

He pushed inside me, bare, raw, deep.

I gasped, nails digging into his back, clinging to him, feeling every inch as he stretched me open, filled me.

"Jesus, Brooks—" His head dropped to my shoulder, his breath hot, uneven, wrecked. "You feel so fucking good."

I rocked my hips, grinding against him, making him groan, curse, grip my thighs even tighter.

He started moving, slow and deep, dragging it out, making me feel every inch, every thrust, every ounce of love and need in his touch.

I tilted my head back, moaning his name, whispering, "Faster."

Jett let out a low, dark chuckle, but he obeyed, his pace turning rougher, harder, deeper.

We moved together, needy, desperate, breathless.

His lips crashed against mine, swallowing my moans, kissing me like he needed me to breathe.

"Mine," he growled against my mouth. "My fiancée. My wife. My fucking everything."

I shattered again, trembling, breaking apart around him, dragging him with me.

Jett let out a low, wrecked groan, his body stiffening, pulsing deep inside me, filling me up, claiming me completely.

He collapsed against me, his breath uneven, his heart racing against mine.

For a long moment, we just lay there, tangled together, his forehead against mine, his body still inside me, as if he couldn't bear to let go.

I ran my fingers through his hair, soft, loving.

"I love you," I whispered.

Jett smiled, pressing a lazy kiss to my lips. "Yeah?"

I nipped at his lower lip, smirking. "Yeah."

His grin was pure bliss.

"Good," he murmured. "Because I'm never letting you go."

BONUS CHAPTER

The snowstorm was in full force by the time I pulled into the driveway. The wind howled, thick flakes coating the windshield faster than the wipers could clear them. It had been a long damn day, and the idea of stepping into a warm house—of stepping into her—was the only thing keeping me sane.

I killed the engine, grabbed the bags of groceries I promised to pick up from the passenger seat, and jogged to the front door, shaking the snow from my shoulders as I stepped inside.

The house was quiet, dimly lit by the glow of the fireplace. And there, curled up on the couch, wrapped in one of my sweatshirts, was Brooks.

My wife.

That word still did something to me. *Wife.*

It had only been a month since we stood in front of a courthouse judge, her in a black dress, me in a suit I barely had time to put on before she was dragging me down the steps to celebrate in the best way she knew how.

One week of being engaged. That's all it had taken.

Because when you've already almost lost each other, why the fuck would you waste time?

I stepped closer, setting the bags on the counter, my gaze locked on her soft, sleeping form. One leg was kicked out from under the blanket, the sweatshirt slipping just enough to tease a bare shoulder, smooth and inviting.

My cock twitched.

Christ.

Even asleep, she did something to me.

I leaned down, brushing a kiss against her temple. "Brooks," I murmured against her skin, my lips trailing lower, teasing the edge of her jaw. "Wake up, sweetheart."

She stirred slightly, shifting under the blanket, making a soft, sleepy sound that had no damn right being as sexy as it was.

I smirked, brushing my mouth over hers—just a light tease of a kiss, but then she sighed, her lips parting slightly. I deepened it, sliding my hand under the blanket, finding the bare skin of her thigh and lifting her up, just to set her back down in my lap.

Brooks hummed against my lips, shifting to press closer, her fingers threading into my hair. "Jett…"

Fuck.

The way she said my name—husky, half-asleep, needy.

I was already hard.

I slipped my fingers beneath the sweatshirt, palming her bare waist, sliding lower, feeling the soft warmth of her skin against mine.

She arched into me, grinding against my thigh, her breath hitching.

I pulled back slightly, grinning down at her. "That's one hell of a way to say welcome home."

She smirked, her eyes still heavy with sleep but dark with heat. "You should get home earlier then."

I chuckled, but it faded fast when she slipped her hand between us, palming my cock through my jeans.

I groaned, hips jerking into her touch.

"Shit, Brooks—"

She was already pulling at my belt, her fingers quick, practiced, shoving my jeans down just enough to free me.

And then she dropped to her knees.

My chest heaved, my breath coming ragged as she wrapped her fingers around me, stroking slow, teasing.

"Fuck, sweetheart," I muttered, watching as she licked her lips.

She glanced up at me, eyes gleaming, her mouth so fucking close.

Then she took me in.

The first hot, wet pull of her mouth had my head slamming back against the couch.

"Jesus—" My fingers dug into her hair, my hips jerking forward before I could stop myself.

She moaned around me, the vibration shooting straight through me.

I gritted my teeth, trying to hold back, but she was already working me deeper, her tongue teasing, swirling, her fingers gripping my thighs.

It was too much.

I grabbed her chin in my hand, tilting her face up.

Brooks frowned. "What?"

I exhaled, cupping her jaw, brushing my thumb over her lips.

"I only want to come inside you," I murmured, low and firm.

Her breath hitched.

I dragged my fingers through her hair, tugging lightly. "You remember why, don't you?"

Her pupils blown wide, she nodded.

We'd been trying for a baby for weeks. No IUD. No pulling out. Just me, deep inside her, filling her up, over and over.

Brooks swallowed, her voice coming out breathless. "Jett…"

I didn't let her finish.

I grabbed her, lifting her off the floor, crashing my mouth to hers.

She wrapped her legs around me as I carried her to the bedroom, her hands buried in my hair, her lips hungry, desperate.

I didn't slow down.

Didn't stop.

Because this was ours.

I laid her on the bed, stripping the sweatshirt from her body, baring her to me completely. Jesus Christ.

Every fucking time, she took my breath away.

Brooks arched up, impatient, reaching for me. "Jett—"

I flipped her onto her stomach, pinning her beneath me.

She gasped, fingers fisting in the sheets.

"You want it, sweetheart?" I murmured against her ear, grinding my cock against her soaked entrance.

She whimpered, pressing back into me. "Yes. God, yes."

I didn't make her wait.

I grabbed her hips and slammed into her, deep, hard, raw.

Brooks cried out, her body tightening around me, taking me in completely.

Fuck, she was so wet.

So perfect.

I pulled back and thrust into her again, harder, deeper, my hands gripping her hips so tight I'd probably leave bruises.

But she liked that.

She loved that.

"Jett—" she gasped, fisting the sheets, her body clenching around me.

I groaned, my fingers sliding up her spine, gripping her shoulders, pulling her back onto my cock.

"You like that, baby?" I growled.

She nodded frantically, breathless. "Yes. Yes. Just like that."

I fucked her harder, each thrust pushing her into the mattress, her moans turning into breathless, wrecked cries.

I reached between us, finding her clit, circling it, teasing, pressing just right.

Brooks shattered.

Her whole body tightened, trembled, and broke apart, her orgasm crashing over her as she moaned my name like a prayer.

But I wasn't done.

I flipped her onto her back, hooking her legs over my shoulders, driving into her again, watching her fall apart beneath me.

"Jett—" she gasped, her fingers digging into my back, her nails raking down my skin.

"Mine," I growled, kissing her deep, swallowing her moans, driving into her with everything I had.

I felt it building, the tight heat in my spine, the need to fill her, claim her, give her exactly what she wanted.

"Take it, baby," I gritted out, thrusting deep, spilling inside her, filling her up.

Brooks moaned, her body clenching around me, milking me dry, taking every last drop.

I collapsed against her, breathing hard, tangled together, my forehead pressed to hers.

She cupped my face, her lips brushing mine. "You really want this?" she whispered. "A baby?"

I smiled, my thumb brushing over her cheek. "I want everything with you."

Her eyes softened, her fingers twisting in my hair.

I brushed damp strands of hair from her face, pressing a kiss to her temple.

"Think it worked this time?" she whispered.

I smirked. "Guess we'll find out."

She grinned, pulling me closer. "Then I guess we should keep trying."

Yeah.

I kissed her again, slow, deep, lingering.

Because we had all the time in the world.

I kissed her again, slow, deep, lingering.

And as the snow fell outside, the heat between us refused to fade. I knew—this was everything.